THE BRASS RING

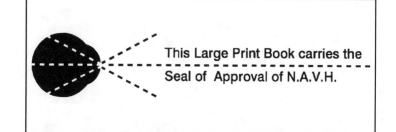

This Large Print Book carries the
Seal of Approval of N.A.V.H.

A HIDDEN FALLS ROMANCE, BOOK 2

THE BRASS RING

AMANDA HARTE

THORNDIKE PRESS
A part of Gale, Cengage Learning

GALE
CENGAGE Learning™

Detroit • New York • San Francisco • New Haven, Conn • Waterville, Maine • London

GALE
CENGAGE Learning™

LIBRARY OF CONGRESS CATALOGING-IN-PUBLICATION DATA

Harte, Amanda.
   The brass ring / by Amanda Harte.
     p. cm. — (A Hidden Falls romance series ; no. 2.)
   (Thorndike Press large print clean reads)
   ISBN-13: 978-1-4104-1398-7 (alk. paper)
   ISBN-10: 1-4104-1398-5 (alk. paper)
   1. Large type books. I. Title.
   PS3515.A79457B73 2009
   813'.6—dc22
                                  2009002204

Published in 2009 by arrangement with Thomas Bouregy & Co., Inc.

Printed in the United States of America
1 2 3 4 5 6 7 13 12 11 10 09

In loving memory of my mother-in-law, Gladys Tayntor, who never passed up an opportunity to ride a merry-go-round and who reached for — and caught — the brass ring of love.

CHAPTER ONE

November 1908

She had been certain he would come. After all, he had sent a gift accompanied by a gracious note, and she had glimpsed him standing in the back of the church. There was, however, no sign of him here. Jane Moreland tried not to frown. Today was a day for smiles, and so she pasted one on her face, hoping that no one would realize just how false it was.

The smile firmly in place, she walked around the room, greeting guests, ensuring that everything was in order and looking for the man who, if dreams had come true, would have been at her side. Fairlawn's ballroom had never seemed so beautiful. It had taken days of hard work to restore it to its former glory, but, judging from the comments she overheard, the effort had been worth it. The oak floor gleamed with polish, the small-paned windows sparkled, and the silken draperies, freshly cleaned and once more lemon yellow, gave the room the appearance of early morning, though the autumn sun had already set.

The preponderance of smiles and the ever increasing volume of the conversation told Jane that the guests were enjoying themselves. Most important, the guest of honor looked more radiant than Jane had ever seen her. Anne Moreland, now Anne Ludlow, glowed with happiness. Her blue eyes, so like Jane's own, had shone brighter than the afternoon sky when she and Rob had exchanged vows. Her face, though no longer a mirror of Jane's, was softened by a smile, the scars visible only to those who knew where to look. At long last, Anne's nightmare was over. Jane's twin had found true happiness and a chance at the life she had dreamed of for so long. Only a curmudgeon could begrudge her that. Jane was not a curmudgeon; still, she wished that Matt had come. If he were here, it would be a perfect day for her as well as her sister.

"Yes, it was a beautiful wedding," Jane agreed. "No, I've never seen my sister look happier." Jane's replies were mechanical. Though she did her best to focus her attention on the guests, she could not stop glancing around the room, looking for Matt. He should have told her that he wouldn't attend the reception. Then she wouldn't be searching for him, wishing he were with her.

"They're traveling to Niagara Falls for their wedding trip," Jane told the mayor's wife. "Rob has been offered a position as the head carver at a carousel factory near Lake Ontario, so they're combining their wedding trip with the move there. Yes," she agreed, "it's a wonderful opportunity for them."

Jane wouldn't think about the fact that she and her sister, who had never been separated for more than a few days, would soon be living on opposite sides of the state. If she thought about that, her smile would falter, and she couldn't let that happen, not at Anne's wedding reception. Instead, she moved closer to the French windows, planning to close the drapes before the dancing began.

The musicians had arrived and were tuning their instruments. In a few minutes, Anne and Rob would lead the first dance. Jane grasped one of the drapery panels, then stopped, her pulse beginning to race. Surely it wasn't her imagination that she had seen motion in the yard. She looked again, trying to appear casual, but this time the smile that she had pasted on her face became genuine.

He was there!

Moving as cautiously as she had done countless times before, Jane made her way to the door, then hurried along the hall. In the past, she had slipped down the servants' staircase, carrying her shoes, lest the sound of footfalls alert someone to her exit. Tonight there was no need for silence; the gaiety in the ballroom would mask most noises, but still she moved with care, not wanting to attract notice and be delayed with explanations of why she was leaving the party. It was only when she was on the grass that she began to run.

"Matt!" Even from a distance she had known it was him. Though there were many tall, dark-haired men in Hidden Falls, no one else held his head at that precise angle and no one else had shoulders as broad as Matt's. He was standing on the site of the old gazebo, the place where he and Jane had met so many times in the past. Jane wondered whether he had chosen the spot out of nostalgia or simple habit, for the gazebo was gone. Just a few months earlier, Charles had demolished the fanciful white edifice to make room for the carousel. Now that the merry-go-round had been moved to the town park, the empty concrete circle cried out for a building.

"Matt!" Jane repeated when she reached him. "The party's inside." Though the sun had set, the moon provided enough light that she could see that he still wore the formal clothing he had donned for the ceremony. She reached for his hand and tugged. "Come back with me." If they hurried, they would not miss the first dance. How wonderful it would be to share that with Matt!

"I'm sorry, Jane, but I can't ruin Anne's day." As he shook his head, a lock of dark hair tumbled over Matt's forehead. Impatiently, he brushed it back. "She deserves to have a perfect wedding."

Jane tightened her grip. One of Matt's worst characteristics was his stubbornness. "Having you there would make the day perfect," she insisted, for Jane as well as her sister.

Matt shook his head again. "You're deluding yourself. You know Charles doesn't want me to set foot inside Fairlawn."

Jane tried not to sigh. Though neither Matt nor her brother would divulge the origin, their childhood enmity had not diminished with maturity. She gestured toward the platform where Anne's carousel of dreams had once stood. "We rode the merry-go-round together that first night.

Charles didn't protest then."

His lips thinning, Matt's expression appeared little less than a grimace. "It doesn't matter what he said. I saw Charles's eyes that night, and nothing had changed. The only reason he didn't order me off the grounds was that he couldn't resist Susannah's and Anne's pleas." A nocturnal animal scurried past the platform, rustling the fallen leaves at the same time as Matt turned Jane's hand over and laced his fingers with hers. "I can't go inside and risk another argument. I won't do that to Anne and Rob."

His voice told Jane that the decision was final. Nothing she said would change Matt's mind, but still she had to try. "Please, Matt. I want to dance with you." The sound of music carried through the still night, telling Jane that the dancing had begun. She was missing Anne's first waltz as a married woman, the one Jane had dreamed of sharing with Matt.

"It's cold. You need to go inside."

Matt was right. Her evening gown was not designed for a November evening, and she had started to shiver. Still, Jane could be as stubborn as Matt. "I won't go back without a dance." She gestured toward the platform. Though it wasn't as smooth as the ballroom floor, they could dance here.

This time when Matt shook his head, he was smiling, and Jane realized that he was shaking his head at himself rather than denying her request. "I guess that's one thing Charles and I have in common. Neither of us can resist a Moreland woman's pleas." Matt slipped off his jacket and draped it over Jane's shoulders. "Put this on," he urged. "I don't want you catching cold."

Though far too large for her, Jane savored the coat's warmth and the smell of hair tonic and shaving cream that clung to it. They were ordinary scents, made special by the fact that they belonged to Matt. Jane smiled. Matt smiled. And then he opened his arms.

In all the years Jane had known him, she and Matt had never danced. They had walked together, fished together, even learned how to climb rocks together, but never before had they danced. Perhaps it should have felt awkward, his coat flapping against her as they twirled on the cement. Perhaps it should have been difficult, straining to hear the beat of the music. Perhaps there should have been a need to learn how each other moved. Instead, Jane felt as if she and Matt had done this a hundred times before. There was no awkwardness; rather, their movements seemed as fluid as if they had practiced together, and for the length of a song, Jane felt herself relax. No matter what tomorrow brought, this was where she was meant to be.

As the last strains faded, Matt released her. "The ball's over, Cinderella."

He wouldn't run. He'd done that before. Though it shamed him to admit it, the first time he had run away had been Jane and Anne's birthday many years before. Matt clenched his fists as he thought of how he'd stood among the trees, watching the workmen set up the carousel that Mr. and Mrs. Moreland had rented for their daughters' party. Matt had read about merry-go-rounds, but — like most of the citizens of Hidden Falls — he had never seen one, much less ridden on one of those painted ponies. He'd remained concealed in the forest while the guests arrived and those beautiful animals began to revolve, their gilded trappings shining almost as brightly as the myriad lights that outlined the carousel's canopy. It had been a scene out of one of those storybooks that the schoolmarms used to read to them, something so magical that Matt could scarcely believe his eyes.

He could still recall how his heart had filled with longing to ride one of the painted ponies. As he watched the other children clamber onto the wooden steeds, some clinging to the manes with obvious fear, Matt knew that he could do what no one else had done. His arms were long enough that when he reached out, he could capture the brass ring that had eluded the others. But when he had stretched his right arm, all he had touched was the bark of another tree, a reminder that Matt Wagner wasn't invited to the Morelands' party. He might attend the same school as the Moreland children, but he was a mill worker's son.

Everyone in Hidden Falls knew that mill hands' children did not receive invitations for this or any other event at one of the houses on the hill. Though his father helped manufacture the textiles that had made the Morelands the wealthiest family in Hidden Falls, in the Morelands' eyes, Matt was not fit to associate with their children. Charles Moreland had made that as clear as the glass that filled the mill's windows.

From his vantage point in the forest, Matt had watched the carousel revolve, his foot tapping in time to the music that filled the afternoon air. He had seen Anne move from horse to horse, apparently determined to ride each one. He had watched Jane, the shy twin, have to be coaxed onto a pony. And he had seen Charles's gloating expression. Charles shouldn't have been able to see him, but the way he looked at the trees and the smile that seemed to say, 'Stay away, poor boy. You don't belong here,' pierced through Matt like the lances they'd read about in school. It was that expression that had caused Matt to run, lest someone see the moisture that had gathered in his eyes. It wasn't tears, of course. Big boys didn't cry, but they did run, and so he had run home, refusing to tell his mother where he'd been or why she'd seen wet streaks on his dirty face.

Matt was no longer a boy from the wrong side of the river. He was a grown man, a man who could hold his own with Charles Moreland or anyone else on the hill. Instead of being excluded, he had been invited to the party today. It had been his choice not to attend, and so he wouldn't run tonight. But as he strode down the road, Matt realized that his legs were not listening to his brain. He would be home in record time.

As he rounded the corner onto Forest and approached the small house that served as both his residence and office, Matt saw a man sitting on his front step. Why was Al

Roberts visiting him?

"Evenin', Mr. Wagner." The man rose and extended his hand to Matt. "Or should I call you Esq?"

Matt chuckled. Though he had heard that some of the townspeople used that sobriquet in what he suspected was a mocking tribute to the law degree that gave him the right to add "Esquire" to his name, it was the first time anyone had addressed him that way.

"Matt will do." He opened the door and ushered the man inside. "Is this a social call?" Al was one of the mill hands, and while social calls were not unheard of, they were rare. That same law degree that Matt hoped would benefit the workers appeared to have created a barrier between him and them.

Al Roberts straightened his shoulders. "It's business," he said with obvious pride. "I need myself a lawyer."

"Then sit right here." Matt gestured toward one of the two chairs that fronted his desk. The house was so small that its main room had to do for everything except sleeping. He had placed his desk and book-case on one side. The stove shared the other half of the room with a small table and one comfortable chair. When he ate, Matt dragged one of the wooden chairs from the desk to the table. It was a far cry from most Harvard law graduates' offices, far different even from the office of Hidden Falls' senior attorney, Ralph Chambers. But Matt hoped that this room, unlike more pretentious ones, would not intimidate his clients.

He stoked the fire. It was one thing to present a spartan appearance, another to cause chilblains. "What can I do for you, Al?"

The mill worker propped his elbows on the desk and leaned forward. "I aim to buy a farm. Need to do it legal like." His gaze was fixed on the bookcase, leading Matt to suspect that his client was evaluating his expertise by the weight of his tomes. Biting back a smile, Matt recalled one of his professors insisting that every new attorney needed an impressive set of books shelved behind his desk. Perhaps this was the reason. "Me and my gal heard tales of folks gettin' swindled," Al Roberts announced.

"I can ensure that that will not happen," Matt promised. "You'll have a properly signed bill of sale, and I'll register the transfer of the land." When Al Roberts began to relax, Matt continued, asking for the details of the proposed transaction. Half an hour later, his client nodded and pushed back his chair.

"How much do I owe you?" When Matt stated his fee, Al Roberts raised an eyebrow. "I reckon that's a bargain. Thanks, Matt." The previously taciturn young man leaned toward Matt. "Me and my Millie sure do appreciate this." Before Matt could reply, he continued, "She's my sweetheart, you know, a real pretty gal. A man couldn't ask for anyone better than Millie. Why, she's been right patient, waiting three years while I saved my money." Al Roberts' smile faded a little as he said, "It ain't bad, workin' at the mill, but a man wants a place of his own when he settles down. It ain't right for women and children to be cooped up in a boardinghouse."

It also wasn't right for men, women, and children to risk injury or death simply to increase the Morelands' wealth. Al Roberts was one of the lucky ones, leaving Hidden Falls with the money he sought and no serious injuries, unlike Matt's father, who had paid the ultimate price for the Morelands' perfectly woven textiles. There was no need to mention that, not tonight, and so Matt forced the corners of his mouth to turn upward. "My felicitations to you and your bride."

Al Roberts grinned again. "Me and Millie would be mighty pleased if you'd come to our wedding."

Matt's smile faded. Weddings. Was that all anyone thought about? He closed the door behind his client, then strode toward the kitchen area and opened the cupboard. The loaf of bread he had found there and some cheese would be supper tonight. A veritable feast. Matt's laugh sounded brittle, even to his ears. Jane would tell him he was a fool, giving up the delicacies that were being served to the wedding guests so that he could sit here and dine on slightly stale bread and cheese that he hoped hadn't grown mold.

Perhaps he was a fool, but if there was one thing Matt knew, it was that he could not have gone to Anne Moreland's wedding reception. It wasn't simply that he wanted to avoid an altercation with Charles, although that was part of it. More important, Matt didn't need to be reminded that everyone around him was entering into the state of holy matrimony. It had started with Charles and Susannah. Today it was Anne and Rob. Soon Al Roberts and his Millie would be reciting those same vows. Would Matt Wagner and his bride ever pledge their love before God and the congregation? It didn't seem likely.

Matt sawed the bread with more force

than necessary, heedless of the crumbs that littered the floor. A year and a half ago, he had been certain he'd be married before summer's end. He had never deluded himself that the future would be easy, but he had been confident that with his bride at his side, he could surmount any obstacle. How wrong he had been! That naïve certainty had vanished on the night that had changed so many lives, the night that had parted him from the woman he loved, the night that a fire had killed Jane's parents and burned her sister so badly that Anne and Jane had spent close to a year in Switzerland while one of the world's foremost doctors sought to restore Anne's beauty. It wasn't simply the thousands of miles and the months that had separated Matt and Jane. Those miles and months had translated into experiences that had driven a wedge between them.

Matt carved a slice from the chunk of cheese and tossed it onto the bread, then poured himself a cup of the coffee that had been left from breakfast. This was hardly gourmet fare, but it would ease hunger pangs. Other pangs were not so easily satisfied.

Jane was back. Matt sighed as he chewed the bread. The future had not turned out

21

the way he'd envisioned. He had believed that when Jane returned from Switzerland, they would resume their relationship, then take the next step, the one he had dreamed about. It hadn't been as simple as Matt had anticipated. Unlike Anne, who bore physical changes, Jane looked the same. The blond hair, the blue eyes, the beautiful face were just as he remembered them. But inside, there were differences that Matt couldn't quite define, changes the dozens of letters they'd shared over the past year had not revealed. Jane was older, of course. He'd expected that. She wore more fashionable clothing. That, too, was to be expected. The other changes were not. Matt hadn't expected Jane's shyness to disappear. Nor had he expected that the shyness would be replaced by a protective shield. That worried him most of all.

Though he saw her almost every day now, the old camaraderie, the sense that Jane was his best friend as well as the woman he loved, was gone. The new Jane might laugh with him, but he doubted she would ever again cry in his presence. She might discuss the latest happenings in Hidden Falls, but he suspected she would no longer confide her deepest longings and fears to him.

Matt didn't know the reason. All he knew was that Jane had changed, and he didn't like it.

They would talk about it for years. Jane knew that as surely as she knew that she missed the warmth of Matt's coat around her shoulders. It wasn't simply the fact that this was the first time Fairlawn had been opened to guests in well over a year that would provide fodder for the rumor mill. It wasn't simply that this was Fairlawn's first wedding. This was also the largest, fanciest party Hidden Falls had ever seen. The dining table was laden with platters of food; waiters circulated with trays of champagne glasses; the band that had almost everyone dancing was reputed to be one of the finest in all of New York State. No expense had been spared, for Charles had declared that nothing was too good for Anne. It was truly a night to remember, and Jane knew it was one that would be engraved on her memory, for — no matter what else happened — tonight was the night she had first danced with Matt.

"May I have this dance?"

For a second, Jane thought her fondest wish had come true and Matt had joined the party. But this wasn't Matt's voice, and the man with the red hair and green eyes was most definitely not Matt.

"It would be my pleasure." If she couldn't dance with Matt, at least she knew that Brad Harrod would not crush her toes as some of the older gentlemen had. Though Jane could remember how Brad and Charles had protested when their mothers had insisted they take dancing lessons and how those protests had escalated in both volume and frequency when the boys had been instructed to practice with Anne and Jane, those much dreaded sessions had resulted in Brad and Charles becoming accomplished dancing partners.

As she moved into Brad's arms, he murmured, "You're the most beautiful woman in the room."

Jane smiled, remembering all the times her brother's best friend had teased her and Anne, telling them they were little pests. "You, my dear sir, are the most outrageous flatterer in Hidden Falls. Don't you know that the bride is always the most beautiful woman on her wedding day?"

She and Brad danced with the ease that came from years of practice, their feet moving instinctively. Since Jane didn't have to guess which way he would turn, normally she could relax and enjoy his conversation, but normally Brad did not indulge in flattery.

"As long as Rob believes that, my opinion doesn't matter. I stand by my statement."

Though his words were light, the expression in Brad's eyes startled Jane by its intensity. This was not the Brad who had been her partner so many times before. "You're impossible. What on earth am I going to do with you?"

"Marry me."

Jane's gasp owed nothing to the increased tempo of the music. He was joking. Of course he was joking. Hadn't Charles claimed that Brad had been the practical joker at school? And wasn't he the man who had instituted the pact with Charles and their friend Anthony, that none of the men would marry before they were thirty? Jane tried not to frown at the fact that both Anthony and Charles were now married, though they had yet to reach that milestone birthday.

She gestured toward the elaborate decorations. "I'm afraid the Moreland accounts have been stretched to their limits. Alas, I regret to inform you that we cannot have another wedding for at least six months."

"Then I'll ask you again in six months."

"You're incorrigible!" But, of course, he

was only joking. Thank goodness he was only joking, for Jane did not want to think about marriage. At least not to Brad Harrod.

As the music ended and Brad returned her to the edge of the dance floor, Jane smiled and gave him her fanciest curtsey. As he moved away, Jane's eyes narrowed at the sight of the young woman on the other side of the room.

Though Megan O'Toole hadn't worked at Fairlawn in close to two years, she and her mother had been hired to help serve refreshments tonight. Dressed in her neat black uniform with the crisp white apron, her luxuriant dark hair pulled back in a tidy knot, Megan was the picture of the perfect servant. All except for her expression. Though house staff were schooled to display no emotions, Megan's face bore such a look of longing that Jane's heart ached with compassion. Poor Megan! She looked as if her heart were about to break. What — or, more likely, who — could have caused such anguish?

Hoping there might be something she could do to help the woman who had once been a friend as well as a servant, Jane tried to follow the direction of Megan's gaze. Oh, no! As her heart stopped for an instant, Jane feared her expression was as sad as Megan's. It couldn't be. But it was. Charles was the object of Megan's affection. No wonder Megan looked so morose, for her love was destined to be unrequited. Surely Megan knew that Charles was happily — deliriously happily — married and thrilled to be expecting his and Susannah's first child. Surely Megan knew there was no hope that Charles would ever return her feelings. Or did she delude herself into thinking that things would change?

As she struggled to compose her face, another thought assailed Jane. Did Susannah know of Megan's infatuation? The fact that Megan now served at Pleasant Hill, Charles and Susannah's home, made the situation particularly awkward. Though there was nothing she could do tonight, Jane resolved to have a conversation with Susannah. Soon.

Jane smiled as one of the guests asked her to dance, and for the next hour, she moved from one partner to another, her smile firmly in place, her eyes scanning the room, trying to ensure that the guests were all enjoying themselves. As she whirled around the room, she noticed that Philip Biddle and Ralph Chambers remained on the sidelines. As was typical for them, while the two older men sat next to each other, there appeared to be no conversation.

"Gentlemen," Jane said as she approached the men who had been her father's closest friends, "I seem to be without a partner for this dance." Though there was no familial relationship, she and Anne had always referred to Philip and Ralph as uncles.

Both men rose and bowed slightly, reminding Jane of their differences. Almost ascetically thin, with white hair and piercing blue eyes, Philip stood a head taller than Ralph, whose girth was kindly referred to as portly. Ralph had always been the more serious of the two, although, unlike Philip, he could occasionally be convinced to join the Moreland children in a game. Though Philip had retired from his position at the bank years earlier, Ralph was still practicing law on Main Street. The one thing the two men had in common was ownership of a motor car.

"Nothing would give me greater pleasure than to dance with you," Ralph said, "but I'm ashamed to admit that I twisted my ankle." He gestured toward his bandaged right foot. "I'm afraid I'd mangle your toes worse than ever."

"My dear, I would love to oblige you." Philip took Jane's hand in his and squeezed it. "As our esteemed attorney said, nothing would give me greater pleasure, but I made a promise to Rosemary that I would not dance with another woman." It was the response Jane had expected. Both she and Anne had speculated that the reason why Philip, an accomplished dancer, had sat on the sidelines after his wife's death was because of a promise to Rosemary. Still, Jane could have sworn that Philip had danced with her sister just a few months ago at the Harrods' party. She must have been mistaken.

Pulling up another chair so that the two older men need not remain standing, Jane spent a few minutes talking to them. Then she saw her sister beckoning to her and knew that it was time to ready the bride for her wedding journey.

"Oh, Anne, I'm so happy for you!" Jane said as she helped her sister remove her veil and gown. Anne would don a simple navy blue traveling suit for the train trip west. Jane gave her sister a quick hug. It was wonderful to see Anne's eyes reflecting joy rather than pain and to have the worry lines erased from her face. Rob Ludlow was not simply the most talented carousel carver in the country. He was also a miracle worker. Though he might think that the painted ponies he designed were his greatest work, the happiness he had brought to Anne was far more precious.

"I only wish you weren't going so far away." Though Jane hadn't meant to say it, the words slipped out.

Anne nodded slowly, and for a second, her smile faded. "We'll be back for visits, and you can come stay with us. Rob has promised me that wherever we make our home, it will have plenty of room for you."

It was Jane's turn to nod. "I've always wanted to see Lake Ontario," she admitted, trying to force her lips to curve upward. The truth was, she did want to see the lake and Niagara Falls, but it would be different, visiting Anne there, for Anne was no longer simply Jane's sister. She was now Rob's wife.

Keeping her false smile firmly in place, Jane adjusted the angle of her sister's hat, then pronounced it perfect. "Mrs. Ludlow," she said with mock formality, "your groom awaits."

Though the bridal couple had departed, the party continued, and as one of the hostesses, Jane remained in the ballroom until all the guests had left. She must have said the right things, for no one looked askance at her replies to their questions. Still, she could recall none of the conversations. All she knew was that while she was smiling and nodding, she had longed for the evening to end.

At last the guests departed, and Charles and Susannah returned to Pleasant Hill, leaving Jane alone. As she had countless times before, she climbed the stairs to her bedroom. Tonight was different, though, for this was the final night she would spend here. Other than the year she and Anne had lived in Switzerland, Jane could not recall a night she hadn't slept in this room. It was so familiar, and yet it wasn't.

She ran her hand over the intricately carved bedpost. It hadn't changed. Her mind told her that at the same time that her heart cried out that it was different. The truth was, it wasn't only Jane's room that seemed different. All of Hidden Falls did. Though Anne had insisted that nothing had changed, she had been so caught up in her love for Rob that Jane doubted she would notice anything short of an earthquake.

Drawing her favorite chair next to the window, Jane gazed outside. Perhaps the sight of the stars and the moon would help calm her thoughts. When Anne had asked what she thought had changed, Jane had found herself unable to pinpoint any one thing. The buildings in town were the same;

there were few new residents. The only major change was the addition of Anne's carousel to the town park. That wasn't what disturbed Jane, but something else was, something she could not identify.

Ever since she had stepped off the train with Anne, Jane had felt as if something were wrong. Unlike Anne, who had dreaded the homecoming, Jane had been eager to be back in Hidden Falls. This was her home. It would always be her home. But, oddly, it no longer felt the same. *She* no longer felt the same. It seemed as if she were looking at everything through a thick glass. Familiar buildings, trees, even people appeared wavy and distorted when viewed through that glass, and her sense of equilibrium seemed off-kilter. Both were unexpected and decidedly unpleasant sensations.

So, too, were the changes Jane had found in Matt. When she had last seen him, he had still been a law student, coming to Hidden Falls only for brief visits. Now that he had finished school, he'd once again taken up residency here and was quickly establishing himself as the town's junior attorney. Matt had traded the cast-off clothing he used to wear for fancy suits. He had started rolling cigarettes, although Jane had never seen him smoke one. He greeted the townspeople with more confidence than before. Though those differences had startled her, they hadn't disturbed Jane. Matt's new position in Hidden Falls could account for them. Unfortunately, the changes were deeper than new clothing or mannerisms, and that disturbed Jane more than she had dreamed possible.

For years Matt had been her friend. He'd been the one who had understood that, unlike Anne, she wasn't comfortable with the limelight. He'd been the one who had taught her how to fish and how to tell the difference between a spruce and a pine tree. He'd been the one who had breached her shyness, convincing her that she could trust him. And she had trusted him. Matt had become not just her friend, but her best friend. And, because he was such a special friend, Jane had confided secrets to him that even Anne didn't know. In return, Matt had shared his dreams with her. All that had ended when she arrived home.

Jane didn't know what had happened to Matt while she was in Europe, but something had. Though his letters had seemed the same as the ones they'd traded during his years at college, something had changed. Matt still treated her with the utmost courtesy, but the easy camaraderie, the sense that they were more than friends, was gone. At times, Jane felt as if he regarded her as a stranger, and that was wrong, so very wrong.

She closed her eyes, then blinked desperately. It was no use. No matter how hard she tried, the tears began to fall. It wasn't supposed to be this way.

CHAPTER TWO

Charles looked at the pile of boxes and the
two trunks outside Jane's door. "Are you
sure this is all you want to take?" His skeptical expression told Jane he was remembering the number of trunks he and Susannah
had brought back from Paris. There had
been so many that Anne had been certain
they would overload the wagon. In comparison, Jane's belongings must look paltry.

She nodded. Though both Charles and
Susannah had urged her to bring some of
her furniture if it would make Pleasant Hill
feel like home, she had refused. "It needs to
stay here," Jane had insisted. The truth was,
she doubted anything would make Pleasant
Hill feel like home. Fairlawn was her home,
or it had been. She had dreaded this morning almost as much as she had Anne's move
to the other side of the state, and the sullen
gray day only heightened Jane's sense of
uneasiness.

"Let's get started." Oblivious to her mood, Charles hefted the first box and began to descend the stairs. Jane followed him, carrying one of her small valises. "It seems strange to think of Fairlawn being closed up," she said when they reached the landing. They were the third generation of Morelands to live in the house, and even though Fairlawn now held unhappy memories, Jane had never considered that Charles would not continue to make it his home. "I didn't think you'd leave," she told her brother.

"It would cost too much to repair the south wing," he said. Though Jane knew that the work would be costly, Charles's expression hinted that there were other reasons that he chose not to live in their childhood home but that those reasons were not open for discussion. The reasons, Jane suspected, were related to what she called the Moreland Mystery, the argument Charles and their father had had the day of the fire that had caused him to leave Hidden Falls without so much as a good-bye. It did no good to ask Charles about what had happened that fateful afternoon, for he refused to answer.

Charles pulled the front door open, then descended the steps toward the wagon. "Susannah and I agreed that we should use the insurance proceeds for the mill." A wry smile lit his face as he positioned the box. "Of course, we might be forced to move back here if we outgrow Pleasant Hill." Susannah's family home had only three bedrooms, while Fairlawn boasted six.

"Planning for the future, are you?" Jane wrinkled her nose, glad to exchange her gloomy thoughts for happier ones. "I'm still having difficulty envisioning you as a father. Does Susannah know what she's gotten herself in for, joining this family?"

Charles's eyes sparkled the way they always did when he thought of his wife, and somehow the gray day no longer seemed so gloomy. "I warned her that you and Anne were meddling little girls and to beware if this baby is a girl."

"Did you also tell her you were an obnoxious big brother and that a baby boy would be much, much worse?"

As they reentered the house, Charles feigned disdain. "Of course not."

"It's as I thought. Poor Susannah has no idea of what life will be like with a little Moreland underfoot."

"It will be blissful."

"I might have used a different adjective." Jane's smile faded as she considered the reason she and Charles were loading boxes into the wagon. "Are you certain you want me living with you?" Jane knew that if she were as recently married as Charles and Susannah, she wouldn't want another person in the house — not even a sibling, perhaps especially not a sibling.

Charles picked up another box and started to descend the stairs. "You can't stay here alone. Even in a town as small as Hidden Falls, that would make you the object of unpleasant speculation, and I can't allow that to happen." Jane tried not to bristle at Charles's tone. Once more her brother was asserting his role as the oldest child and, since their parents' death, the patriarch. "Besides," he added, "you know Mrs. Enke is ready to retire." The housekeeper who had been with them since Charles's birth had told them she wanted to spend what she called her autumn days with her cousin but had agreed to remain at Fairlawn until they could hire her replacement. Closing the house now would eliminate the need to find someone who could take Mrs. Enke's place and would allow her to celebrate the winter holidays with her cousin.

When they were once more outside, Charles gestured toward the rose brick house with the crenellated towers that had been the Moreland residence for over sixty years. "Even before the fire, somehow I could never picture myself living here as an adult. The truth is, I always thought either you or Anne would make this your home once you married."

Marriage! This time Jane did bristle. She was growing tired of every conversation revolving around marriage. It was understandable, of course. Charles and Susannah were newlyweds, and Anne's wedding plans had occupied them all for the past six weeks. But that didn't mean that Jane wanted the trend to continue. The last thing she needed was Charles playing matchmaker. He and she had very different ideas about the ideal bridegroom for Jane. As if he knew he had annoyed her, Charles grabbed the remaining trunk and carried it to the wagon. Thank goodness that discussion was over.

Jane's relief was short-lived. When he returned to the house, removing his hat and gloves as he entered the hallway for his final farewell to the housekeeper, Charles continued as if there had been no interruption. "Since Anne has left Hidden Falls, that leaves you to carry on the tradition of a Moreland living at Fairlawn. Once you marry, that is."

The house was silent, save for the loud ticking of the longcase clock at the far end of the hallway. Jane took a deep breath, reminding herself that this was vintage Charles, deliberately baiting one of his sisters. She wouldn't respond with anger, for that was what he had always sought. "There's only one flaw with that theory," she said in the coolest voice she could manage. "I don't expect to marry any time soon." The fact that she had once been confident she would be married by now was something she had no need to tell Charles. Those hopes, those dreams, that sense of certainty had been destroyed along with the south wing of Fairlawn.

Charles shrugged, his expression telling Jane that he had anticipated her response. "As I recall, Anne said the same thing just a few months ago, and look at her now."

They were walking toward the kitchen where, if the faint rattling of pans was any indication, Mrs. Enke was washing breakfast dishes. Jane stopped and faced her brother. "I am not Anne." She forced the words through clenched teeth. "We may be twins, but we are not alike." Was Matt the only one who had realized that while the Moreland sisters appeared identical, the similarities were all on the surface? Inside, they

40

were two very different women.

"Okay. Okay." As Charles raised his hands in mock surrender, Jane saw that his right hand was bare.

"Where's your ring?" she demanded. Since their parents had given it to him on his eighteenth birthday, Charles had worn the Moreland signet ring. Family legend said that when their grandfather, the first Charles Moreland, married, he had given Fairlawn to his bride as a wedding present. Her gift to him had been a ring. Larger than many, this one was intricately carved on the edges and had an 'M' outlined in rubies on the top surface. Though Charles had once confided that he found it overly ornate and wore it only because of its sentimental value as a family heirloom, he had never to Jane's knowledge removed it from his finger. Where was it now?

Charles glanced at his hand almost as if he hadn't noticed the absence of the ring. "I instituted a new safety rule at the mill," he said. "We've had too many accidents when people's rings get caught in a piece of machinery or tangled in the yarn, so I've decreed that no one can wear anything other than a plain band. Like this." Charles pointed toward his wedding ring. "The reason I don't wear Grandpa's ring is that I didn't think it was right to ask the workers to do something I wasn't willing to do."

Brushing aside her earlier annoyance with him, Jane realized that this, too, was vintage Charles, concerned about doing the right thing. Though she knew he would have preferred to remain in New York City where he'd had a profitable business of his own, when their parents had died and he had inherited responsibility for the mill, Charles had returned to Hidden Falls. He hadn't simply assumed the helm at Moreland Mills; he had been determined to make it the best textile factory in the country. And, though it had been a difficult task to escape from the quagmire of overwhelming debt and deliberate sabotage of the operations, he had succeeded.

After an emotional farewell to Mrs. Enke, Charles helped Jane into the wagon. It was foolish, Jane told herself, to feel such sorrow over leaving. Fairlawn was only a house. The other changes in her life were of far more importance. Though she couldn't help regretting them, there was no reason to infect others with her doldrums. For what seemed like the hundredth time in the past few days, she forced a smile onto her face.

"I'm so glad you're here," Susannah said a few minutes later as Jane and Charles climbed the stairs to Pleasant Hill. Charles's bride, a tall brunette with warm brown eyes and a smile that was obviously not forced, stood in the doorway, welcoming her. "Down, Salt! Come here, Pepper." Susannah reached for the dogs whose exuberant greeting involved attempting to leap into Jane's arms. Jane recalled Charles's letter, describing how he'd found two orphaned dogs — one black, the other white — on his doorstep one evening and how they'd adopted him. Now, he claimed, their primary loyalty was to his wife. "I apologize for these rascals," Susannah continued, "but they're as happy as I am that you've come."

Jane looked around the house that was her new home. Smaller and less formal than Fairlawn, it seemed to exude a friendly welcome, just as its mistress did. "It's good of you to say that when I'm almost interrupting your honeymoon," Jane told her sister-in-law.

"Nonsense." Susannah hung Jane's coat. "We're old married folks now. Besides," she said, grinning at her husband, "I've always wanted a sister. I told Charles that was the reason I married him, because then I'd be part of your family."

"And I thought it was so you could have Salt and Pepper." Charles gave his wife a smile that startled Jane with its intensity. Never before had she seen him looking so happy. The worry lines that had furrowed his brow and bracketed his mouth were gone, replaced by an unfamiliar expression. It was happiness, but there was more to it than that, something that made his smile luminous. Jane had the feeling that Charles had finally found what he needed to make his life complete.

"I'd better unpack a few things," she said, suddenly uncomfortable. It was the coward's way, running away from a difficult situation, but Jane could not stop herself. As she climbed the stairs to the room Susannah had given her, Jane told herself that she didn't begrudge her brother his new found happiness. It was true. She didn't. Heaven knew Charles deserved happiness after everything he'd endured. Jane wanted him to be happy. She was thrilled that he was happy. But there was no denying it. When she'd been downstairs, she had been the outsider. Charles and Susannah and even those silly dogs of theirs were part of a family, just as Anne and Rob now formed a family. Of all the Morelands, Jane was the only one who was alone. Not simply alone, but as unnecessary as a fifth wheel on one of Henry Ford's Model Ts.

It wasn't what she had expected. Jane had thought that when she returned from Switzerland, she would be able to help Charles and Anne. Perhaps it had been wishful thinking, but she had believed there would be something she could do to atone for the night when she hadn't been at Fairlawn. But Charles and Anne, it appeared, needed no help. They had established lives that were complete without her. They had managed to banish the ghosts of the past, and in doing so, they had found the thing that continued to elude Jane: happiness.

Although her room was bright and cheerful, Jane was frowning as she looked out the window. From here, she could see neither the burned wing of Fairlawn nor the scorched spot on the ground where the stable had once stood. All she could see of her childhood home were the chimneys. That was enough, she told herself. The reason she was feeling so miserable had nothing to do with moving out of Fairlawn. It wasn't even seeing Charles and Susannah's happiness and feeling as if she were an outsider. The problem, Jane knew, was deep inside herself. While Anne had been the happy twin, the one who was always smiling and who could make others laugh so easily, Jane had been the quiet one, the child who preferred to be alone, the one who rarely smiled. And there had been times when, even on a sunny day, she had felt as glum as others did on a dismal day.

Reaching for her hat and gloves, Jane straightened her shoulders. When they'd been growing up, Matt had always been able to coax her out of these moods. Perhaps, even though so many things had changed, he could do that again.

Feeling better than she had since she'd wakened, Jane descended the stairs. Though Susannah offered the use of one of her horses or the wagon, Jane shook her head. It wasn't simply what she told Susannah, that it was a good day for a walk. The truth was, since Jane and Matt had always felt the need to keep their meetings secret, they went on foot to the rendezvous spot. Horses, Matt had pointed out, were difficult to hide, carriages even more so.

Jane was partway down River Road when she heard the unmistakable sound of an automobile behind her. She turned, wondering why someone was driving on this particular stretch of road. There were no other houses on this end of River, and with only three automobiles in Hidden Falls, it was unusual to see one at all. Could a stranger have gotten lost? As the car drew closer,

Jane saw that it belonged in Hidden Falls. She smiled when she recognized the driver as Brad rather than Philip or Ralph.

"Would you care for a ride?" Brad asked as he stopped the motorcar beside her.

"I never pass up the opportunity to spend time in one of Henry Ford's inventions." Both Uncle Philip and Uncle Ralph knew that and would occasionally invite her for a ride. Brad's invitations were less common. Though she didn't have a dust coat or the veiled hat that were considered the proper attire for riding in a Model T, Jane didn't care. Perhaps a drive was what she needed to chase away the doldrums. Brad's jokes, though sometimes directed at her, rarely failed to entertain her, and — if the grin that wrinkled his freckled nose were any indication — Brad was in a jolly mood today.

He waited until she was seated, then closed the passenger door behind Jane. "You may soon have more opportunities to ride. Charles told me he wants to buy one of these black beauties." Brad patted the side of the car before climbing behind the steering wheel.

The November day was cold and damp, causing Jane to shiver slightly. "I think he's planning to wait until spring. Susannah is

47

worried about him driving on the hills here in the winter." Jane shivered again. "Although I doubt she phrased it exactly this way to Charles, Susannah told me she fears he'll be the worst driver in the country."

Brad's laugh was as merry as his grin. "For the sake of my friendship with Charles, I won't add my opinion." His left foot pushed the first pedal at the same time as he moved the hand lever forward. Jane wasn't certain which action was responsible, but the Model T began to accelerate. She turned slightly in the seat, preferring to watch Brad rather than think about the fact that they were passing Fairlawn. Rose Walk, Brad's home, was next, the last of the three houses on the hill. He had reached his driveway when he turned to look at Jane again. "If I were a jealous man, I would probably be bothered by the fact that you're paying more attention to this automobile than you are to me."

Jane's eyes widened as she realized that she'd been observing the way Brad pressed the pedals and how he moved the lever rather than looking at him or the scenery that was passing far more quickly than it did when walking. Her mother would have been appalled at her rudeness. "I'm sorr—"

Before she could complete her apology, Brad interrupted. "Don't worry, Jane. I'm not a jealous man." He wrinkled his nose. "At least not when my rival is a Model T. They really are marvelous creations." He slowed the car again. "Do you want to learn to drive?"

"Oh, yes!" Brad was a lifesaver. That was the only way to describe it. Somehow he had sensed that she needed something different to think about. Learning to drive was the perfect antidote to Jane's malaise. Fiddling with those pedals and the lever, not to mention holding the steering wheel, would keep her from thinking about things that were best forgotten.

Brad stopped the car and gestured toward the stretch of River Road they had just traversed. "We could practice here. There's almost no traffic." Both Ralph and Philip lived on the other side of the river and had few reasons to climb the hill to River Road, and with only three houses, one of which was now uninhabited, there was little pedestrian or horse traffic. This was the ideal spot for a novice driver.

Despite all that, Jane shook her head. "Charles might see us. If I ever do master the art of driving, I'd like to surprise him."

His green eyes sparkling with mirth, Brad

nodded. "An excellent idea, Miss Moreland. And don't worry. You'll be an accomplished motorist before you know it." He put the car in gear again and headed across the river. "We'll use the west side of Forest. There's hardly anyone there."

Although the street extended for over a mile, there were few houses and no stores on Forest west of Bridge Street, a dramatic contrast to the eastern half of Forest. That was where the workers who could not afford the boarding houses' rent lived in tiny buildings, little better than shacks. That was also where Matt had established his home and law office. Jane would never have agreed to drive on East Forest. It was far too dangerous, and the danger was not simply the fact that children played in the middle of the street. Jane did not want Matt to see her driving any more than she wanted Charles to learn of her endeavor.

Once she was in the driver's seat, there was no time to think of anything other than how quickly to move her feet on the three different pedals and just how far to move the hand lever. Driving an automobile, Jane discovered, was far more difficult than driving a team of horses.

"That's because you had trained horses," Brad told her when she voiced her opinion.

"Someone spent months teaching them to work together and to obey commands."

That someone had been Brian O'Toole, Megan's father and the man who had been reputed to be the best horse trainer in the state. He was also the man who was widely believed to have . . . Jane pushed those thoughts aside. There was nothing to be gained by reviving ugly rumors.

"Do you suppose this black beauty will ever obey me?" she demanded when she had stalled the motor for what seemed like the hundredth time.

Brad laid his hand on hers and began to pry her fingertips from the steering wheel. "Just relax," he said. "It's supposed to be fun."

And, after a while, it was. Though the vehicle moved more like a balky mule than a finely trained race horse, Jane had to agree that there was nothing quite so exhilarating as the feeling of being in control of this mechanical masterpiece. There was also nothing quite so exhausting as attempting to remember all of the motions that had to be carefully coordinated if the car were to move. When Brad suggested that they continue their lesson another day, Jane surrendered the steering wheel without a protest.

"I'm amazed at how tired I am," she admitted as Brad drove toward the center of town. She was also amazed at how carefree she felt. The problems that had plagued her all morning were still there, but there was a difference. Now they felt surmountable, and that realization made Jane laugh in sheer delight.

"Were you going somewhere in particular when I distracted you?" Brad asked as they approached Bridge Street.

"Dr. Kellogg's. I want to talk to Bertha." That would be Jane's first stop and her ostensible reason for coming into town. After that, if she just happened to meet Matt . . .

"I'll take you there." Brad continued down Forest, turning onto Rapids. If they had gone a few more yards on Forest, they would have passed Matt's office and saved Jane a short walk. But she had no intention of telling Brad that meeting Matt was the real reason she had come into town. Besides, it was true that she wanted to ask Bertha if she needed assistance with the nursery, now that Anne was gone.

"I always wanted to aid a damsel in distress." Brad's green eyes sparkled with mirth.

"Alas, kind sir, I hesitate to mention that I

was not in distress."

"But this is a mighty steed."

Jane chuckled. "That's one way to describe it." She was still smiling when she reached Matt's house a few minutes after discovering that Bertha was not at home. "It's a nice day for a walk," Jane said as Matt opened the door. Propriety dictated that she not enter the building, but nothing stopped them from walking in the forest that gave the street its name.

"I would hardly call this a nice day." Matt gestured toward the leaden sky. "Still, I suppose walking is preferable to sitting inside."

His expression was little less than a scowl, his tone almost surly. Though Jane kept a smile fixed on her face, she was puzzled by Matt's mood. He was normally the most even tempered person she knew. "If you'd rather not walk, I can go alone."

"No." He shook his head. "I'll get my hat and gloves." The words were ordinary, but, again, the tone was not. It was almost as if Matt were sulking, and that was something Jane had never seen.

They walked in silence for a few minutes until they were outside the town limits and had entered the small forest where they had met so many times before. While casual observers might think that all evergreens were the same, Jane had been there often enough to distinguish between spruce and pine and to identify specific trees. They walked all the way to the tall pine that Jane thought of as the Old Man before Matt spoke.

"Are you lonely with Anne gone?" he asked.

Though the question was logical, it surprised Jane. She had thought that Matt's unusual mood might have been caused by personal worries. Was it possible that he had realized how difficult the day had been for her, and that that was why he was morose? Jane would have thought it unlikely, but the past few months had taught her how little she understood Matt. "I am lonely," she admitted. Jane laid her hand on the tree trunk. Even through her gloves, she could feel the rough bark. "I guess I never thought we would be separated."

Though Matt nodded, the sadness in his eyes did not lessen. "A lot has changed."

Jane murmured her assent. *Including you,* she added silently. *Especially today.* Though she hadn't meant to voice her concerns, the words came out, as if of their own volition. "Is something wrong?"

"Why do you ask that?"

She noticed that Matt didn't deny it.

Instead, he had taken the lawyer's tactic of responding to a question with another, putting her on the defensive. "You seem different today, as if something is bothering you." And that worried Jane. In the past, Matt would have confided in her. But the past was exactly that: past. As Matt said, much had changed.

"You're mistaken. Nothing is wrong."

A prudent woman would have heeded the dismissal in his voice and changed the subject. Today Jane was not prudent. "I don't think so. Matt, I've known you for years. I can read your moods as easily as my siblings and . . ."

"I am not one of your siblings!" This time there was no mistaking Matt's emotion. His words seethed with anger, and for the first time that Jane could recall, that anger was directed at her.

"I'm well aware of that," she said softly, trying to defuse the fury. Matt was not her brother. He had been her best friend for years, and for almost that long she had dreamed that one day they would be more than friends. What she felt for him was most definitely not brotherly. "I want to help you," Jane told Matt, stretching out her hand to lay it on his arm. "A wise man — I believe his name was Matt Wagner — once told me that it helps to talk about problems."

A gust of wind rustling the pine boughs and a blue jay's raucous cry were the only sounds that disturbed the silence. Jane waited. Though he did not brush her hand away, Matt was looking at it as if it were a poisonous object. "There's nothing you can do," he said at last. Her face must have registered her dismay, for he added, "It's not just you, Jane. There's nothing anyone can do. The problem is me."

Jane almost smiled when she realized that Matt's words mirrored her thoughts earlier that day. But she kept her expression neutral, not wanting to do anything that would cause him to stop talking. Perhaps now that he had begun, he would confide in her the way he had so many times before.

"I came back to Hidden Falls with grand aspirations," he said softly. Though she hated to break the connection, Jane drew her hand away. The looks Matt had given it told her that her touch was causing him discomfort. "The reality isn't what I expected."

How well Jane understood that! She had had the same sense of disappointment, or perhaps it was disillusionment, since she'd returned from Europe. "What were you expecting?"

Matt stared at the forest floor for a long moment, his toe brushing acorns away from a tree trunk with an intensity that made Jane think he had no intention of answering her question. At last he raised his eyes to meet hers.

"I probably suffered from the same delusions as every other new attorney. Oh, I never thought I would change the world, but I did expect to be handling more important cases than I've seen so far."

Jane knew that Matt's professors had been concerned when he, who had graduated close to the top of his class at Harvard Law, had announced he would establish his practice in Hidden Falls. This, she suspected, was the reason. A town as small as Hidden Falls simply did not have a great need for an attorney. But, still, there had to be something Jane could say to help Matt.

"Who was your last client?" she asked.

Matt shrugged, his expression indicating that the answer did not excite him. "A mill worker who wanted to purchase a farm for himself and his bride."

Jane thought quickly. Though the case was hardly one that would have challenged Matt's skills, she had to show him that it wasn't a waste of his talent. "I dare say that making sure that the farm is legally his is the most important thing in that man's life right now."

This time it was a pinecone that Matt kicked. "You're probably right." The words were grudging.

"Of course I'm right." As Jane tossed her head to emphasize her assertion, she felt her hat shift. She probably looked disheveled, but if that, combined with the words she planned to utter, made Matt smile, she didn't mind. She placed her hands on her hips and stared at him. "Haven't you noticed that I've grown into a wise old woman?"

Though the corners of Matt's mouth threatened to curve, his reply was delivered in a tone that would not have been out of place in the summation of a murder trial. Jane's heart began to sink. "The evidence would appear to contradict that particular assertion." Matt raised his hand and began to unfurl his fingers as he addressed each of her points. "Number one: you are not old. Number two: your wisdom is in doubt." He straightened a second finger. "As proof thereof, I enter the evidence that a wise woman would not be seen in the company of a man like me." Straightening a third finger, he nodded slowly. "I will, however, grant the fact that you are a woman."

He was joking, Jane told herself. Though his voice was solemn, he must be joking. But, why, oh why, did he make being a woman sound as if it were an epithet? *Oh, Matt! What's wrong?*

Jane shivered and wrapped her arms around herself. Matt's expression was so bleak that it chilled her more than the November day.

"You're cold." Matt took Jane's arm and turned her toward the edge of the forest. "It was a mistake to come out here. We won't do it again."

Jane stopped and stared at Matt, not wanting to believe he was serious. Though his words and the way he pronounced them brooked no dissent, Jane could not accept them. She and Matt had met here in every season. Why was this year different?

"I have warm clothes. So do you." She punctuated her sentence with a sneeze.

"Don't you see, Jane? This is not a good idea. You're suffering from the cold. Besides, we both have other things to do. We can't continue to waste time here."

Jane felt warmth rise to her cheeks. "I do not consider this a waste of time," she said, her tone as steely as Matt's had been. "I will be here tomorrow at our regular time. I hope you will, too."

He waited until he was certain she would have crossed to her side of the river before he ventured onto Main Street. Like it or not, he needed food. Matt scowled. What he needed more than nourishment was to leave Hidden Falls. At least if he were hundreds of miles away, he wouldn't have to see Jane with Brad Harrod. He wouldn't have to endure the pain of stepping outside his office and watching her come his direction, totally oblivious to him.

Matt turned right on Rapids, his stride longer than normal, as if the timely acquisition of bread and beans would somehow improve his life. The truth was, nothing was going to improve his life until he learned to live with his jealousy. He could find a euphemism, but why deny it? The sight of Jane and Brad in the automobile had filled him with that ignominious emotion. Though in the past Jane had treated Brad as nothing more than a pesky older brother, today she'd been laughing and looking at him as if he were the one person on earth who could make her smile.

Matt's frown deepened as he entered Hidden Falls' general store. There had been a time when Jane had smiled for him. Unfortunately, those smiles had been rare since she had returned from Europe. Matt regretted that more than he wanted to admit. There had been a time when Jane had told him details of her life and — more important — she'd confided her innermost thoughts. Today she hadn't even alluded to her ride with Brad. Matt had given her the opportunity by asking why she'd ventured out on a cold, damp day. Her response had not been what he'd expected. Jane had shrugged, as if the answer should be apparent, and claimed she wanted to walk with him. As much as he wanted to believe that, Matt the lawyer noted that she had not told the whole truth. Matt the man didn't want to think about the reason for her omission.

He nodded a greeting at the store's proprietor, afraid to say anything until he managed to control his jealousy. That had come when he had seen Jane in that motor car and had realized how right Brad was for her. Everyone in Hidden Falls would agree that they belonged together and that theirs would be the perfect marriage, uniting the town's two leading families. Their parents had been close friends, and judging from the expression he'd seen on the other man's face, Matt knew that if Brad had his way, he and Jane would be more than friends. As for Jane, though the thought wrenched his heart, Matt was afraid that newfound feelings were the reason she'd seemed so different since she'd returned from Switzerland.

"Three cans of beans." Matt forced the words out from between clenched teeth. He didn't want to think of Jane and Brad together, and he most definitely did not want to think about how wrong he had been to come back here. What he had told Jane had been the truth, if not the whole truth. He had returned to Hidden Falls with grand aspirations, but those aspirations weren't related solely to his law practice. The grandest of Matt's aspirations was Jane.

The cliché about magnets and iron filings was trite. Matt knew that, but he also knew that it was a good description of the attraction Jane held for him. From the first day he had attended school and seen her, he had been drawn to her. She had been so quiet, so obviously flustered whenever the teacher called on her. Jane would blush and stammer and look as if she wanted to hide beneath her desk, but she always knew the answer. That was more than you could say about Charles.

Matt tucked the sack of groceries under his arm and strode out the door. He didn't want to think about Charles. As a boy,

Jane's brother had done everything in his power to make Matt's life miserable, and he had succeeded more times than Matt wanted to admit. Though they were grown men now, he saw no sign of Charles changing.

Charles's father had been different. Had Mr. Moreland lived, Matt believed he would have achieved his aspirations. Charles's father had nodded slowly the afternoon that Matt had asked permission to court his daughter, his only stipulation being that Matt say nothing to Jane until he finished law school. Matt had done that. He had graduated from law school, distinguishing himself in the process. There should have been no more obstacles.

Matt ought to be able to tell Jane of his feelings. He ought to be able to ask whether he had a chance of winning her heart or whether she'd already given it to Brad. But how could he, when he knew how much marriage to him would cost her? It wasn't simply that they'd be flouting the caste system that still flourished in Hidden Falls. Somehow they'd overcome the raised eyebrows and the potential shunning that would result from the marriage of Hidden Falls' leading heiress to a man from the wrong side of the town.

The problem was deeper than that. Matt knew what family meant to Jane. After her parents' tragic death, she'd clung to Anne and Charles. That was natural, as was the fact that she'd gone to Europe to help Anne through the endless rounds of surgery. Now Anne was gone. Matt had seen how disturbed Jane was that her twin had moved so far away. Charles was all that was left of Jane's family in Hidden Falls, and that was a problem. A big one. Not only would Charles would never, ever approve of Jane's marrying Matt, but he might even refuse to see his sister if she dared to defy him. That would leave Jane with no family at all. Matt couldn't let that happen to the woman he loved. He couldn't deprive her of her brother. And that brought him full circle. He should not have returned to Hidden Falls.

When he saw a gaggle of women approaching on this side of the street, Matt crossed it, only to discover that he had exchanged one problem for another.

"Good afternoon, my boy." Ralph Chambers stood in the doorway of his office. Since he wore no hat or coat, Matt realized Hidden Falls' senior attorney must have seen him enter the general store and had been waiting for him to emerge. That supposition was confirmed by Ralph's next words. "If you have some time to spend with an old man, I'd like to talk to you."

"Certainly, sir." Though Matt doubted he would be congenial company, the older attorney had served as his mentor during the difficult years. He couldn't snub him today. And so he followed Ralph into his office, marking — not for the first time — the differences between it and his own. It wasn't simply the greater size and the polished wood furniture, nor was it the fact that all the chairs were comfortably upholstered in leather. The biggest difference was intangible, but Matt was certain that even a casual visitor would recognize that this office belonged to a trustworthy man. His own, he was afraid, did not have the same aura. For all too many people, no matter where he located his office or how he furnished it, it would always be the office of Matt Wagner, Hidden Falls' hellion.

"I had thought to see you at Anne Moreland's wedding," Ralph said as soon as they were seated. He never had minced words, Matt reflected, and had, in fact, told Matt more than once that a direct question was the best way to elicit a candid response. Today, however, Ralph would learn no more than Matt chose to tell him, even though he had eschewed his normal seat behind the desk and sat at Matt's side.

"I didn't think it wise to attend," Matt said. "There are still many in Hidden Falls who can't forget the past." Charles Moreland first among them.

"I believe there are fewer every month. In fact, my boy, that's the reason I wanted to have this conversation." The attorney removed his spectacles, polished them carefully, then slid them back on his nose before he continued. He was, Matt knew, delaying deliberately to heighten Matt's interest. That was another technique his mentor had taught him.

"When you returned from Harvard," the older man said, "you asked me to take you on as my junior partner."

"And you refused." At the time, it had seemed a devastating blow, the first hint that returning to Hidden Falls would not be the answer to Matt's dreams.

"So I did. The reasons seemed prudent at the time, but now . . ."

Matt couldn't let him continue. "I am no longer interested in a partnership."

"I thought you'd say that." Behind his spectacles, Ralph's gray eyes seemed to shine with approval. "I had no intention of offering you a partnership. The fact is, I can't avoid noticing that I'm getting older." He touched his hair, which was now completely gray. "I've spent a lot of time thinking about what I want to do before I die, and I realized that I want to travel. Before I can do that, I need to be certain my clients will have someone they can trust." Ralph leaned toward Matt. "Let me get to the heart of this. Would you be willing to take over my practice next spring?"

Matt blinked. A year ago, he would have agreed with no hesitation. He would, in fact, have been elated. But that was a year ago, before he had realized how much had changed.

"I'm not sure, sir."

"You look as if you need a cup of tea." Susannah's smile was as warm as the beverage she offered. Jane suspected her sister-in-law had been waiting for her return, because no sooner had she entered the front hall than she heard the sound of Susannah's footsteps on the staircase. The smudge on her cheek and the flakes of paint on her fingers told Jane that her sister-in-law had been in her attic studio, painting. That didn't surprise Jane. What did was the fact that Susannah had interrupted her creative time to greet her. "My mother used to claim tea would cure everything," Susannah explained.

"Hot chocolate was Mrs. Enke's panacea." Jane bent her head to rub Pepper's belly. The black dog's need for attention was a good excuse to keep her all too perceptive sister-in-law from reading her expression. Jane sneezed once and then again.

"*Gesundheit.* Would you prefer cocoa?"

Jane shook her head. "Tea is fine. I am a bit chilled," she admitted, although the reason for the chill was not the weather but Matt's parting words.

"Men can do that to you."

This time Jane looked up, startled. "So can a November afternoon." Today the temperatures hovered at the freezing level.

"I didn't want to admit it, either," Susannah said when she had ordered a pot of tea and some scones. "I'm the last person to give you advice, Jane. After all, I was engaged to the wrong man and would have married him if he hadn't come to his senses and realized that he loved someone else."

His need for attention apparently sated, Pepper fell asleep, leaving Jane with the uncomfortable feeling that she was alone with the Grand Inquisitor. "That's a fascinating story, but I'm not sure why you're telling me it."

Susannah raised one perfectly arched eyebrow, her expression saying she didn't believe Jane. "Because I saw you and Matt Wagner the night we opened the carousel and because I saw the way you watched the door at Anne's reception. You were looking for someone, and I'm willing to bet that that someone was Matt."

"You'd lose the bet." Jane noted with pleasure that her lie sounded sincere. "Matt was a friend once," she admitted, "but that's over now." And that, unfortunately, was not a lie. Though she could tell herself that this afternoon was an aberration, Jane knew that it was really the culmination of everything that had happened since she had returned from Switzerland. Although they had breached the physical distance between them, there was no ignoring the fact that something divided her and Matt, and whatever that something was, it was greater than the thousands of miles between America and Europe.

"I wish I could believe that." Susannah's expression was serious as she added, "Your brother is more than a little worried that Matt wants to marry you."

Jane shook her head. "If he once did, that's over." And somehow, someday the pain of knowing he didn't love her would subside.

CHAPTER THREE

She wasn't there. Matt had waited in the forest for an extra half-hour, thinking that she might have had more difficulty slipping away from Charles and Susannah's house than when she had lived at Fairlawn. But there was no question about it; she wasn't coming. Matt hurled a pinecone at a tree, trying to defuse his anger. The worst part of it was, it was his fault. He had done many foolish things in his life, but yesterday was the worst. He'd let his jealousy overrule his common sense, and look what he'd gained from that: a miserable morning.

Matt flung another pinecone, his lips thinning with satisfaction as it shattered. Pivoting on his heel, he headed back into town. Though the cold air was the reason his breath was visible, Matt wouldn't have been surprised to see flames of anger shooting from his mouth. How stupid could he be?

"Just as well," he muttered in a vain attempt to convince himself that the emptiness he felt inside would dissipate. Hadn't his mother told him that when something important was taken away, if you looked hard enough, you'd find something of value to take its place? Matt hadn't believed her at the time; it had been impossible to believe that anything good would come from his father's death, although when John Moreland had insisted he attend school and Ralph Chambers had taken him under his wing, Ma had claimed those were positive effects of Pa's death. Matt hadn't believed her years ago and he wasn't certain he believed her now, but this morning he needed all the encouragement he could find.

Perhaps it wasn't coincidence that Ralph had spoken to him when he did. Yesterday's conversation with his mentor had done more than calm Matt. It had also started him thinking about things other than how unsuited he and Jane Moreland were. Even before he'd reached his home, Matt had realized that it was time to make some decisions about his future. There was no ignoring the older attorney's regret that he hadn't traveled while he was young. The reasons why Ralph had never left Hidden Falls once he'd completed his education didn't matter. What did matter was the fact that he wished his life had been different.

Walking home, Matt had found it easy to picture himself thirty or forty years in the future, saying almost the same things to another young man. That was a picture he didn't like. He didn't want to be Ralph Chambers' age and find himself filled with sorrow over things that might have been.

Matt hadn't gotten much sleep last night. He'd paced the floor, trying to decide what it was he wanted to do with his life — besides live happily ever after with Jane, that is. By morning, he had made his decision. He couldn't change everything that was wrong with the world or even with Hidden Falls. Matt was realistic enough to know that. But he knew that, if he tried, he could make a difference. It might not be earth-shaking, but even a small difference could be important. As he strode back into town, Matt knew exactly where he would start.

"You and I have nothing to say to each other." Charles rose from behind his desk and met Matt at the doorway of his office, his stance proclaiming as loudly as his words the fact that he had no intention of allowing Matt to enter his sanctum.

"You disappoint me, Charles. You're so predictable. You always did think you could win every argument by flaunting your name and position in this town." Matt glanced behind him at the clerk who was listening avidly to the conversation. "If you prefer, we can broadcast our business to Hidden Falls; however, I suggest we go inside and close the door."

Grudgingly, Charles ushered him into his office. It was smaller than Matt recalled, though the large potted plant still stood in the corner, and the furniture was what he remembered. Perhaps it was only because he was entering the room as an equal this time that it seemed less impressive than when he'd visited Charles's father here.

"In case you didn't understand me the first time, let me reiterate." Charles remained standing, though without being invited, Matt had taken one of the chairs in front of the desk. "I cannot imagine why you think we have anything to say to each other."

"Once again, you're wrong. And, by the way, intimidation doesn't work against me any more, so you might as well sit down." Matt waited until Charles sank into his chair before he continued. "We have several things to discuss, or at least I have. I had hoped that we could discuss them like two civilized human beings, but if you prefer, I can simply implement my plans without your prior knowledge. I don't need your consent."

Charles blanched, the expression on his face telling Matt he thought those plans involved Jane. If only!

"To what do I owe the dubious pleasure of your presence?" Charles demanded. Though his words were ordinary, the tone left no doubt that his anger was barely under control.

Matt smiled. For once, he felt as if he had the upper hand, and there was no denying the satisfaction that brought. "Your mother would be proud that you've remembered at least some of her etiquette lessons, although she might frown on your inclusion of the word 'dubious' in your greeting."

"Get to the point." His pallor replaced by an angry flush, Charles forced the words through clenched teeth. "I'll listen, but if you think I'll agree . . ."

"Careful, Charles. You don't know what I want."

"Point taken, counselor. Just what is it you want?"

Your sister's hand in marriage. But that wasn't the reason Matt had come here today. He leaned forward ever so slightly. "There was another accident at the mill this week. A worker lost his finger."

Charles raised one brow in the infuriating habit he'd developed as a child. It was designed to show others his superiority, and for a while, it had worked. It did not work today. "This may come as a surprise to you," Charles said in his most acerbic tones, "but I am aware of what is happening in my mill. Aaron Cartwright's ring finger caught when he was adjusting the reed." The reed, Matt knew, was a wire comb that kept the warp even on the looms, ensuring the smooth weave for which Moreland Mills was famous.

"It shouldn't have happened."

"On that point, you and I are in agreement." Charles sounded surprised that they had found common ground. "It will not happen again," he announced, and this time it was Matt who was surprised by his certainty. How could Charles ensure that no one else would lose a finger or sustain a severe laceration? As if he sensed Matt's question, Charles continued. "I have instituted a new policy. Workers will wear no rings other than simple bands. That means there will be nothing to get caught on either the yarn or any of the moving equipment."

Matt wasn't sure which was stronger, his surprise or his annoyance. He hadn't heard about the new policy, and that surprised him. It also annoyed him that no one at the mill had mentioned it to him. What was happening to his group of informants? They were supposed to keep him apprised of everything that occurred at Moreland Mills.

"That's one step," Matt conceded, "and it's a good one." The fact that he did not like Charles was no reason not to give the man credit for what he'd done. "We need additional changes. The work day is too long. People are having accidents because they're tired."

Charles shook his head. "Moreland Mills' workday is no longer than any other mill's, and we have the fewest injuries in the country. This is a good place to work."

"But it could be better." Matt was convinced of that.

Charles rose and pointed toward the door. "Give up, Matt. You're chasing ghosts."

It was the first time he had heard the expression, but Matt couldn't deny that there might be some truth to it. After all, there was more than one ghost in Hidden Falls.

"I'm sorry to be so much trouble." Jane managed to prop herself up long enough to sip the water Susannah had brought her. Though both Megan and Moira O'Toole were working today, Susannah had insisted on caring for Jane herself.

"Nonsense," her sister-in-law said. "What is important is getting you well again."

Jane sank back on the pillows, astonished that the effort to drink had exhausted her reserve of energy. "I've never felt this way, as if my legs won't support me." What she had thought was nothing other than a chill had proven to be considerably more serious. The one time Jane had tried to venture out of bed, she had been so dizzy that she had collapsed on the floor. It was the thump that had alerted Susannah to Jane's illness.

"That's the fever." Susannah's diagnosis was as confident as if she were a physician. "You'll feel better in a few days when it breaks. Meanwhile, the best thing is for you to try to sleep for the rest of today."

The rest of today? The drapes were still drawn, giving Jane no clue to the passage of time. "What time is it?"

"Almost two-thirty."

"Oh!" It wasn't simply that she had missed half the day. More important, she had missed her walk with Matt. Jane tried not to wince at the thought that he might have gone to the forest, despite his insistence that they would not meet again. Perhaps it had been the fever rattling her brain; perhaps it was only wishful thinking, but Jane had tried to convince herself that Matt hadn't meant that.

"Is there something else I can do?" Lines of concern formed between Susannah's eyes as she laid a cold compress on Jane's forehead.

Weakly, Jane shook her head. But the next morning when she realized that she could not walk to the doorway, much less to the forest, Jane nodded at her sister-in-law. "There is something you can do for me today."

"Certainly. What is it?"

"I would prefer that Charles not know about this."

Susannah frowned, her lovely brown eyes dark with consternation. "Charles and I don't keep secrets from each other."

"Please, Susannah. Just this once." The fever had made Jane so miserable that she couldn't bear the thought of arguing with her brother, and he would disapprove if he knew what Jane wanted.

"Tell me what you need done," Susannah said at last, "and then I'll decide."

It was the best she could hope for. "Please phone Matt. Tell him I'm ill."

The clock in the hallway chimed the half-hour. The day was passing, and Matt had to know Jane hadn't deliberately ignored him.

"I thought your friendship with him had ended." Susannah's frown telegraphed her disapproval.

"It has." Or it would, if Matt was serious about what he'd said the last time they had met. "But he's used to seeing me walking around town. I don't want him to worry." Even to Jane's ears, the story rang false; fortunately, Susannah agreed, albeit grudgingly, to make the call.

For the first time all day, Matt was smiling when Al Roberts entered his office. Though he hadn't liked the message Susannah Moreland had delivered and though he worried that Jane's illness was more serious than her sister-in-law claimed, Matt couldn't deny that he was relieved. As worrisome as sickness was, he felt a rush of pleasure that Jane's absence wasn't caused by either his foolish words or her spending more time with Brad Harrod. If luck was with him, she would soon be recovered and — if he was especially fortunate — she would forgive him his hasty words. Even if he never realized his dream of making Jane his wife, Matt couldn't bear the thought of losing her friendship.

Still smiling, he rifled through a stack of

paper. "Everything appears to be in order," Matt told his client as he handed him the bill of sale he had drafted after he'd reviewed the details of the land purchase.

"Thanks, Matt. Me and Millie sure do appreciate it." The man's grin was more eloquent than his words, underscoring the truth of what Jane had told Matt, namely that knowing his farm was legally his was one of the most important things in Al Roberts' life. "I don't reckon it's likely," the mill worker said, "but if you ever need my help, all you gotta do is ask."

Matt nodded slowly. This was the opening he sought. "There is one thing you can do for me." When Al Roberts' eyes widened in obvious surprise that Matt was consulting him, he continued. "Would you tell the workers that I'm going to have a meeting next Sunday afternoon? I want to talk about how we can improve conditions at the mill."

That was, Matt had realized, his best chance of accomplishing something for the mill hands. It was obvious from their conversation that Charles wouldn't listen to him. Whether it was because of personal animosity or the fact that Matt was only one voice didn't matter. The effect was the same. His hope now was that Charles would pay attention if all of his workers delivered the same message.

It was one of the longest weeks Matt could remember. Part of the reason, he knew, was that he was worried about the meeting. He'd outlined the points he wanted to make countless times, trying to find the phrases that would convince the men to join him, only to rip the pages in half and start anew. That had been frustrating, but the major reason the days had passed so slowly was that Matt had not seen Jane. She was, he had learned, recovering from whatever had ailed her, but she still could not leave the house. Matt missed their walks. He missed their talks. Oh, why not admit it? He missed Jane. And this week had been especially difficult because of the way they'd parted.

Though the meeting was set for two o'clock, Matt arrived at the park half an hour early, thankful that the gray weather that characterized so many November days had blown away, leaving clear skies in its wake. That was, he told himself, a favorable omen. There was no one near the carousel pavilion, but that was no surprise. He hadn't expected anyone to arrive this early.

Matt walked slowly, passing the time by looking at the enclosure some of the mill workers had made for the merry-go-round to protect it from winter's winds and snow.

He had heard that it was Anne's idea that they install a few windows, two fairly close to the ground so that children could use them. Whoever's idea it was, it was a good one. Matt looked through one of the adult-height windows, admiring the view. There was no doubt about it. Rob Ludlow had created a beautiful carousel.

Matt's lips curved in a smile as he thought of the night he had ridden that carousel. Magic. That was the only word he could find to describe it. While he and Jane had ridden side by side, their horses moving up and down as the carousel revolved, the infectious music blaring, the hundreds of lights twinkling, nothing had mattered save the fact that they were together. For a few minutes, Matt had felt totally carefree. For a few minutes, he had believed that he and Jane had a future together. And if that wasn't magic, he didn't know what was.

He pulled out his watch for what seemed like the hundredth time and tried to quell his disappointment. It was two o'clock and only half a dozen men had come. Matt had expected no less than fifty, perhaps even a hundred. There were, after all, more than three hundred workers at Moreland Mills.

"Gentlemen, I appreciate your being so prompt. If you don't mind, though, I think we'll wait a few more minutes."

Two stragglers appeared, but by a quarter after the hour, Matt realized that there would be no others. The clear day had not been the favorable portent he'd thought.

"Thank you for coming." Matt took a seat on the edge of the carousel platform, urging the workers to do the same. There was no point in standing when they were such a small group. There was also no point in delivering the speech he'd prepared so carefully.

"The reason I asked you to come," he said simply, "is that I'm concerned about your safety at the mill. To be blunt, there are too many injuries. Some of them are caused by inadequate lighting, others because you are tired." Though there was silence, two of the men nodded. "One person cannot change Moreland Mills, but if we all work together, I believe that we can make improvements."

When he finished speaking, instead of the clamor that Matt had expected, there was an awkward silence. The men looked at each other; they looked at the ground; they did not look at him. Finally one man spoke up. "I don't know, Matt. Mr. Moreland is mighty fair with us."

A second nodded vigorously. "Yeah. He always does right if someone's hurt."

Matt couldn't argue with that. "The point is," he told the men, "people shouldn't be getting hurt."

The first man shrugged his shoulders. "Accidents happen. Always have. Always will. You can't stop them."

"It can be better," Matt insisted. "I know it can." Once again the men shuffled their feet, as if uncomfortable with his stance, and Matt knew he would accomplish nothing more today. He would have to consider this a seeding mission and hope that those seeds would germinate. "Why don't you go back home, think about it, and we'll meet again?"

Maybe next time there would be more workers and more enthusiasm.

"That man has been nothing but a trouble-maker since the day he was born." Charles stabbed a piece of roast beef with such force that his fork clattered on the china.

Susannah laid her hand on his arm in a gesture designed to calm her husband. "I'm sure that's not true."

Though the dining table at Pleasant Hill could seat twenty, instead of sitting at the foot, yards away from Charles, Susannah had placed herself on Charles's left, with Jane on his right. There was, she declared, no reason to shout from one end of the table to the other. Charles appeared to have forgotten that, for he practically bellowed. "I'm sorry, Susannah, but you didn't live in Hidden Falls then, so you don't know all the trouble he caused. He broke windows, cut open bales of cotton, even dumped manure in my father's office."

There was no question about the subject of Charles's tirade. Not only had Jane heard the same litany of complaints before, but there was no one else who could turn Charles's face that alarming shade of red. "Why are you so riled?" Jane demanded. Susannah might placate Charles, but Jane had no intention of letting him continue to malign her friend. "Matt hasn't done anything wrong in the last ten years. Why can't anyone in Hidden Falls forget the past?"

"I might have known that you'd take his side." Charles glared at Jane, his expression so fierce that a year ago Jane might have quailed. Today she did not. "For your information, Jane, we are no longer talking about the past. It's what that despicable cur did today that has me riled, as you put it." There was the briefest of pauses while Charles took a sip of water. "He had a meeting of the workers. He wants them to band together to make the mill safer. Claims they should have more lights and fewer hours of work." Charles shook his head. "I don't know why he won't accept the fact that Moreland Mills is safe."

"You know the answer to that." Jane buttered a roll, wondering if it would have any more flavor than the beef. Before Charles had started his diatribe, the food had been delicious. Now it was as tasteless as the cotton Moreland Mills turned into fine textiles. "If our father had been killed in the mill, we'd probably feel the same way."

Charles shook his head again, clearly not accepting Jane's logic. "Our father was killed in a fire, and we aren't trying to extinguish every flame in Hidden Falls."

"Maybe that's because you and I weren't in the house that night. Anne was, and she's deathly afraid of fire. Haven't you seen the way she shudders at even a candle flame?"

"That doesn't excuse Matt."

"Yes, it does, but I don't expect you to agree. You're too blinded by the past." Though many things had changed since she'd returned from Europe, Charles's attitude, unfortunately, had not.

"Good morning, Matt." Jane smiled as she spoke into the telephone receiver. It *was* a good morning. For the first time in over a week, she felt well enough to leave the house. "It looks like a lovely day for a walk in the forest."

"I'm surprised you called. I thought we agreed to end those walks." Matt's voice was more acerbic than normal, and there was an undertone of fatigue. Jane had encountered those moods in the past, usually when Matt was worried about something and didn't sleep well.

"You suggested that," Jane reminded him. "I never agreed." And today it was more important than ever that she see him. There were things she wanted to discuss, and a telephone conversation that anyone in Hidden Falls could overhear was not the forum for that discussion.

For a long moment, Matt said nothing, leaving Jane with the fear that he would disconnect the phone. "As it so happens," he said at last, "I'm busy now."

"Then tell me a time when you won't be busy."

She heard his sigh. "You're persistent, aren't you?"

"Yes. It's my finest virtue."

As she had hoped, Matt chuckled and agreed to meet her in an hour.

When she reached the forest, he was waiting for her. "I heard you were ill. I'm sorry."

Jane wrinkled her nose, then inhaled the pungent smell of pine needles. "You can't be as sorry as Susannah. The poor woman insisted on nursing me herself, and I'm not a good patient. All I wanted was to be up and doing things." Instead, Jane had been confined to bed, unable to do anything more strenuous than turn the pages of a book.

She paused for a moment, trying to gauge Matt's mood. Would he be receptive to what she had to say? Though she'd spent the week longing to see Matt again, hoping to reassure herself that he hadn't been serious when he'd declared they should no longer meet, she also wanted to broach a certain subject with him. "I hear you've been doing some things," Jane said as evenly as she could.

Though Matt had been leaning against a pine tree, the picture of relaxation, he snapped to attention. "Did Charles send you here?"

"No!" If Matt was angry, so was she. "I'm surprised you'd think that. First of all, no one sends me anywhere. You ought to know that. And, second, Charles would hardly approve of my being here. You're not exactly his favorite person."

Matt appeared to relax ever so slightly.

"But when you said 'things,' you *were* referring to the workers' meeting."

"Yes. And before you ask, Charles is furious about it. He doesn't understand why you think that it is necessary."

"But you do?"

Jane had the feeling that she was sitting in the witness stand and that Matt was the prosecuting attorney. She nodded. The only good thing she could say about being bedridden for a week was that it had given her time to think. She had replayed the last two times she had seen Matt so often that she was convinced both memories were indelibly etched on her memory. The dance and the dismissal, pleasure and pain, opposite ends of the spectrum.

"I know it's not because of the enmity between you and Charles," Jane told Matt. "I believe you want to reform the mill because of your father and the way he died."

Matt looked away, apparently counting the cones on the closest spruce tree. When he spoke, it was so softly that Jane had to strain to distinguish his words. "Charles told me I was chasing ghosts."

She considered that for a moment, shivering at the image. There was no such thing as ghosts, and yet . . . "I might not have phrased it that way, but violent death —

particularly of a parent — can't help but affect us." Jane fixed her gaze on Matt, and this time he returned it, his dark eyes solemn as he heard her say, "I know I'll never forget the night my parents died."

A gust of wind set the tree boughs to singing. Though the sound was anything but ominous, it reminded Jane of how wind had fanned the flames on what should have been a perfect spring night, and she shivered again.

"That was a horrible accident."

Matt's expression told Jane that he was remembering all that had happened, not just that night but also earlier that day. She shook her head slowly. "It wasn't an accident, Matt. Brian O'Toole set the fire."

She heard Matt's intake of breath and saw his eyes widen in surprise. "I knew Brian had set the fire at the mill, but I hadn't heard that he was responsible for Fairlawn burning."

"That's what the investigator told Charles." Jane didn't try to hide her skepticism. Her surprise when she'd learned the result of the prolonged insurance investigation had been greater than Matt's. "I still can't believe it. Brian was such a gentle man." He and his family had worked at Fairlawn for so many years that when he was dismissed because his periodic bouts of drinking had endangered the horses, Jane had been aware of a sense of emptiness. She had missed the man who trained their horses and who, no matter how busy he was, always had a smile and a story for an inquisitive child.

"He might have been gentle with you, but Brian was angry with your father for firing him," Matt reminded her. "Anger can be a powerful motive."

"Perhaps. But it's still difficult to accept." Jane had had several months to reflect on the investigator's verdict, and it continued to bother her. "Charles said the fire was carefully planned, as were the incidents at the mill. The problem is, Brian wasn't a planner. He was the most impulsive man I know. I could understand him setting a fire in a fit of anger. But premeditated arson? That's not the Brian O'Toole I knew."

Matt nodded slowly, as if he agreed with her. "If Brian wasn't responsible for the fire, who was?"

"I wish I knew. Maybe then that ghost would rest." And maybe she would find the peace that had eluded her since the night of the fire. Jane shook herself mentally. She had not come here to talk about her parents. "What would it take to put your ghost to rest?" she asked Matt.

"That's simple. No more accidents at the mill."

Though Jane doubted it was so simple, she said only, "They're decreasing in both number and severity. You may not want to believe it, but Moreland Mills is the safest one in the country."

"Charles claimed the same thing."

"That's because it's true." Jane laid a hand on Matt's arm, willing him to listen to her. "You can try to unite the workers against Charles. You can even organize strikes, but that won't make the mill any safer."

"Spoken like a Moreland."

"No, Matt, that was spoken like your friend." Even before she had heard of Matt's attempt to organize the workers, Jane had spent hours thinking about him, trying to find a way she could help him. Their last conversation had echoed endlessly while she'd been confined to bed. "You told me you weren't happy here," she said, keeping her voice gentle. Though what she had to say was painful for her, it was important that Matt hear her out. "We both know your talents are wasted in Hidden Falls."

"I didn't say that."

Jane tried not to flinch at the harshness of his reply. "But you thought it. Admit it,

Matt. There's nothing here to challenge you. You're no ordinary lawyer. You graduated near the top of your class. With your talent, you could be working for a large firm in New York or Philadelphia. They'd give you a variety of cases and a chance to use your education."

Matt's eyes narrowed until they were little more than slits. "Are you telling me to leave Hidden Falls?"

This time Jane did flinch, but she kept her voice light as she said, "I'd never tell you to do anything. Remember that I've known you for a long time. I know how you react when someone orders you to do something." Jane took a deep breath and continued, "All I'm suggesting is that you think about what you really want." Matt stood there, as silent as one of the trees on a still day. "Remember the night we rode the carousel?" It was a night Jane knew she would never forget. "Every time we passed the ring machine, you stretched out your arm. You were so determined to catch the brass ring and so disappointed when all you caught were the ordinary tin ones." What Matt didn't know was that when Rob's helpers had loaded the rings into the machine, they had forgotten to add the brass ring. That was, Jane was convinced, the only reason Matt hadn't captured it.

She looked up at him, hoping he would understand how difficult it was for her to tell him to leave. More than almost anything, Jane wanted Matt to remain in Hidden Falls. In her dreams, they lived happily ever after in a small cottage on his side of the river. It was a dream that had helped Jane survive the year in Switzerland when she'd been so homesick. Though it was a wonderful dream, the last weeks had made Jane realize it would never come true. Even if she and Matt married, she knew he would be miserable trying to practice law here. Jane couldn't let that happen. Matt deserved happiness, and she would do everything she could to help him find that happiness, even if it meant sacrificing her own dreams.

"No one can do this for you, Matt. You need to decide what the brass ring in your life is and then reach for it."

He looked at her, his expression inscrutable. "You have this all figured out, don't you?" For once, his voice was as difficult to read as his face.

"I spent a week able to do very little other than think," she admitted.

"Well, Jane, if you've done all that thinking, answer one question for me. What is your brass ring?"

It was the question that had haunted her since her return. "I wish I knew."

The night was cool and clear, the perfect weather for a party. Jane clung to the shadows as she hurried along River Road, lest a late-arriving guest see her and ask why she wasn't going to Rose Walk. How could she explain her old dress and her tear-stained face when even she didn't fully understand? All she knew was that she had to escape. She had to be with the one person who could provide comfort.

Lights gleamed in every window of the Harrods' house, and the sound of revelry spilled into the evening air. Jane knew that if she were closer, she would be able to smell the blend of perfume, flowers, and tobacco as all of Hidden Falls' society celebrated the Harrods' silver wedding anniversary. Everyone, that is, except for their closest friends, the Morelands.

Jane gathered her skirt in both hands and ran, anxious to pass the sight of the festivities. The muslin that she gripped was a far cry from the soft silk of the ball gown she had expected to wear tonight. She and Anne as well as their mother had ordered new gowns, and Charles had come home from New York especially for the party. The gowns still hung in their armoires, while Charles . . . Jane didn't want to think about Charles.

The Harrods' anniversary celebration was to be the social event of the year. And, judging from the number of carriages that lined the driveway and the music that filled the air, it was. This was also to have been one of the happiest weekends in Jane's life. It was not.

She stopped to catch her breath, her heart racing as much from the memories as from running. "Don't tell anyone else," Matt had written in his last letter, "but I have an appointment with your father." Jane had clutched the letter to her heart, a rush of excitement filling her as she considered the reasons for Matt's visit. Whatever the appointment was, it had to be an important one, she knew, or Matt would not have spent the money for an extra train ticket to Hidden Falls. His money was carefully budgeted to last until graduation and left little for unplanned expenses like this trip, but something had brought him home today. There could have been a dozen reasons why he wanted to speak with Papa. Jane knew that. But she hoped — oh, how she hoped — that she was right in believing that Matt was coming to ask Papa for permission to court her.

Jane's feet began to move again, a swift walk now that she had turned onto Bridge

Street. It would not be seemly to run through town. But soon — soon — she would be with Matt. He would help her make sense of today's madness, and maybe he would say the words she'd dreamed of for so long.

She and Matt had been friends for more than ten years. At first that had been enough. Jane had needed nothing more than friendship in those early years. But somehow over time their relationship had changed, deepening. Though neither one of them had pronounced the word love, Jane knew that was what she felt for Matt, and she believed with all her heart that he felt the same way.

What she felt was so precious, she didn't want to share it with her mother or even Anne. Jane held it close to her like a rare night-blooming flower that would wilt if exposed to the sun. Thoughts of Matt accompanied her on the most mundane of tasks, and when something wonderful happened, she was filled with an intense longing to share the pleasure with him.

When they were apart, she counted the days until she would see him again and cherished every letter he sent her. When they were together, each moment seemed special. Though her vision of the future was murky, Jane knew that Matt would be there with her, sharing each day. He had to be, or the future would be unbearable.

She climbed the small hill, turning right onto Forest. Soon! Soon she'd be with Matt! It had been so strange, seeing him earlier today but being unable to speak with him. Matt had told her the appointment was at two o'clock and that it would be at Fairlawn, not the mill. At a quarter to two, Jane had stationed herself at an upstairs window where she could watch the driveway. It had been months since she'd seen Matt, and she longed for a glimpse of the man she loved. There he was, his stride as confident as ever. Jane willed him to look up at her, but he kept his eyes focused on the front door. She waited, anxiously wondering how long he would be. Whatever he discussed with Papa, it was a short meeting, for less than ten minutes later, Matt walked back down the driveway. He turned once, and though he did not appear to realize she was watching, Jane saw that he was smiling. It was surely a good omen.

She had started to descend the stairs, intending to run after him, then stopped herself. Matt had insisted that they would not meet until the next morning when the Harrods' party was over. It would be too risky, he had told her, for her to try to slip away from Fairlawn when everyone was preparing for the celebration. She could wait, especially since she had seen that smile on Matt's face. Clutching happiness to her like the doll that had once been her constant companion, Jane went outside, her thoughts focused on the Harrods' party. Though her mother had a garden filled with perfect roses, Jane wanted to weave some of the small wild ones that grew near the old swimming hole into her hair. She slung a basket over her arm and almost skipped toward the pond. Oh, what a beautiful day it had been!

Jane tried not to frown as her feet propelled her down Forest, but memories of how a seemingly perfect day had been transformed into a nightmare would not be ignored. She had been gone from Fairlawn no more than half an hour, but by the time Jane returned to the house, the world she knew had shattered. No one was certain what had happened other than that Charles had come home earlier than expected, and something had provoked a violent argument between him and Papa. That in itself was strange, for Charles and Papa never argued, not even when Charles had declared his intention of establishing his own business in New York City rather than taking what Papa considered his rightful role at Moreland Mills. Mrs. Enke had told Jane she heard the shouting but could not distinguish the words. Whatever caused it, the argument was serious, for Charles had left, and nothing had been right after that.

Dinner that night was the worst hour Jane could remember. Mama's face was still tear-stained, and Papa's had been gray with worry. Neither would say why Charles had left, simply that he had needed to return to New York, and that under the circumstances, the family would not attend the Harrods' party. Anne had been distraught, taking no comfort from anything Jane said. Finally, unable to bear the tension that filled the house, Jane had slipped out as she had so many times before. That was why even now her feet were carrying her to her friend. Though Matt wouldn't be expecting her, she knew where she could find him.

"What's wrong, Jane?" Matt's forehead furrowed when he opened the door and saw her on his step. "Why aren't you at the party?"

At the sight of his familiar, beloved face, the tears Jane had tried so hard to hold back began to fall. "Oh, Matt! I'm worried!" He waited until she had pulled a handkerchief from her pocket and had blotted her tears before he took her arm and led her to the forest. Though the sun had set, they had come that way so often that their feet needed little illumination to find the path.

"I don't know what's wrong," Jane said when

she and Matt were seated on a fallen log. "All I know is that it's something horrible, and nothing will ever be the same again." She blinked furiously in an attempt to keep her tears from falling.

Matt pressed her hand between both of his. "Tempers cool," he said softly. "Even Charles's."

Though his words and his gesture were meant to be reassuring, they provided little comfort. "You didn't see the way Mama and Papa looked. I've never seen them that way."

Matt was silent for a moment, and Jane knew he was searching for the right phrases. "I know your father, Jane," he said at last. "He loves all of you. He'll mend whatever is broken." Matt squeezed Jane's hand. "It will be all right."

But it wasn't.

She was the first to see the eerie glow that lit the eastern sky. Jane leaped to her feet and ran to the edge of the forest. "It's Fairlawn!" she cried, her voice shrill with fear. "Fairlawn's on fire!"

Matt grabbed her hand, and together they raced through the town and up the hill, but by the time they reached Fairlawn, it was too late. Jane's parents were dead, and Anne had been horribly burned trying to rescue them.

Nothing had been the same since that night.

CHAPTER FOUR

"Brad Harrod is here." With the familiarity they'd developed when her family worked at Fairlawn, Megan O'Toole gave only a perfunctory knock, entering the small library without waiting for Jane's response. "Sure and it looks like he's come courtin'."

Jane refused to be annoyed either by the fact that Megan's interruption had startled Jane so much that she'd left an ink blot on the letter she'd been writing to Anne, or by Megan's impertinent comment. Jane could copy the letter and still have it ready for tomorrow's post. As for the ridiculous assertion about courting, it seemed likely that Megan couldn't help herself. Judging from the way she looked at Charles every time they were in the same room, it was clear that the lovely brunet had romance on her mind. But just because Megan had misinterpreted Brad's actions didn't mean that everyone in Hidden Falls was equally preoccupied with thoughts of love and marriage.

"Nonsense." Jane wrinkled her nose in an attempt to tell Megan how mistaken she was. She glanced out the window. The afternoon was sunny, a rarity for this part of November. Brad probably wanted an excuse to be outdoors. Though she owed Megan no explanation, Jane said, "Brad is bored. He doesn't have much to fill his days, since his father doesn't need his help with the railroad. I'm sure he came here because he wants some companionship."

"If you say so." Megan sketched a saucy curtsey and backed out of the room in a parody of the perfect servant, leaving Jane smiling. The smile was still on her face when she greeted Brad. Though normally she would have met him in the parlor, today Jane ushered him into the small morning room where she'd been writing. Despite its name, the room received afternoon sunshine and was pleasantly warm today.

"You're more lovely than a day in spring," Brad announced.

His green eyes seemed serious, and a faint flush stained his cheeks. Courting. Megan's words echoed in Jane's head. It couldn't be true. Jane raised an eyebrow as she motioned Brad toward the chair facing hers.

She needed to show him, as diplomatically as she could, that she had no desire to be courted. "Why, Brad, I didn't know you read poetry. I told Megan you were bored, but I hadn't realized how extreme the situation had become. Memorizing poetry. Oh, my."

Brad seemed unfazed by her lightly mocking tone. "Can't a man compliment a beautiful woman?"

Jane tried not to sigh. Megan was right. Brad was acting as if he were a suitor, not simply a friend and neighbor. Jane didn't want to hurt him by telling him how uncomfortable that made her feel, but she couldn't let him continue. Brad was not the suitor she wanted. "Is this the boy who used to put frogs in my desk at school, the same one who declared he'd rather dance with a porcupine than with me?"

A wry grin lit Brad's face. "Boys grow into men. They change."

Indeed they did, and it wasn't only Brad. Jane tried not to think of how very much Matt had changed.

"The reason I came was I thought you might be ready for another driving lesson." As if he sensed that she wanted to change the subject, Brad gestured toward the window. "The snow has melted."

As happened almost every year, Hidden Falls had experienced an early storm. Fortunately, like most of the early snowfalls, this one had melted quickly, leaving the roads clear, though muddy.

"That would be wonderful!"

Wrinkling his nose, Brad rose when Jane did. "I wish you'd show that much enthusiasm over my visit."

The relief that had washed over Jane when Brad mentioned driving vanished. They had returned to a topic she did not want to discuss. "You're a dear friend, Brad," she said, emphasizing ever so slightly the word *friend*. "I'm always glad to see you, and I'm more grateful than I can express that you're teaching me to drive." Jane smiled her thanks as Brad held her coat for her. "Do you realize this will be the first time I've been able to do something before Charles? He may never forgive you, but I'm so thankful you've given me this opportunity."

As he had the previous time, Brad drove to the western half of Forest, then surrendered the steering wheel to Jane. Though she feared that she had forgotten some of the techniques Brad had shown her, to Jane's relief, the car responded to her pressure on the pedals and hand lever. Today there was less lurching, and she stalled the motor only once.

"You're doing well." Brad's expression was so woebegone that Jane wanted to pat his head, the way she patted Susannah's dogs when they were feeling glum. "Soon you won't need any more lessons."

Though she knew he wouldn't appreciate a pat on the head, Brad sounded so disappointed that Jane felt the need to reassure him. "Even if that were true — and it isn't — I'd still enjoy going for a ride with you." She accompanied her words with a warm smile, and that appeared to mollify him. Jane returned her attention to the motor car as she continued driving back and forth on the now familiar stretch of road.

Although Brad normally turned the Model T when they reached the end of their route, after an hour, he told Jane that she could try the intricate maneuver. This would be the first time that Jane had attempted to drive the car in reverse. "Go to the edge of the road," he directed. "Then put the car into reverse."

Jane was following Brad's instructions, frowning as she discovered it was more difficult than she'd expected, when she heard the unmistakable sound of another automobile. Her concentration broken, she looked over her shoulder and saw Philip Biddle approaching, his face shaded by his hat, his muffler streaming behind him. Jane muttered in exasperation as she inadvertently stalled the motor.

"I can hardly believe my eyes." Philip pulled his car next to Brad's and leaned across the passenger's seat. "I never saw a lady driving."

Jane tried to hide her chagrin. It had been too much to hope for that no one in Hidden Falls would see her. She suspected that others had observed the driving lessons, but — fortunately for her — they had not mentioned it to Charles. She might not be so lucky this time. "I wouldn't exactly call this driving," she said, wrinkling her nose in a dismay that was only partially feigned. "Despite Brad's expert tutelage, I managed to stall the car again."

"It happens to all of us." Though Philip's words were directed at her, Jane noted the way he appeared to be studying Brad.

"Please don't tell Charles about this," she said, nodding toward the car. "I want to surprise him."

Philip leaned forward. "I won't do anything to spoil your surprise," he promised. "Your brother needs a little jolt every so often to shake him out of his complacency."

It was Jane who felt jolted by Philip's

words. She would not have described Charles as complacent. Though she wondered why Philip had used that word, she forbore asking, reminding herself that people's views differed.

"I drove past Fairlawn." Obviously unaware of the effect his previous statement had on her and the fact that he was introducing a potentially painful topic, Philip continued. "I wonder what your parents would think, knowing no one lives there any longer. There's been a Moreland at Fairlawn since it was built."

Though the sun shone brightly, Jane felt as if a cloud had obscured it. Philip was a family friend. As such he deserved to know their reasons for moving out, but still Jane hated to speak of her home. "It would be different if we could afford to repair Fairlawn, but we used the insurance money to improve the mill." And to recoup the losses from last year's sabotage, although Jane saw no need to mention that. "In its current state, Fairlawn holds too many reminders of the fire." Despite her efforts, Jane's voice trembled. "Both Charles and I agreed that it would be easier if we didn't have to see the damage every day." When Brad laid a comforting hand on Jane's arm, she turned to smile at him. While she was uncomfortable with the idea of Brad as a suitor, there was no doubt that he was a good friend, and good friends were what she needed today.

"It was such a tragedy." Philip's voice deepened as he intoned the words, but his frown eased as he said, "At least now that Brian O'Toole is dead, you no longer have to worry about another fire. You must be thankful for that."

Jane tried to hide her surprise that Philip knew about Brian's alleged role in the fire, then reminded herself that the former banker had been one of her father's closest friends and advisers. Hadn't she just told herself that as a family friend Philip was entitled to be privy to family affairs? It was likely that Charles had told him of the investigator's verdict.

Jane focused on Philip's final words. "I cannot be thankful that anyone is dead." Especially a gentle man like Brian. No matter what the insurance company believed, she could not believe that he had deliberately set Fairlawn on fire.

"We won't be able to do this much longer," Matt said as he and Jane started to descend the path to the falls that gave the town its name. Though visible from the opposite bank of the river, trees and bushes obscured the view from Fairlawn's side. The only way to see them was to take the frequently treacherous path that led from River Road to an overlook. Mist from the cataract could turn the path slippery in any season, but winter's ice made it too dangerous for all but the most intrepid. Jane, who had broken a leg on the path one winter when she had failed to heed her parents' warning, was no longer intrepid.

She stopped and looked up at Matt. "Snow is beautiful, but I hate the idea of being cooped up inside for so many months." Her walks with Matt were by necessity less frequent during the winter. How she wished they were free to meet in public or that Matt could visit her at Pleasant Hill without incurring Charles's wrath. Unfortunately, neither of those was likely to happen any time soon.

"Do you remember how we came here one winter?"

Jane caught her breath at the kaleidoscope of memories Matt's words evoked. How could she forget that day? There had been a January thaw. Though the sky was still the lead-gray that made winter so bleak, Jane's spirits had soared when Matt told her that he'd walked the path, and it was safe.

"Let's go there tomorrow," he suggested.

"I'll bring hot chocolate." Though part of her daily diet, Jane knew it was a luxury for Matt. Somehow she would convince Mrs. Enke that she needed to take a jug of cocoa on her walk, carefully omitting the fact that she would be accompanied on that walk. Mrs. Enke might be her ally in many things, but the woman who served as their housekeeper and cook would feel compelled to tell Jane's parents of the clandestine meetings if she knew of them. Though Mama and Papa might not forbid her to see Matt, that was a chance Jane was unwilling to take. Walks with Matt were too important to jeopardize.

Matt was waiting when she reached the path, and judging from the color of his face, Jane could tell that he had been waiting for quite a while. Even during the thaw, a January day was cold.

"Here, Matt." As soon as they were out of sight of the road, she took the insulated jug from the sack. She had planned to save the treat until they reached the overlook, but Matt's obvious chill made her reconsider. "Let's have some cocoa." Jane pulled out the small blanket that she'd brought with her and spread it on the ground. Though the cold would soon seep through it, the blanket would allow them to sit for a few minutes as they drank the fragrant beverage.

"This is delicious!" Jane smiled at Matt's obvious pleasure and poured him another cup. Perhaps she could convince Mrs. Enke to teach her how to make hot chocolate. Then she wouldn't have to invent stories each time she wanted a thermos of it. She could bring some for Matt whenever they walked. Jane sipped her own beverage slowly. Though she wanted to see the falls, she found herself reluctant for this moment to end. Surely nothing could be better than watching Matt's smile as he savored the cocoa.

When he drained the last drop, he rose and extended his hand to her. "The falls await, m'lady."

To Jane's surprise she found herself blushing. It was not like Matt to use such flowery phrases. When he didn't call her Jane, his favorite nickname seemed to be "hoyden." It was a far cry from hoyden to m'lady, and Jane couldn't help wondering what had wrought the change. Was there something magical in the hot chocolate?

Perhaps she was distracted by the idea. Perhaps it would have happened anyway. When she thought about it afterward, Jane wasn't certain. All she knew was that she stepped on an icy patch, and suddenly she was slipping, sliding forward, certain to land face first in the mud.

"Jane!" Matt shouted the word, then grabbed her, wrapping his arms around her waist in an attempt to break the fall. It should have worked, but the momentum was too great, and before Jane knew what was happening, they were tumbling together, rolling down the hill. Their heavy winter clothing saved them from all but minor bruises, and with Matt's arms around her, Jane's fear vanished. Matt would keep her safe, she knew instinctively, and so she did nothing to break the fall.

When they stopped, their faces only inches apart, Jane could smell the sweet scent of chocolate on Matt's breath and see the spatters of mud that had landed on his nose. She heard his rapid breathing and felt the strength of his arms around her. But most of all, she saw his expression as he looked at her. Though she'd known Matt for years and had seen him in many different situations, today his brown eyes were filled with an unfamiliar warmth, a warmth that sent shivers along Jane's spine.

Neither one of them spoke, and yet Jane knew that they had reached a turning point. No longer could she claim that what she felt for Matt was simple friendship, for in that moment when she had gazed into his eyes, she realized that she loved him.

An icicle fell from one of the pines, shattering when it hit the ground, the soft clinking of the ice shards bringing Jane back to the present. "I'm afraid I didn't bring any cocoa today," she said, hoping that her voice did not betray the emotions her memories had raised.

Though they had been walking, Matt stopped and faced her. "Is that what you remember most about that day?"

"No." There was no reason to deny the truth. Jane only hoped that he wouldn't ask her what her most vivid memories were, for though she did not want to lie to him, she was not ready to declare her love. Before the fire she would have gladly told Matt her deepest thoughts, but that was the old Matt. She wasn't certain the new Matt Wagner wanted to know them.

To Jane's relief, Matt shook his head. "Me, neither. What I remember is how much I wanted to take your hand in mine and hold it while we walked."

In the distance, Jane heard the falls. They were muted now, the result of autumn's diminished water levels.

"Why didn't you?"

Matt raised an eyebrow, as if to tell her she ought to know the answer. "Oh, Jane. We were so young then. I was afraid you'd refuse, and I didn't think I could bear that."

"I wouldn't have refused." Jane stretched out her hand. It was too late to change what had happened then, but there was no reason not to grant Matt's wish today. Though he'd seemed unwilling to have her touch him when they were in the forest, today was different. Today she sensed the touch of her hand might make him happy, and there was nothing Jane wanted more than to bring Matt happiness.

He stared pointedly at her hand and shook his head. "My fantasy was to hold your hand. Not your glove."

"Oh!" Jane's eyes widened. No wonder Matt had feared that she would refuse. Mama would have been shocked at the very idea. After all, a lady did not permit such liberties, not to a man who was not her husband. Gloves, Mama had insisted, were never to be removed outside of the home. But Mama wasn't here, and Jane was no longer a young girl. Hadn't she said she would do anything she could to make Matt happy? Jane started to unbutton her glove, then, as Matt followed suit with his, she slipped the glove from her hand.

In the moment before their hands touched, the air chilled Jane. An instant later, all thoughts of cold were banished by the warmth of Matt's hand on hers and the smile he gave her. The smile made Jane feel that it was Christmas morning and Matt had just opened her present to him, discovering it was the gift he'd dreamed of all year. The smile made Jane's skin tingle with pleasure.

Then there was his hand. Ah, his hand. Matt's skin was rougher than Jane had expected, his muscles firmer than hers, his fingertips blunt rather than rounded like hers. Her mind registered the differences while her heart reveled in the glorious sensation of having her palm pressed to his, her fingers laced with his. It was, Jane tried to remind herself, nothing but a hand. There was no reason to feel this way, as if something special, something monumental, was happening. Jane tried not to shiver with delight, but she failed utterly and completely. This was Matt's hand, and having hers clasped in his was more wonderful than she could have dreamed.

"I wish today would never end," she said softly.

Matt squeezed her hand, sending fresh waves of pleasure up her arm. "So do I."

"You're looking much better," Susannah said. She and Jane were seated in the parlor, accompanied as always by the two dogs. When she had returned from her walk with Matt, the dogs had sniffed Jane's skirt and boots with more interest than normal. Was she carrying Matt's scent, or was it simply the fresh smells of the path that intrigued the dogs?

"So are you." Jane tried to keep her attention focused on the woman seated across from her rather than dwelling on the memory of Matt's hand holding hers. Susannah's bouts of morning sickness had ended, and she fairly glowed with health and happiness. Jane wondered if her own face betrayed her excitement. The time she and Matt had spent together had been unforgettable.

Susannah patted Pepper's head, then smiled at Jane. "I told Charles this baby had better be worth all the trouble he's causing."

"*She* will be." Salt, obviously jealous of the attention his sibling was receiving, nudged Jane's shoe. Obligingly, Jane stroked the white dog's head so that he would not feel excluded. Envy was something she understood. Though she was happy for Susannah and Charles, when she saw how radiant Susannah was, Jane couldn't help but wish she were the one who was happily married and expecting a baby. It was so very easy to imagine herself holding a small child, a child with Matt's dark hair and eyes, and when she did that, pangs of longing swept through her.

"Then you agree that you would prefer kerosene to cream in your tea."

"What?" Jane stared at her sister-in-law. Why was she suddenly spouting nonsense?

"I was only teasing." Susannah's smile was a knowing one. "You were engaging in what my mother would have called wool-gathering."

Jane couldn't deny that she'd been lost in a dream world. "I'm sorry. I was caught up in my thoughts."

Megan O'Toole knocked firmly, then carried the tea tray into the room. Taking advantage of Susannah's momentary distraction, the black dog jumped onto the settee. "Down, Pepper." Susannah lifted the dog and placed him firmly on the floor. When Megan had left, Susannah faced Jane. "They looked like deep thoughts," she said. "And, if I'm not mistaken, the object of those thoughts was a man." Though Susannah continued to smile, her eyes were serious. "If the man in question is who I think it is, you needn't worry. That's one secret I will not share with Charles. He won't be pleased if he learns that you're still seeing Matt, but it's your life and your happiness that are at stake, not Charles's."

Relief flowed through Jane. She wanted — no, she needed — to talk to someone about her feelings. If Anne were here, she would have been Jane's confidante, but Anne was hundreds of miles away. And though Jane valued Susannah's advice, she hadn't wanted to place her in the awkward position of choosing between her friendship with Jane and her loyalty to her husband.

"Thank you," Jane said simply. "I feel as if I'm bursting, wanting to speak of him but being afraid to put my thoughts into words."

Susannah nodded, encouraging Jane to continue. "I thought you said your friendship was ending."

"I'm so confused," Jane admitted. "Before I was sick, Matt acted as if he didn't want to see me again, but now things seem back to normal." Better than normal, for today's walk and the touch of his hand had been so special. "I don't know what to do. I want Matt to be happy, but I know that life in Hidden Falls will never be enough for him. His talents are wasted here." Jane took a sip of tea, hoping it would calm her nerves. "I know Matt needs to live in a big city. The problem is, I don't know how I'll bear it when he leaves." Squeezing her eyes closed, Jane tried to block the image of a life without Matt.

"Oh, Susannah, I love him so much that it hurts. It's wonderful and yet it's awful, and I'm so afraid that he doesn't love me." Jane knew that she was babbling, but once the gate was opened, her words rushed out.

"I know how you feel." Susannah reached out to lay her hand on Jane's. The glow had faded from her cheeks, and her eyes were dark with remembered pain. "We all believe that falling in love will be easy, but it's not. It's a path with so many obstacles that sometimes we wonder if we'll ever reach the end or if the dream of happiness is just that — a dream." Susannah squeezed Jane's hand, her touch reminding Jane of another hand, one that felt far different.

"If you knew how much I worried about your brother and how many sleepless nights I spent —" Susannah sighed. "It wasn't only that I worried Charles might not love me. At one point, I thought he loved someone else."

"Megan?"

Susannah looked up from the tea she was pouring, her surprise evident. "How did you know? You weren't here."

"I've seen the way she looks at him. I

don't know whether it's love or simply infatuation, but Megan cares for Charles."

Susannah nodded. "Charles told me that as a very young man he made the mistake of kissing her once, and in her mind Megan turned that into a declaration of love. Whatever feelings she harbors, I can assure you that they're one-sided. Charles feels nothing for her other than pity that her father died." Susannah handed Jane a teacup. "That's why, even though I think she would be happier somewhere else, I cannot dismiss Megan. It would be cruel."

"And you're not cruel."

"Neither, despite what Matt thinks, is Charles."

"You're looking dejected, my boy," Ralph said within seconds of Matt's arrival at his office. That was one of the things that made Ralph Chambers such a successful attorney. He was able to delve to the heart of the matter with no difficulty. "Are you still brooding over the poor attendance at your meeting?" Without waiting for a reply, Ralph said, "The workers have a great deal of loyalty toward the Morelands."

Matt shook his head, wishing it were that simple. "I recognize that, and I'm not done yet. I know people need time to accept new ideas, so I'm planning to hold another meeting. The outcome of the next one will be different. I'm certain of that."

"Then if it's not the workers, what is making you so unhappy?" Tenacity was another of Ralph's most notable characteristics. Matt had once compared him to a terrier digging for a bone, declaring that Ralph wouldn't stop until he had retrieved it. At the time, his mentor had nodded and pointed out that tenacity had served him well. Today Matt wished that trait were a little less developed. Short of leaving the office, which he had no intention of doing, there was nothing Matt could do but answer the question. The truth was, he had come here today, hoping that Ralph could offer advice.

"There's this woman I . . ." Matt swallowed deeply. He hadn't thought it would be so difficult to pronounce the word. He swallowed again, then finished the sentence. ". . . care for." It wasn't what he had meant to say, but there was less danger in using that phrase than in speaking the single, powerful word that his lips refused to utter.

"And she does not . . ." Ralph's pause mirrored Matt's. ". . . care for you." Surely it was Matt's imagination that the older man was biting back a smile. There was nothing amusing about this situation.

"I don't know, sir. I haven't asked her."

"Why not?" Ralph asked the question as easily as if he were cross-examining a witness.

Matt tried not to squirm as he responded. "Her family would not approve of me. They believe she ought to marry someone of their social class." *Someone like Brad Harrod, a man who's been spending far too much time with Jane.*

Ralph was silent for a moment, making Matt wonder whether he had somehow read his thoughts. "This is America, Matt," he said at last. "I won't tell you we don't have classes. Of course we do. But what makes this country great is that we have the opportunity to transcend the class structure. Just because you're born into one doesn't mean you can't move into another." It was the same speech Ralph had given Matt several times before, and it was, to a large extent, the reason Matt had attended law school. He had wanted what Ralph called upward mobility. He'd wanted to be more than a mill hand.

"Intellectually, I know that," Matt admitted. "But I can't dismiss the fear that her family regards me as 'the bad boy.' "

Ralph leaned back in his chair, a pose that

Matt knew meant he was pondering something. Soon he would polish his spectacles.
It was a routine Matt had seen countless
times. "It seems a bit ludicrous," Ralph said
a moment later, "a bachelor like me advis-
ing you on matters of the heart, but I urge
you not to make the same mistake I did."

To Matt's surprise, Ralph did not polish
his spectacles. Instead he rose and walked
slowly to the window. Though his back was
turned to Matt, Ralph's words were clearly
audible. "When I was about your age, I
loved the most beautiful woman in Hidden
Falls." Matt saw the clenched his fists and
knew how much this admission was costing
his mentor. "I wasn't alone in that. At least
one other man felt the same way. Philip
made the same mistake."

"Philip Biddle?"

Ralph turned, his face ashen. "I shouldn't
have said that. It was an unfortunate slip of
the tongue." For the first time in Matt's
memory, the older man was visibly disturbed. "I beg you to keep that information
in strictest confidence."

"Certainly, sir." Matt was an expert at
keeping secrets. "But what was your mistake?" Surely Ralph didn't regard falling in
love as a mistake.

Though he stood a few yards away, Matt

saw the anguish on his mentor's face. "I never told Mary of my love. I believed she loved my best friend, and so I said nothing. Like a fool, I forced myself to remain at a distance, loving her but not admitting it."

The older attorney clenched and un-clenched his fist, his distress obvious. "To this day, I regret it. I wish I had had the courage to tell Mary how I felt. She might have rejected me, but there's a chance she might not have." Matt knew he would long remember the pain that radiated from Ralph's eyes as he said, "Now I'll never know which answer Mary would have given me. All I can tell you is that the saddest day of my life was when she married John Moreland."

For a second Matt was speechless as the identity of Ralph's true love became clear. "You loved Jane's mother?"

"I did, and I still do, even though she's gone." His voice was husky with emotion. "I think about Mary every day and wish I knew whether she had ever — even if only for a moment — regarded me as something more than a friend." Ralph laid a hand on Matt's shoulder. "Don't repeat my foolishness. Tell Jane you love her."

Chapter Five

Tell Jane you love her. The words had echoed inside Matt's head ever since Ralph had pronounced them, an endless refrain that tantalized at the same time that it frustrated. Matt poured hot water into the basin and readied the rest of his shaving equipment. *I love you.* It sounded so simple. Three words. Three syllables. Simple. But it wasn't.

He wrung out the cloth and laid it over his face, wincing at both the heat and the thought of telling Jane he loved her. Ralph's advice had merit. Matt wouldn't deny that. He didn't want to find himself in his mentor's situation, regretting his silence, wondering whether his love was returned. He didn't want to stand on the sidelines, watching Jane marry someone else. Matt wanted to tell her how much he loved her. The problem was, a declaration of love should be followed by a proposal of marriage. That was what a woman had a right to expect.

Why would a man declare his love if he didn't want to marry her? Matt wanted to marry Jane. Indeed, he did, but it wasn't as simple as Ralph implied.

Swirling the brush through the shaving cream, Matt frowned. How could he marry Jane? Even if he could overcome the obstacle of Charles's disapproval — and Matt wasn't certain he could — but, even if that miracle happened, there was still the problem of where he and Jane would live. Matt reached for his razor and frowned again. Finding a home for Jane wasn't the only problem. There was also the not inconsequential question of how to pay for that home. He earned enough to support himself in this spartan building, but his clients' fees would not stretch far enough to pay for food, clothing, and the niceties that a wife deserved. Especially a wife like Jane. She had grown up at Fairlawn with servants, pretty clothes, a beautiful garden. How could he ask her to live with anything less?

Matt peered intently into the mirror as he shaved his face, wishing the problems would disappear as easily as whiskers. There was an answer. He just wasn't certain it was the right one. When he started to frown, Matt forced himself to relax. The last thing he needed was to slice his cheek. The prospect of accepting Ralph's offer and taking over his practice when the older attorney retired in the spring shouldn't elicit a frown. It could be a good solution. Although Ralph had never discussed his annual income, Matt surmised that it would allow him to give Jane a decent home, perhaps even one servant. Though she wouldn't have all the luxuries of Fairlawn, she would still have her standing in Hidden Falls society, for her husband would be counselor for what Matt referred to as the landed gentry as well as the shopkeepers. It would be a good life for Jane, and there was no doubt that marrying her would bring Matt incalculable happiness.

Patting his face dry, Matt glanced out the window. The street teemed with workers, hurrying toward the mill. The workers. This time Matt did frown. If it weren't for them, his decision would be easy. There would be no dilemma. Somehow Matt would convince Charles to consent to his and Jane's marriage, and they would live happily ever after. It was a lovely fantasy, but it ignored the reality of the three hundred men and women who worked for Moreland Mills.

What would happen to them if Matt assumed Ralph's practice? It had taken some persuasion to convince them to consult him here, in a house that was little better than the ones where they lived. Would they even consider coming to a law office on Main Street, or would the fancier surroundings intimidate them? Matt sighed, afraid that he knew the answer. The workers were why a simple declaration of love wasn't simple. As dearly as he loved Jane, Matt couldn't abandon them. After all, they were part of the reason he had returned to Hidden Falls. Charles had claimed Matt was chasing ghosts. Perhaps there was some truth to that, for Matt was still haunted by the memory of his father's lifeless body being carried home from the mill and of his mother's sobbing in the night when she thought Matt wouldn't hear. The day he'd started law school, Matt had vowed he'd do everything in his power to ensure there were no more needless deaths at Moreland Mills.

He closed his eyes for a second, envisioning the scales of justice with Jane on one side, the workers on the other. How did a man weigh those choices? How did he find a compromise that would satisfy everyone?

The knock on the door provided a welcome distraction, and as Al Roberts entered his office, Matt greeted him with more enthusiasm than normal.

"I'm leavin' town," the young man told

Matt. "Just want to tell you again, me and my Millie sure do thank you for all you done."

Matt shook Al's hand and gestured toward one of the visitors' chairs. "It was my pleasure." Jane was right. Though arranging for the purchase of a farm was not a precedent-setting case, it was important to this man and his betrothed, and that knowledge brought a sense of satisfaction. How could Matt abandon Al Roberts and all the others? The answer was simple: he could not.

Though the chair had a sloping back, Al Roberts kept his spine straight, his feet planted firmly on the floor. "I tole the men what you said about working conditions at the mill." The solemn expression on his client's face told Matt that the outcome of those discussions would not be to his liking. "Most of 'em agree with you," Al continued, "but they're worried about their families. Don't want nothing to spoil the younguns' Christmas."

Matt nodded slowly. "I hadn't thought of that." Ever since his mother had died, Christmas had been nothing more than another day on the calendar. There had been no reason to celebrate, but Matt knew that his sentiments were not shared by the rest of Hidden Falls. "Good advice, Al. I'll wait until after New Year's to schedule the next meeting."

And in the meantime, he would speak with Ralph, asking for more information about assuming his practice. There had to be a way to marry Jane without abandoning the workers. All Matt had to do was find it.

Did he love her? That was the question. Jane wandered toward the first shelf of books. Though she had no desire to read this morning, she needed something to occupy her mind, something other than wondering whether Matt loved her. The question echoed endlessly in her mind. Did he or didn't he? Jane pulled a book from the shelf, frowning when she saw it was a treatise on archeological digs in Egypt. That wouldn't hold her attention. Did Matt love her? Jane railed at the strictures of society that declared she couldn't simply ask him. A lady couldn't do such a scandalous thing. Jane frowned again. There had to be some way to learn Matt's true feelings.

"Sure and you look like you've lost your best friend." Megan entered the small library, a dusting rag in her hand. Without waiting for Jane's response, she continued to speak while she flicked the rag across a row of books. "You must be lonely with Anne so far away and you here in a strange house."

As excuses went, it wasn't a bad one, for there was a grain of truth in it. "I do miss my sister," Jane admitted. Had Anne been here, she might have been able to advise Jane. "It's the first time we've been parted." As twins, they had always been close, but the year that they had spent together in Switzerland while Anne endured months of treatments for her burns had made them not just sisters, but allies in the battle against pain.

Megan gave Jane an appraising look, as if she didn't accept her explanation. "Me mam would say you need a man to fill your heart." Megan's eyes sparkled as she added, "And the town folks would like to dance at another wedding."

Images of church bells ringing and herself walking down the aisle made Jane's heart ache. Though it was what she wanted, only Matt knew whether that dream would ever come true. "Perhaps someday," Jane said, pleased that her voice did not reflect her dismay. Perhaps someday she would be Matt's bride. In the meantime, she needed to find something to fill her days. If she were busy, surely she wouldn't spend so much time dreaming of life with Matt and wondering whether he loved her. She needed a purpose for her life. Charles had the mill, Susannah her painting. While she had been here, Anne had had the nursery. Jane smiled. The nursery. That was the answer.

"Thanks, Megan." Though the lovely brunet looked confused by Jane's words, she said nothing more as Jane hurried from the library. Half an hour later, Jane opened the door to the house that Anne had turned into a nursery for the mill workers' youngest children. The first story was a cheerful room filled with children, toys, the aroma of warmed milk, and the sound of laughter. The second floor, Jane knew, contained beds and cribs for the children's naps.

"Good morning, Bertha." Although the scene appeared chaotic, Jane saw no sign of distress on the young woman's face. The daughter of Hidden Falls' physician, Bertha Kellogg had been Anne's assistant and had assumed full responsibility for the nursery when Anne had married. Judging from her serene expression, she was a natural caregiver.

Refusing the coffee that Bertha offered, Jane looked around the room, smiling when she saw that an enterprising child had draped a cloth over a table, creating a fort.

How many times had she and Anne done the same thing in their playroom? What fun it would be to come here every day. Perhaps one day she'd even join a child inside a makeshift fort.

Jane turned back to Bertha. "I remember Anne telling me how much work twelve children can be, and I wondered if you'd like my assistance. It would," she added quickly, "still be your nursery, and, of course, I wouldn't expect to be paid."

To Jane's surprise, Bertha appeared uncomfortable with her suggestion. "It's a very generous offer," she said at last, "but I hired Rachel Wallis last week." Bertha gestured toward the far corner of the room where a young woman sat on the floor, reading to a group of children.

Jane tried to bite back her disappointment. "That was an excellent idea." She couldn't deny it any more than she could deny that she envied Rachel. Bertha had chosen wisely, hiring the daughter of one of the mill hands. By having Rachel here, the other workers would feel as if it were truly their nursery, not the Morelands'. It was the right decision for the nursery, for the workers and for the town as a whole, but it did nothing to ease the emptiness inside Jane. What was she going to do with her days?

She knocked on Matt's door, hoping he'd be able to chase her doldrums. Though the day was cold, there was no reason they could not meet in the forest, unless Matt had a client. He did not. But when he arrived at the big pine tree a few minutes after Jane, he wore a preoccupied expression.

"Is something wrong?" Matt looked the way she felt, alone and confused.

He shrugged, then leaned against an oak tree. If it hadn't been for the tension she saw in his neck and shoulders, Jane might have believed that he was at ease, but she knew him too well to accept his charade. "I'm trying to make a decision," he said, his eyes reflecting his inner turmoil.

Jane's heart leapt at the thought that the decision might involve her. A second later she shook herself mentally. How silly! Matt either loved her or he didn't. There were no decisions involved. "Have you set a date for the next meeting of the workers?" That was, Jane suspected, the cause of Matt's uneasiness. She knew how unhappy he'd been at the poor turnout the last time and how much he worried about the workers. Though he was wrong in thinking Charles would deliberately risk injuries to the mill hands, Jane knew that improvements were always possible, and she couldn't help admiring Matt's commitment to the workers.

"It'll be after New Year's. I think people will have fewer distractions then."

Jane nodded. Matt's logic was solid. She took a deep breath of the cold air, exhaling slowly before she spoke. Would Matt approve of her idea? She didn't know. "I'd like to attend the meeting."

"Why?" Matt abandoned all pretense of being relaxed, taking a step closer to Jane and staring at her as if she had suddenly gone mad.

"I want to show my support." For days, Jane had thought about Matt's plan to organize the workers and her brother's opposition to the idea. Though the two men were too stubborn to admit it, there was some validity to each of their positions. Knowing that it would take a mediator to get them to agree on anything, she had sought a way to reconcile their points of view. "I'm a Moreland," she said.

Matt nodded shortly. "That is precisely why you should not come. The meeting is about convincing the Morelands to change."

Though Matt's tone left no doubt that he opposed Jane's suggestion, she wasn't ready to concede. There were good reasons for her to attend Matt's meeting. He simply needed to understand them. "If I heard what the workers said, perhaps I could use that to persuade Charles. He might listen to me."

Matt raised an eyebrow. "Do you really believe that?"

"Yes." Jane kept her eyes fixed on him, willing him to listen. The man she loved could be just as stubborn as her brother. That was, Jane suspected, part of the reason they'd always been adversaries. "Charles is not an ogre," she told Matt. "He opposed Anne's plan for a nursery at first, but when she insisted, he finally agreed." And, if Jane phrased her arguments for improved mill conditions carefully, Charles would agree with her.

"That was different." Matt looked away, as if he were trying to formulate his response. It was clear that he didn't like the idea of Jane attending the meeting and was seeking reasons to dissuade her. "Anne was arguing for something she wanted. You'd be pitting yourself against your brother for something you don't believe in."

Though Jane wanted to refute that, she could not. She didn't feel passionately about changing the mill. "I believe in you," she said simply.

"Then believe me when I tell you it's best

you not attend the meeting. It would only anger Charles and confuse the workers."

There was no way to counter that argument.

When Megan and Moira had finished serving dinner that evening, Jane turned toward Charles. She hadn't mentioned her idea to Susannah, in part because it had only occurred to her this afternoon. "Next week is Thanksgiving."

Charles's lips curved into a faintly mocking grin. "I cannot help but be aware of that when every conversation in this household seems to center on the size of the turkey." The fond smile he gave Susannah told her he wasn't complaining. Jane suspected that, though he might be loath to admit it, Charles was looking forward to his first Thanksgiving as head of the household. He had told her that, other than attending services at the church last year, he had done nothing special in honor of the day, since he'd been alone at Fairlawn. This year was different.

"How do you suppose the mill hands will celebrate?" After she had left Matt, Jane had deliberately walked by the mill, trying to imagine how she would feel if she worked there. Perhaps Matt was right. Perhaps

Jane's attendance at a meeting would confuse the workers, making them wonder if there were divisions within the Moreland family. That was possible. Jane didn't want to create confusion, but she did want to ensure that everyone who worked at the mill knew that the Morelands cared for them as human beings, not simply a source of wealth.

Charles accepted the gravy boat from Susannah, pouring a generous amount onto his mashed potatoes. "I've given them a half-day off with pay," he said. Then, as if anticipating Jane's protests, he added, "No other mill does that."

"I'm not disputing that, Charles. I simply thought we might do something extra this year." Remembering Megan's comment about the villagers wanting to dance at another wedding, Jane turned to Susannah. "If you and Charles had been married here, there would have been a wedding celebration for the whole town. Since they missed that, I thought we might arrange something special for Thanksgiving instead."

Charles and Susannah exchanged looks. Though she knew her brother well, Jane could not interpret the silent communication. "What did you have in mind?" he asked.

"A nice dinner." When Charles made no comment, Jane continued, "We could use the church hall and have dinner right after the services."

When Charles remained silent, Susannah laid down her fork and knife and smiled first at Jane, then at her husband. "I remember my mother talking about the year President Lincoln declared a day of thanksgiving and how it helped to unite the nation. Perhaps a special celebration will remind the workers of how fortunate they are to be employed by Moreland Mills."

"I don't deny that there is some merit to the idea." Jane's spirits began to soar. From Charles that was high praise. "But," he continued, "it seems to me that preparing and serving dinner for the entire town would require a lot of work. I do not want my wife exhausted, particularly not this year."

He hadn't refused! Jane tried not to grin at the realization that she'd surmounted the largest obstacle. She'd anticipated Charles's concern for Susannah and their unborn child and had an answer for it. "I'm confident Mrs. Harrod and the other women would help if I asked them, and I can enlist the quilting society. Every one of those ladies is a wonderful cook."

Though Jane hadn't grinned, Charles did. "You have everything planned, don't you? What would you have done if I had refused?"

"Found another way to convince you."

Shaking his head, Charles reached for a roll. "What happened to you and Anne in Switzerland? I put two girls on a ship one year, and the next time I saw them, it was almost as if they were strangers. You both changed so much."

It wasn't only she and Anne who were different. So was Charles. So was Hidden Falls. Most of all, so was Matt. Though Jane had no intention of mentioning Matt and raising her brother's ire, her expression was somber as she said, "The girls turned into women."

"Stubborn ones."

"Like their brother."

Charles's chuckle warmed Jane almost as much as his approval had and helped dispel the gloom that always accompanied the realization of how much Matt had changed. "I can't deny that," Charles said. "Susannah would be the first to attest to the fact that I have more than my share of that particular virtue." He gave Susannah one of the special smiles that made Jane feel as if she were an outsider, watching a play but not being able to share in the magic that was unfolding on the stage. Would Matt ever smile at her that way? Would they ever sit at their table, sharing a meal, a smile, a life? Though it was Jane's fondest dream, today it seemed more distant than ever.

"All right, Jane." Charles's words brought her back to the present. "Plan your Thanksgiving dinner."

Will you come? Jane's words echoed in his head. Matt had sensed her hesitation when she invited him, and it had reminded him of the shy girl she had once been, the girl who had been afraid to ask for something she wanted, lest she be refused. He had thought that girl had vanished, that the year in Switzerland had transformed her reticence into confidence. But it seemed that, for reasons he could not fathom, though Jane wanted him to attend the Thanksgiving dinner, she was afraid to issue more than a casual invitation.

Matt's steps slowed as he approached the church hall. He hadn't planned to come. Indeed, he had not. Oh, he couldn't deny that the dinner was a generous gesture. From the day they had first heard of it, the workers could talk of little else. The women worried about what they would wear, and

Matt had even overheard some of the men declaring that they would give their boots an extra polish on Thanksgiving morning. It would be one of the most important events in Hidden Falls this year, a day that no one wanted to miss. No one except Matt.

It wasn't that he wasn't willing to give thanks. He was. It wasn't that he didn't like turkey and squash and all the other foods that were part of a traditional Thanksgiving feast. He did. The problem was that Matt couldn't bear the thought of seeing Jane — his Jane — in the church hall, playing her role as lady of the manor. With her new-found confidence, she would do it well. She would be the perfect hostess, graciously dispensing bounty to the less fortunate. Matt knew that. He also knew that would remind him of thoughts he preferred not to remember, namely the differences that separated them. Jane was the lady of the manor; he was the boy from the wrong side of the river.

Matt gripped the door handle, more than a little surprised to find himself at the side entrance to the church. He hadn't planned to come, but here he was. He might as well go in, only for a moment, of course. He'd take a quick look, then leave. He entered the church hall as quietly as he could. As long as he was here, he would stay a few minutes. It would be good for business, he told himself. He would greet some of the workers, perhaps even share a plate of food with them.

Matt took a deep breath. The workers. They were the only reason he was here. It wasn't to see Jane, and it most certainly wasn't to see Charles Moreland. He would do his best to avoid Charles. Today was supposed to be a happy occasion, and since there was no guaranteeing what he and Charles would say if they encountered each other, Matt would try to ensure that there were no encounters. That was wise. So too was his resolution not to speak to Jane. He had told her that it would confuse the workers if she attended his rally. How much more confusing would it be if Matt gave in to his longings and took his place at Jane's side? He couldn't — he wouldn't — do that.

Matt hung his coat on one of the hooks in the vestibule, then walked into the main room. He wouldn't look for Jane. She was not the reason he'd come. But Matt's eyes refused to listen to his brain. Though there were more than a hundred people in the hall, his gaze moved unerringly to the woman who haunted so many of his dreams. There she was! Matt blinked in surprise.

He had expected a lady of the manor, but not this.

Jane looked like a princess from one of the books the schoolmarm used to read. An incredibly beautiful princess. She was more beautiful than Matt had dreamed possible, but, then, he had never seen her dressed like this, not even on the day of Anne's wedding. Today she wore a blue velvet gown that was more suited to a formal ball than an afternoon meal. Her hair was piled high on her head in some intricate arrangement, and Matt saw the sparkle of jewels around her neck and at her wrists. If this were England, Matt would have said she was about to be presented to the Queen. But this was not England. It was Hidden Falls, New York, and these were mill workers, not royalty. Surely she was overdressed.

Matt looked around. Susannah wore an equally formal gown, as did Mrs. Harrod. It appeared that the three ladies on the hill thought this was a regal occasion. If he lived to be a hundred, Matt knew he'd never understand women and their sense of fashion.

"Isn't Miss Moreland's dress the most beautiful thing you've ever seen?"

Matt wheeled at the sound, thinking the

question was directed at him. Instead, he saw two of the young girls who worked at the mill, deep in conversation. They stood on the perimeter of the room, presumably waiting for the dancing to begin. Though his instinct was to flee, Matt paused, curious about the second girl's response.

"Oh, Virginia. It looks so soft! Do you suppose it came from Paris, France?"

Virginia. That was right. The girls who resembled each other so closely were Virginia and Deborah Sempert. Matt had met them one of the days he had visited the main boarding house. They had come from a farm and were saving their wages so they would have the dowries their parents could not provide.

Virginia nodded solemnly. "It might have. Lydia said Mrs. Moreland brought back trunks and trunks of fashions from Paris."

"I never thought they'd wear their fancy gowns here," Deborah told her sister. "I was sure they saved them for special occasions."

Matt stopped as the realization hit him with the force of one of the Harrods' train engines. How wrong he had been! Jane wasn't overdressed. She was honoring the workers by wearing her best gown to their dinner.

She hadn't seen him yet. Matt was certain

of that. He was also certain that the time wasn't right for him to approach her. He needed a few minutes to stop berating himself for his idiocy before he greeted the most beautiful, perceptive woman in Hidden Falls — perhaps in all of New York State. Matt moved into the corner where he could stand behind a thick pillar. Here he would be hidden from view but could still watch Jane.

"Yes, the gown is from Paris. It's silk velvet." She had been moving slowly around the room, greeting the workers as if they were guests in her drawing room, and had reached Deborah and Virginia. She held out a fold of her skirt. "Have you ever felt anything so soft?"

"You want me to touch it?" Virginia's amazement was reflected in her voice. Matt suspected his own amazement was only slightly less than the girl's.

"Of course. What good is something if you don't share it?" As the two young women fingered the velvet, Jane continued, "I've been admiring your coiffures from across the room. I wondered how you formed those curls." Though Matt knew Virginia and Deborah were not twins, their hairstyles were identical.

Virginia nodded toward her sister. "It's

Deborah's doing. She has a clever hand with hair."

"So I see." The words were simple. They could have been condescending, but they were not. Matt watched the two sisters' faces flush with pride. The story that Jane — Miss Moreland — had complimented their coiffure would be repeated countless times over the next few weeks, undoubtedly embellished in the retelling.

"Hello, Matt." He started, his pulse beginning to race at the sound of Jane's voice. Somehow she had seen him, though he thought the pillar had provided adequate concealment. "I'm so glad you could come." Matt smiled. He wouldn't tell Jane that he hadn't planned to come; there was no reason to confess that when he had obviously changed his mind. And now that he was here, he was glad his feet had ignored his brain's command not to approach the church.

He and Jane spoke for a few moments before she asked if he would mind visiting with four men. Jane pointed toward a table at the other side of the room. "It will be a while before I get there, and I want to make certain that they have enough food. They took only one serving." Matt wondered how, with all these guests, Jane knew who had not returned for a second helping of food. "There's plenty left," she told him. "Enough for you, too." Something in Jane's expression told Matt that she'd been aware of him from the moment he'd entered the hall. He only hoped she hadn't been able to read his thoughts.

As she moved to the next table, Matt crossed the room toward the men that Jane feared were hungry. She was, without a doubt, the most wonderful woman he had ever met. Not only was she the perfect hostess, but she had displayed a sensibility toward the workers that shamed Matt. How wrong he'd been! His step faltered as another thought assailed him. If he'd underestimated Jane's understanding of the workers, might he also be wrong about their reaction to her? Was it possible that they would not be intimidated if he married Jane and took over Ralph's practice?

Buoyed by that possibility, Matt convinced the four men whose modest food consumption had worried Jane that he needed their assistance in choosing the best items from the buffet table. It was all the encouragement they needed to take second helpings of almost everything. Jane would be pleased.

Matt found himself enjoying both the meal and the men's conversation when he saw Charles approach Jane. Though he'd been aware of Charles, he had kept himself as far away from his nemesis as possible. As Matt watched, Charles spoke for a moment. When he was finished, Jane shook her head. As if in response, Charles returned to his wife's side. Mildly curious about the exchange, Matt saw that when one of the workers stood on a chair and announced that the dancing would begin in five minutes, Charles and Susannah left. He guessed that Susannah's fatigue had been the reason for the early departure and that Jane had insisted she would not need their assistance for the remainder of the evening.

It was hours later and the brief November daylight was gone when the townspeople started to drift home. Matt looked at his watch, astonished that the few minutes he'd intended to stay had turned into hours. But then, nothing about today had been what he'd expected. Especially Jane. Other than the short conversation when she had first seen him, Matt had not spoken to her. He approached her now.

"I saw Charles and Susannah leave. Is he coming back to drive you home?"

Jane shook her head. "There's no need. I'll probably collapse tomorrow, but today I feel as if my energy is boundless. Walking will be good for me."

Deciding that a light approach was the best, Matt sketched a quick bow. "May I have the honor of escorting you, Miss Moreland?"

She laughed, and the smile she gave him made Matt's pulse race. "I accept with pleasure, kind sir." The pleasure, Matt suspected, would be his.

The night was cold, the clear sky sprinkled with stars. If Jane had been able to choose the weather for her Thanksgiving party, Matt doubted she would have picked anything different. "The town will be talking about this afternoon for a long time," he told her. "And everything they'll be saying is good. No one I spoke to had anything but praise."

They had reached the bridge. To Matt's surprise, Jane stopped and looked down at the water. Stars reflected in the surface, their light diffused by the slow current.

"I'm so thankful for that. I wanted today to be perfect." She turned and leaned her back on the railing, tipping her head up toward Matt. "I can't take credit for everything. The dancing wasn't my idea. One of the workers volunteered to bring his banjo. The next day, someone else said he'd bring a harmonica. Before I knew it, I had an orchestra."

Matt grinned. It had been obvious that the men had never played together, but the occasional lack of harmony had not appeared to bother anyone. To the contrary, Matt had overheard guests pointing with pride to a neighbor, acting as if the music were the best they had ever heard.

"It was good of you to accept the men's offers," he said. "It meant that they were able to contribute something to the day."

Jane's smile was sweet. "That's why I was so pleased when they volunteered. I know they work for Moreland Mills, but we're all part of Hidden Falls. Having the dancing turned dinner into a whole day of festivities. That was perfect."

It was she, Matt decided, who was perfect. Not even Susannah, whom Charles had once derided for being egalitarian when she'd treated Matt with courtesy, was as genuine in her beliefs. Jane's concern for the workers and her admiration of their talents was not feigned.

As much as he wanted to linger, Matt could not ignore the cold that nipped his nose. Jane's coat was not as heavy as his, and her boots were not meant for lengthy strolls in late November. Though she wasn't shivering yet, she must be chilled. Unwilling to risk having her be ill again, Matt laid Jane's hand on his arm and turned to climb the hill.

They walked in companionable silence until they reached the drive that led to Fairlawn. There was no need to turn here, and yet by unspoken consent, their steps slowed. In the distance, Matt saw the hulking building that had been Jane's home. It was empty now, its windows dark, and if he closed his eyes, Matt could imagine that the acrid odor of smoke still clung to it. What must Jane feel, knowing that her childhood home had been abandoned, at least temporarily? Matt had never had a permanent home, and so he could only guess at the thoughts that must be coursing through her.

He stopped, laying his hand on Jane's arm. "Jane, I . . ." She looked up at him and smiled, a smile that drove every thought from Matt's head. Her smile was warm and caring and filled with so much promise that Matt could hardly breathe. He swallowed, trying to catch his breath. What had he meant to say? It didn't matter. All that mattered was that he was here with Jane, the most beautiful woman in the world, the woman he loved, the woman he wanted to marry.

"I . . ." Matt searched for the words but

could find none that expressed the wonder of being with the woman who filled his dreams, the woman whose smile made him believe dreams just might come true. "I . . ." Matt shook his head, unable to form a coherent thought. And then, as if they had a mind of their own, his arms reached for Jane.

He'd held her once, the night they had danced at Fairlawn. This wasn't like that. Then they'd been constrained by the rules of the waltz. Tonight there were no rules. Matt drew Jane closer, wrapping one arm around her, while the other cupped her chin, turning her face toward his. She smiled again, that breathtaking, heartbreakingly sweet smile. Matt returned her smile. And then slowly, ever so slowly, his lips descended until they met hers. He had dreamed about kissing Jane. Thoughts of holding her in his arms had filled his days. But dreams and daylight fantasies could not compare to the reality of this, their first kiss. There was nothing that could compare to this.

Jane fit into his arms as if she were made for them, her soft sigh sending tremors through him. Her lips were sweeter than he had dreamed, smaller and smoother than his, the faint taste of cinnamon and apple lingering on them, the heady scent of her perfume tantalizing his senses. Not even in his dreams had anything been so perfect. He was holding Jane in his arms, kissing her sweet lips, and if he had his way, he would never stop.

Matt closed his eyes, drawing Jane closer and savoring the moment. Today was Thanksgiving, and for the first time in his life, he was truly thankful, for today he was with the woman he loved.

Though it was late, Jane did not extinguish the light. Instead, she stared into the mirror at the face that no longer looked familiar. It seemed like a lifetime ago that she had told Matt that the excitement of the day had given her boundless energy. That had been true, then. She had been exhilarated by the success of the Thanksgiving party. But now . . . Jane laid two fingers on her lips, remembering. The pleasure and the undeniable satisfaction of the afternoon paled in comparison to the way she felt now.

Jane stared at her face. Was that really her? Though she'd seen the reflection thousands of times before, never before had her eyes sparkled like this; never before had her cheeks borne such a rosy glow; never before had her lips felt like this. It was all because of Matt and that magical kiss.

Jane smiled at the memory. If she closed her eyes, she could feel the touch of Matt's lips on hers. She didn't know how it was possible, but they'd been firm and soft, sweet and spicy, exciting and reassuring all at the same time.

She opened her eyes and twirled, holding her arms over her head as she had once seen a ballerina do. Though the dancer's pirouette had been more graceful than Jane's, the twirling helped express her happiness. Today's celebration had been designed to make the day special for the workers. Jane had worked hard to turn that goal into reality, but in all her planning, she had never thought that today would be the most special day of her life. Never had she dreamed that this day would end with Matt kissing her. But he had, and it had been the most wonderful thing that had ever happened to her.

Her first kiss. She and Anne had spent countless hours, speculating about their first kisses. Who would the man be? Would it feel awkward? Where did the noses go? They had laughed, imagining bumps, certain that kissing was overrated. It was not.

Jane touched her lips again, remembering that magic moment. There had been no awkwardness, nothing but the most wonderful feeling of rightness. For a few moments, she had been in Matt's arms, her lips pressed to his, and for those moments, there had been no doubts, only the unshakable certainty that that was where she was meant to be.

If only it hadn't ended!

"You look tired." Susannah's eyes darkened as Jane joined her in the small office.

"I was too excited to sleep." Jane pulled out the chair on the opposite side of the desk and settled herself there. Though she knew there were circles under her eyes, she was still buoyed by the thrill of Matt's kiss. Why had no one — her mother, Anne, even Susannah — told her how wonderful a kiss could be?

"Yesterday was a great success."

"Yes." *Especially last night. I'll never, ever forget that.* But Jane wouldn't tell Susannah about Matt's kiss. Instead, she reached for one of the vellum cards. Susannah had already begun writing invitations to the Morelands' annual Christmas party. Though the celebration would be held at Pleasant Hill this year, it continued a tradition that had been broken only once, last year.

"Thank you for volunteering to help with

this," Jane's sister-in-law said as she handed her half of the guest list. "You're welcome to invite any of your friends who aren't already on the list."

"Even Matt?" Though he hadn't said the words, Jane wanted to believe that his kiss meant that he cared for her. Oh, why mince words? She wanted to believe that he loved her, and if he did, she wanted him by her side at the party.

Susannah nodded. "Even Matt. I can promise that Charles will be civil to him." When Jane raised an eyebrow, wondering how Susannah could make such a promise, her sister-in-law continued, "I'll tell him it can be his gift to me."

Gifts. Jane frowned as she inscribed another invitation. What could she give Matt for Christmas? She wanted something personal, something that would remind him of her whenever he looked at it, but it couldn't be too personal, either. After all, no matter what had happened last night, in the eyes of the world they were only friends, and etiquette constrained what gifts friends could exchange.

Matt was only one of her concerns. "I haven't been able to think of anything for Charles," Jane said. "Do you have any suggestions?"

Susannah nodded. "Your needlepoint is beautiful, and I probably shouldn't tell you this, but he has cold feet. Perhaps you could make him a pair of slippers."

Jane smiled, delighted with the suggestion. Not only would it be the perfect gift for Charles, but it had also given her an idea of a present for Matt. He was a lawyer with more books than anyone in Hidden Falls other than Ralph Chambers. She would craft needlepoint bookends for him.

By midafternoon Jane's hand had begun to cramp. "If you don't mind, Susannah, I'll deliver some of the invitations." Although it was true that her hand needed a rest, Jane had ulterior motives. It had been more than eighteen hours since she'd been with Matt, since he'd held her in his arms and kissed her. She wanted to see him, if only to reassure herself that she hadn't imagined last night. Delivering invitations gave her a reason to see Matt. Jane smiled with anticipation as she headed toward the door.

"Is it out you'll be going?"

As Jane entered the front hall, Megan stopped her dusting and folded her hands behind her back. Though it was a gesture she had seen Megan make countless times, there was something furtive about it today, almost as though Megan was hiding some-

161

thing. Jane thought quickly. What could Megan be hiding? There'd never been any problem with missing items, so she doubted Megan concealed a theft. "Yes," Jane said, wondering whether she'd imagined the unusual behavior. "Would you get my coat for me?"

Megan reached into the closet, and as she did Jane saw the gleam of gold and the sparkle of rubies on her left hand. Was Megan wearing a ring? Was that why she'd hidden her hand? Surely not, for Megan wore no jewelry. Still, the fleeting glimpse Jane had had reminded her of Charles's signet ring. What an absurd thought! Charles would never have given Megan his ring.

"Megan . . ."

The beautiful brunet turned away from Jane for a second, burrowing her hands into Jane's coat before she draped it over Jane's shoulders. "Would you be needing something else?"

Jane looked down at Megan's hands, then shook her head. Both hands were bare. It was amazing what a sleepless night could do to a person. Fatigue must have made her imagine the ring.

CHAPTER SIX

Matt looked at the two men sitting on the opposite side of the desk. Although their chairs were still pushed as far apart as the small room would allow, their hands were no longer fisted. "All right, gentlemen. Are we in agreement? Mr. Black will return Mr. Grunwald's pistol; Mr. Grunwald will refund the three dollars Mr. Black paid for it." The men nodded solemnly. Within minutes, the exchange was complete and the men left his office, having grudgingly consented to share the cost of Matt's fee.

When he was certain they were out of sight, Matt opened the door and stood on the front step. Though the November day was cold, he needed fresh air to sweep away the memory of his clients. Wouldn't his professors laugh if they could have seen him? There he was, a man with a diploma from Harvard Law School, settling a dispute between two men who had drunk too much one night and made an agreement that neither of them wanted. Rather than admitting they had made a mistake, the plaintiff and the defendant had squabbled like children, each threatening the other with bodily harm, until one of the other mill hands had insisted that Matt intervene.

Knowing what was expected, Matt had taken copious notes as the men had related their versions of the events, and he had quoted several particularly impressive sounding sections of the law. All the while, he had felt as if he were playing a part in a third-rate play when what he really wanted was to be with Jane.

As he'd been leafing through law books, searching for citations with a sufficiently sonorous ring to convince his clients of the legality of his proposed solution to their argument, Matt's mind continued to drift back to the memory of how right it had felt to hold Jane in his arms, how wonderful it had been to kiss her. This morning it was difficult to remember that he was an attorney. All that mattered was that he was a man in love. Jane was the most important part of his life, and somehow he had to find a way to make her his wife.

He smiled, remembering the workers' reaction to her at the Thanksgiving dinner.

Surely that was a good omen, a portent of future success. The obstacles he'd imagined were simply that: imaginary. He would talk to Ralph.

He wasn't there. Jane tried to bite back her disappointment when she saw the small sign in Matt's window, announcing that he was out of the office. Though she had delivered a dozen invitations, making polite conversation at each stop, her mind had been focused on this particular house. Anticipation mingled with apprehension. It would be wonderful to see Matt, to relive the special moment they had shared. And yet she could not dismiss her concerns. What would they do? They couldn't kiss, not here where any curious passerby could observe them. What would they say? No one had coached Jane on the etiquette of the day after a kiss, but she was certain she should not blurt out the fact that she had hardly slept because she'd been so excited by their embrace. She wanted to see Matt, to let her eyes feast on the sight of his beloved face, and yet she couldn't help wondering whether the magic of their kiss might disappear in the daylight. Would it evaporate like evening dew?

She stared at the sign. Though she had feared there might be some awkwardness in their first meeting, she hadn't expected this. Where was Matt? Surely he hadn't left Hidden Falls. Jane shook her head at her foolishness. There were a hundred places Matt could be, and no reason to think he had left, no reason to worry. The sleepless night was making her see chimeras where none existed. Chiding herself for her overactive imagination, Jane slid the invitation under Matt's door and retraced her steps. She had one more stop before she returned home.

"Good afternoon, my dear." Philip Biddle's light blue eyes lit with pleasure as he opened the door. "To what do I owe the pleasure of your company?"

Jane stepped into the house that she had visited so often as a child. Though Uncle Philip and Aunt Rosemary had no children of their own, they had furnished one room on their first floor with books, toys, and small-scaled furniture. The whimsical paintings and the brightly colored carpet turned the room into a child's fantasy, making this one of Jane and Anne's favorite places to visit.

"I brought you an invitation to our Christmas party." Jane preceded Philip into the parlor and settled into one of the comfortable wingbacked chairs. "Both Charles and

I hope you'll come."

Philip smiled with what appeared to be approval as he fingered the envelope. "Charles is continuing the tradition. I'm glad. The Fairlawn Christmas party has always been the highlight of the season."

"It will be at Pleasant Hill this year."

Philip stared at Jane, surprise etched on his face. At length, he nodded. "Of course. Fairlawn is closed." He ran a hand through his hair. "Forgive an old man's forgetfulness. I shall indeed attend the party at Pleasant Hill." They chatted for a few moments; then Philip asked whether Anne would be coming home for the party.

"I'm not certain. It's a long distance for them to travel, and Rob is still getting settled at the carousel factory."

Philip stretched his legs in front of him, crossing them at the ankles. "You must miss her. I know I do."

The wistfulness in Philip's voice reminded Jane that he had once courted Anne. At the time, she hadn't understood why he wanted to marry a woman young enough to be his daughter, and she still didn't, but since Philip had attended Anne's wedding to Rob, perhaps that had been nothing more than a passing fancy.

"I think of Anne every day," Jane told

Philip. *But not as often as I think of Matt.*
Thoughts of him accompanied her every-
where she went, and today — with the
memory of their wonderful kiss so fresh —
it seemed as if everything she saw or did
reminded her of Matt. Where was he?

Though Jane was tempted to retrace her
steps and see whether Matt had returned, a
glance at her watch told her she could afford no detours if she was to reach Pleasant
Hill by supper time. The train was whistling
in the distance, signaling its approach to
Hidden Falls, as Jane turned onto Bridge
Street. If she hurried, she would be able to
cross the tracks before the train arrived.
That would mean one less delay on her way
home.

"Jane!" She turned at the sound of the
familiar voice, surprised that Brad was in
town at this hour. She noticed his car
parked near the depot and saw that he was
striding toward her. "You're more beautiful
than ever," Brad said when he no longer
had to shout.

"And you're more silver-tongued than
ever." Jane gestured toward the Model T. "If
you're going out of town, I don't suppose
you'd like me to take care of your car. Susannah is expecting me for supper in just a
few minutes, and this black beauty will help

me get there on time."

As she'd hoped, Brad chuckled. "Though the offer is generous, I fear I must decline. Besides, I'm not going anywhere; I'm meeting someone." He linked his arm with Jane's. "Will you keep me company? I'll drive you home once the train arrives."

"Thank you." Relieved that there was no longer any need to hurry, Jane answered Brad's questions about the Christmas party while the train chugged into the station. With a whoosh and a squeal, it shuddered to a stop. Seconds later the door opened and a familiar figure began to descend the steps.

"Anne!" Forgetting every one of her mother's decorum lessons, Jane gathered her skirts and ran toward the train. "Oh, Anne! What a wonderful surprise! Why didn't you tell me you were coming? How long will you be able to stay? Oh, I'm so glad to see you again!" Jane knew she was babbling, but she couldn't stop herself. She flung her arms around her sister, directing a brief smile at Rob. He had followed Anne off the train and was now shaking hands with Brad.

"This isn't a visit," Anne said as she and Jane walked toward Brad's car, their arms wrapped around each other's waist. "We're back permanently."

Jane's heart skipped a beat. This was better news than she had dreamed possible. Anne was home again, and Jane's family was once more complete. "What changed?" She glared at Brad. "Why didn't you tell me?" Though he hadn't lied, he'd acted as if the person he was meeting was a business associate.

Raising both hands in the classic gesture of surrender, Brad insisted that he was innocent. "Rob asked me to meet them at the train station. That's all I knew."

"We wanted to surprise you," Anne said.

"You certainly succeeded at that." Jane let her sister climb into the car first. "I'm thrilled that you're back, but why did you leave the factory? Your letters sounded as if you were happy there."

It was Rob who answered. "Working at the factory made me realize that your sister was right. I want my own company. I want to control every part of the carousel-making process, not just the design of the horses."

"We're planning to rebuild the stable," Anne said, confirming that this was a joint decision. "It'll be bigger than before, with everything Rob needs to make it a real workshop."

The sparkle in Anne's eyes told Jane how

happy her sister was about the changes. "Are you planning to live at Fairlawn?" Though it was clear that Anne and Rob had discussed many aspects of their return to Hidden Falls, Jane wondered whether Anne was ready to move back into the house where she had been so badly injured. Jane knew that Anne had sustained wounds beyond the burns that had scarred her face and arms. She had also been plagued with nightmares. The dreams that had accompanied them to Switzerland had intensified when they had first come back to Hidden Falls, and Jane had rushed to her sister's room countless times, holding her and trying to banish the terrible thoughts the dreams brought with them. Why would Anne willingly live in the place that caused such agony?

"We want to live at Fairlawn," Anne said, her voice firm. She nodded slowly as she added, "Unless you and Charles object."

They had reached Pleasant Hill. When Brad switched off the motor, Jane turned to her sister. "I don't object, and I can't imagine that Charles will, but are you sure this is what you want?"

In response, Anne squeezed Jane's hand. "The ghosts are gone," she said softly, "and so are the nightmares."

There was nothing Anne could have said that would have made Jane happier. Anne was home again, her wounds healed. Truly this was a reason to give thanks.

"My boy, I applaud your decision." Ralph peered over the top of his spectacles, his grin underscoring his words. "When would you like to announce it?"

Though Matt wasn't sure Ralph would be as approving of his next statement, it was the result of careful deliberation. "Next spring," he said. "And, before you ask, I have two reasons for wanting to wait. First, I don't want anyone to regard you as a lame duck, and second, I have several matters to attend to first."

Leaning back in his chair, Ralph's expression was guarded. "Might I ask what they are?"

"You might." Matt matched the grin he had seen on Ralph's face just seconds before. "And I *might* answer." When his mentor smiled, Matt continued. "I need to hold another meeting with the workers. Even though they may not all agree at this point, they need my assistance in improving conditions at the mill. The problem is, I'm not certain how they'll view my assuming your practice, so I'd rather not confuse the issue."

Ralph nodded. "It's a valid concern. I must admit that I've been surprised that not one of the mill hands has consulted me in all the years I've been practicing law." He pushed his spectacles back on his nose. "Until you opened your office, I don't know how they settled disputes."

"With their fists." That was how Messieurs Black and Grunwald had attempted to resolve their problem.

The older attorney's mouth twisted in a wry smile. "It pains me to think that that's the case, but I suspect you're right."

"The workers are one concern," Matt told his mentor, "but I have another. Are you confident that your clients will accept me? You've spent a lifetime establishing your practice and reputation. I don't want to do anything that will jeopardize either one of those."

Ralph nodded. "I appreciate that, my boy. I can make no guarantees. There are, as you are well aware, few things in life that are certain. But I believe my clients will be amenable to the change." He paused, then picked up a vellum envelope. "We can gauge their reaction at the Morelands' Christmas party. I assume you will be there."

"I have not received an invitation." And, if

Charles had anything to do with the guest list, Matt doubted he would.

Ralph appeared not to share Matt's concerns. "I imagine you will. Jane is delivering the invitations today. In fact, she left here just minutes before you arrived."

Rising, Matt reached for his coat. "I'd better go home. I don't want to miss her."

But he had.

"I wish you'd move back to Fairlawn with us."

Jane reached for a strand of wool, separating the strands and carefully threading one into her needle before she answered her sister. The two women were sitting in the parlor at Pleasant Hill. While Susannah painted in her garret, the sisters remained downstairs. Jane worked on her needlepoint, and Anne sipped tea. "You and Rob would regret your offer within a week," Jane said. "You're practically still on your honeymoon."

Anne shrugged as if that were of no account. "So are Charles and Susannah."

"I told them the same thing, but they convinced me that they were an old married couple, especially since they're expecting a child."

Though the teacup hid Anne's expression,

nothing could hide the color that rose to her cheeks. "Before you ask, the answer is 'not yet.'" She sighed as she laid the cup back on its saucer. "We're both anxious. Rob loves his nephews and can't wait to be a father. Of course, he told me we had to have triplets so that he could outdo his sister and her twins."

Jane kept her eyes on her needlepoint, as if finishing Charles's second slipper was the most important thing in the world. And it was important, for it kept Anne from seeing the tears that, despite her sister's joking tone, were welling in Jane's eyes. She didn't begrudge Anne her happiness any more than she begrudged Charles and Susannah theirs. It was simply that Jane longed for a family of her own. And since Thanksgiving that prospect seemed further away than before.

It shouldn't have been this way. Thanksgiving night had been the most wonderful experience of her life. Jane could not forget Matt's kiss and the way it had made her feel. She relived those magical moments she had spent in his arms a hundred times a day, wishing they could repeat it. Matt, it appeared, did not. Every time they had been together since That Night, he had seemed preoccupied. Oh, he had insisted that nothing was wrong, that he was simply thinking about his clients, but Jane suspected that was a lie. The fact that he had never once referred to the kiss, that he had not so much as touched her hand, told Jane his reaction had been far different from hers. While she cherished the memory, Matt regretted it, and there was nothing she could do.

She worked the end of the yarn into the back of the needlepoint, then snipped it. "Finished," she said, holding the piece up for Anne's inspection.

"It's beautiful." Anne ran her fingers over the design. "I envy you being able to do this. No matter how many times Mama tried to teach me, I never could make even stitches like yours."

Jane tried not to wince. Needlepoint wasn't important. Perfect stitches did not bring happiness. People did, and the one special person who could bring Jane happiness had reverted to his sphinx mode: silent and cold as stone.

"Do you have another project planned?" Anne asked.

"A set of bookends." Although at this point Jane wondered whether Matt would even accept them. The man was so difficult to understand. Difficult? Impossible.

"Bookends?" Anne refilled her teacup.

"How do you make needlepoint bookends?"

This was a safe subject, much better than thinking about the recipient. "All you stitch are the covers. There are bricks inside. That's what provides the shape and the weight."

Anne took a sip of tea. "I can't picture Brad using bookends. I haven't seen very many books at Rose Walk."

Laying the completed slippers on the sofa beside her, Jane raised an eyebrow. "What made you think the bookends were for Brad? He and I have never exchanged gifts." Nor had she and Matt.

"There's always a first time. I know how Brad feels about you, and you both met our train."

Jane couldn't let her sister continue to believe there was anything significant in that. Anne had spent part of the summer trying to make a match between Jane and Brad, despite Jane's protestations that she would never regard Brad as more than a friend. The one good thing about Anne's move to Lake Ontario was that the matchmaking had ceased. Jane did not want it to resume.

"Being at the depot together was coincidence. I was in town delivering invitations for the party when I saw Brad. He asked me wait with him, so I did." Jane poured herself another cup of tea before she fixed her gaze on her sister. "And, no, the bookends are not for him."

"Then who?" Anne's eyes narrowed, and she frowned as she considered the possibilities. "Don't tell me they're for Matt Wagner."

Jane shrugged. "All right. I won't." Though Anne did not share Charles's enmity toward Matt, she had been open in her disapproval of Jane's friendship with him.

"Oh, Jane. I hoped you were over him."

Jane plunked down her cup with such force that tea splashed onto the saucer. "You make him sound like some kind of infectious disease." Not once when Anne had been falling in love with Rob had Jane said anything derogatory about him, and she had been genuine in her admiration for Charles's wife. Why couldn't her siblings afford her the same courtesy?

"I'm sorry." Tears welled in Anne's eyes as she faced her sister. "It's just that he's all wrong for you."

"Why do you say that?" Though the words came out with more bitterness than she had intended, Jane could not regret them. No one, and that included her twin, had the right to tell her who she should love. "You're starting to sound like Charles."

"Don't be angry with me. I can't bear it." Anne brushed away a tear that had started to slide down her cheek. "All I want is for you to be happy." Anne pulled out her handkerchief and dabbed at her face. "I know how much you love living in Hidden Falls and the way you like to arrange parties. Look at how well the Thanksgiving dinner turned out. You're a natural leader, Jane. That's why I always thought you'd be the one who would take Mama's place in society." Anne shook her head slowly, her dismay evident. "You can't do that with Matt at your side. And please don't tell me that he's a successful lawyer. He may have a degree from Harvard, but everyone in Hidden Falls knows he's barely making ends meet and that no one wants him to handle their business."

"That's not true." Jane tried to keep her voice even. "He's not rich because he's not trying to take over Uncle Ralph's practice. Matt is helping the workers."

"And that does not exactly endear him to our friends."

Jane clenched her fists, trying to control her anger and her disappointment. "Oh, Anne, I thought you'd understand. You were the last person I thought would tell me that Matt won't fit into society." Her sister had, after all, married a carousel carver, not a business tycoon.

Anne's face softened. "I'm not saying he couldn't, although it wouldn't be easy for him to gain people's trust. The truth is, I don't think Matt wants to be part of society."

"And maybe I don't want Mama's place in society, either."

Anne laid her hand on Jane's. "What do you want?"

To be Matt's wife.

The party was going well. Less formal than the Christmas celebrations that had been held at Fairlawn, this one had its own charm, thanks to Susannah's careful planning. She had decided to have a wassail party, serving only punch, small sandwiches and gingerbread cookies rather than the traditional roast beef dinner. This, she had told Jane, would give the guests, many of whom were entering Pleasant Hill for the first time, the opportunity to explore the first floor of the house and mingle with others instead of being confined to specified seats for a lengthy meal.

Susannah had also decided to begin a

tradition and had convinced Charles that each of the guests should receive a gift that had been made at Moreland Mills. This year's gifts were towels that incorporated one of Susannah's original designs. To celebrate the town's major event for the year 1908, she had cleverly combined a carousel with pictures of the main buildings, the railroad and the falls themselves. It was a beautiful design, and one almost everyone would appreciate, perhaps even Matt. Jane had no idea how he'd react. Some things, she reminded herself, were outside her control, with Matt being first on that list. It wasn't that she wanted to control him. She did not. But oh, how she wished she understood him.

Jane smiled as gaily as she could and tried her best not to watch the door. Was Matt coming? Though he had accepted the invitation, it had been with reservations, since he wasn't sure he would be back from New York in time. Jane wasn't certain which concerned her more: the fact that Matt was going to New York or that he would not tell her why he had to go. Though there could be many reasons why he'd traveled to the city, when Jane coupled his refusal to divulge the reason with the preoccupation she'd noticed since Thanksgiving, one answer seemed most likely. Matt must have taken her advice and was meeting with one of the law firms there, probably interviewing for a position with them. If that was the case, and Jane suspected it was, it appeared he did not want to tell her until he had made his decision.

Jane kept a smile fixed on her face as she greeted guests. Going to New York would be a good move for Matt. She knew that. That was why she had suggested the idea in the first place. But Jane also knew that Hidden Falls would be almost unbearably lonely without him.

"I'm disappointed that there's no dancing tonight." Brad touched Jane's arm lightly as he moved to her side.

She turned and smiled. Though as a boy he had been the brunt of teasing because of his red hair and freckles, Brad's features were finely chiseled, and Jane had always considered him handsome. Tonight, dressed in his formal clothes, he was the picture of a successful man.

"It would be a bit difficult, since Pleasant Hill has no ballroom." The smallest of the three houses on the hill, the old Ashton estate had been designed as a family residence, not a home for entertaining.

"I know, but I'm still disappointed."

Brad's smile was warmer than normal, and the gleam in his eye made Jane wary. "I enjoy dancing with you." He smiled again, and this time there was no ignoring the fact that this was not a casual smile. Brad's smile was the one Charles gave Susannah, the same one Rob bestowed on his wife. "I enjoy doing many things with you," Brad said.

Jane tried not to let her dismay show. Brad was her friend. Though she wanted nothing more, she did not want to jeopardize that friendship. "I enjoy your company, too. Our friendship is important to me." She started to say something more, but as she looked past Brad, her eyes widened. "Oh, no!"

"Is there a problem?"

Jane nodded. "Look at Ralph and Philip." If their pugilistic stances and red faces were any indication, the two men were close to fisticuffs. "I need to separate them."

"I can help."

Jane and Brad walked toward the men as quickly as they could without alarming the other guests. "Uncle Philip, I'm so glad you could come." Jane took the former banker's arm and led him a short distance away while Brad addressed the attorney. "I know this is a social occasion, sir," Brad said, "but I would like your advice."

Jane spent a few minutes exchanging pleasantries with Philip, not wanting to leave his side until she was certain that Brad had successfully lured the older attorney to the opposite end of the room. Though she knew that there was antagonism between Philip and Ralph, Jane had never learned the cause, nor had she seen the antagonism escalate this far. Tonight was not the night to search for reasons. All she would do was try to ensure that the two men remained separated.

When another guest claimed Philip's attention, Jane excused herself and resumed her mingling. She was on the far side of the room when a new guest arrived. Matt! Jane's heart sang with joy. No matter why he'd gone to New York, he was here. She tried not to run, but it was difficult to contain her excitement as she crossed the room. "Matt! It's so good to see you. I was afraid you wouldn't get back in time." The last train of the day should have arrived an hour ago. When Matt hadn't come, she had believed him delayed overnight.

Matt shook his head in mock dismay. "The train was late. You know it's almost never late, so why did it choose today to have a problem?" He wrinkled his nose. "Perhaps Brad Harrod had something to do with that."

Jane couldn't help laughing. "I doubt Brad would know how to sabotage the schedule. You know his father doesn't let him come near those trains except to ride them. But," she added, "you're here now. That's what matters." The Morelands' Christmas party had become a success, at least from Jane's view.

Matt looked around the room, obviously searching for someone. "I need to greet Charles and Susannah." When Jane started to walk with him, he stopped. "It's probably wiser if I go alone."

Though Jane was soon engaged in conversation with another guest, she positioned herself so that she could watch Matt as he approached her brother.

Susannah smiled and nodded, the picture of a gracious hostess. Her husband, however, was not so welcoming. Whatever Matt said to him, it caused Charles to frown as he responded. Jane saw Susannah lay her hand on his arm and say something, perhaps reminding him that he had promised to be civil. In apparent response, Charles stretched his lips in what Jane assumed was meant to be a smile. Unfortunately, it looked more like a grimace than any sign of cordiality.

She tried not to sigh. Her parents had told her that this was the season of miracles. That might be so, but the miracle she had hoped for, Charles's acceptance of Matt, showed no sign of appearing. It was also supposed to be a season of joy, but as she looked around the room, Jane saw less of that than she had expected. Half an hour ago, she would have said that the guests were filled with holiday gaiety, but now . . . Now there was an unmistakable sense of tension. Perhaps it had started with Ralph and Philip's argument. If so, then whatever had transpired between Charles and Matt had served to fuel the fire. Jane watched Matt making his way around the room, greeting the other guests. Though no one snarled at him as Charles had, their expressions were guarded, their smiles forced.

Why? Jane clenched her hands, then reminded herself that she was one of the hostesses. It was her duty to keep smiling, no matter what happened. Still, she couldn't help contrasting the townspeople's reaction to Matt with the way they had greeted Rob at his first social event. Rob had been welcomed. Matt was being tolerated. Much as she hated to admit it, Jane knew the reason. Rob had been a newcomer to Hidden Falls. Matt had a past, and that past was badly tarnished. A new suit, a law degree, even ten years of exemplary behavior did not outweigh memories of his rebellious years.

As Jane conversed with other guests, she tried to watch Matt without being obvious. The cautious reactions, the obviously stilted greetings, continued, confirming Anne's statement that it would be difficult for Matt to assume a role in Hidden Falls' society. How wrong Jane had been when she'd declared the evening a success. Though she wished it otherwise, memories were long, particularly in a town this size, and no one seemed willing to admit that Matt had changed. If only they would. If only his youthful behavior hadn't been so egregious.

No one knew what Rob had done when he'd been growing up. No one cared, because he hadn't lived here. Unfortunately, Matt did not have the luxury of coming to Hidden Falls as an adult. And yet Jane could not wish that he had no past, for it was in the past, when he had been the Bad Boy of Hidden Falls, that she had learned to love him. Anne and Charles might not believe it, but Jane loved Matt because of, not despite, his past. It was that past that had given him the strength of character she admired.

Jane watched as Matt moved from group to group, greeting and being greeted. Though his smile remained constant and a casual onlooker would not suspect that anything was amiss, she knew him well enough to see the strain on his face. She alone knew how much he wanted to be accepted. She alone knew how painful tonight must be for him, and her heart ached, wishing there were something she could do to change the townspeople's opinion of him.

As the guests began to leave, Jane stood in line with Charles and Susannah and Anne and Rob. As the last one to bid the guests farewell, it was her responsibility to ensure that they took one of Susannah's towels with them. "Don't open it until Christmas," Jane said a hundred times, knowing full well that the beautiful wrapping would be torn off within minutes.

Matt was among the last to leave. As he accepted the package from Jane, he spoke so softly that no one could overhear him. "Will you meet me in the stable in half an hour?"

She nodded, grateful that she would have a chance to talk to him. The party had not turned out the way she'd expected. In her dreams, she and Matt had circulated among the guests together, meeting only friendly faces. Sadly, the reality had been different. Though Jane could not undo the past few hours, perhaps there was some way to ease the pain of the evening.

No one looked askance when Jane pled fatigue and climbed the stairs to her room. Her smile was wry as she slid her arms into her coat and reached for the bookends that she had completed only this afternoon. Though this was Pleasant Hill and not Fairlawn, she was doing what she'd done so many times before: slipping out the back door to meet Matt. This time she moved more slowly than normal, lest she drop the heavy bookends. While she'd waited for the designated half-hour to pass, Jane had decided not to wait until Christmas Eve to give them to Matt. He needed something happy to think about tonight. Perhaps her gift would be that something.

Matt was waiting when she slid open the door to the stable. Unlike Fairlawn's stable, which had been turned into a workshop for Rob, this one still housed horses. The two animals stood in their stalls, looking curiously at the humans who had disturbed their rest. The horses clearly were not accustomed to having lanterns lit at midnight. Jane murmured a few comforting words to them and was relieved when they lost interest in her and Matt. If only all concerns could be erased that easily!

"Oh, Matt, I'm so sorry."

Before she could finish her sentence, he placed his forefinger over his lips in the classic request for silence. "Let's not talk about yesterday. It's over."

Jane's eyes widened as she realized that Matt was correct. The clock had struck midnight, and a new day had begun. She couldn't change what had happened, but perhaps she could make today a better one.

"Merry Christmas, Matt." Jane reached into her bag and withdrew the heavy package. As Matt took it, his expression betrayed both surprise and a faint sense of wonder. Was he so unaccustomed to receiving gifts? Jane's heart wrenched at the thought that that might be the case, and she realized that though Matt was her dearest friend, there were portions of his life that he had kept hidden, even from her.

"Do I have to wait until Christmas Day?"

"No. I'd like to watch you open it." *And I hope that this will help to salvage the night.*

Matt gestured toward a bale of hay, waiting until Jane was seated before he sat next to her. He made a process out of unwrapping the gift, slowly untying the bow, then unfolding the paper with as much care as if

190

it were the gift, not simply the wrapping. When the needlepoint was revealed, he picked up each bookend and examined it at length.

"You made me bookends!" There was a note of awe in his voice.

Jane nodded. "I wasn't certain you'd know what they were. Anne didn't." *And I was hoping you'd realize how much love I put into them.*

Matt's forefinger traced the design in a gesture that was almost reverent. "One of my professors had a set. I always admired his, but they were not as beautiful as these."

There was no doubt about it. Matt's voice rang with sincerity. Her gift had pleased him, and that made Jane's heart fill with happiness. *Oh, Matt, I love you. I want you to be happy.* But she said only, "I'm glad you like them."

A few yards away, the horses nickered, perhaps reminding the humans of their presence. Matt smiled. "The bookends are perfect, Jane. I'll think of you every time I look at them." He touched them once again, then laid them on the bale next to him. "Thank you."

He rose, and for a second Jane thought that he was going to leave. She tried to quell her disappointment. Perhaps it was silly of her, but she had hoped that he would kiss her again. That, it appeared, was another miracle that was not going to happen. Matt would say good-night, and the evening would be over.

But he didn't leave. Instead, he stood in front of her, his expression solemn. "I brought you something from New York," he said slowly. "It's not a Christmas gift, though."

Gift? New York? Jane's heart began to race. Was that the reason Matt had taken the trip? Perhaps she had been mistaken in believing he was visiting one of the law firms there. Perhaps he wasn't planning to leave Hidden Falls. Perhaps it truly was the season of miracles.

Jane's heart sang with happiness at the possibility that the man she loved would not leave her. The happiness grew as she let herself hope that he loved her. Why else would he go all the way to New York to buy something for her? The disappointment she had felt only moments before turned to anticipation. What had he brought?

Matt reached into his pocket, then bent one knee as he sank to the ground in front of Jane, holding out a small velvet box. Her eyes widened at the realization that there was only one thing that was kept in a box that size and shape.

"This is probably not the way you imagined it." Matt gestured toward the stable and the horses that were once again watching them. "This is hardly a romantic spot." To Jane's surprise, Matt's voice quavered ever so slightly, and the expression in his eyes said that he was not sure of her reaction. "I probably should have spoken to Charles and picked a better location, but I couldn't wait any longer." Matt's eyes darkened as he looked at her, and she saw uncertainty reflected in them. "Jane, will you do me the very great honor of becoming my wife?" Matt opened the box, revealing a simple gold band with a diamond in its center.

Though she'd known the box contained a ring, Jane felt the blood drain from her face. "You want to marry me?" Was it possible that dreams really did come true?

Matt smiled, a smile so full of joy that Jane knew this was not a dream. Never before had she seen him looking like that, not even the night he had kissed her. Never had she dreamt that a smile could contain so much love.

"I want to marry you more than anything else on earth. Will you, Jane? Will you marry me?"

"Yes!" The word came out as little more than a croak, but that didn't seem to bother Matt. Slowly, he slid the ring onto her finger, then rose, drawing her to her feet. Matt smiled at her again before he wrapped his arms around her and lowered his lips to hers. At last!

Jane closed her eyes in sheer delight. She had thought that their second kiss would be like the first. It was not. This kiss was sweeter than the first, firmer and yet more tender at the same time. Matt's lips tasted of wassail and gingerbread, and Jane was certain there was nothing more wonderful on earth than this, their first kiss as an engaged couple.

At length, Matt drew away and pressed a kiss on the tip of her nose. "Oh, Jane," he said in a voice that was husky with emotion. "My wonderful, wonderful Jane." And then he lowered his lips to hers again.

Jane reached up, wrapping her arms around his neck, drawing him even closer. Never, ever, not even in her most vivid dreams, had she imagined happiness like this. It filled her heart and began to over-flow, streaming throughout her body, touch-ing every fiber, sending shivers of delight through her. Her parents had been right. This was the season of joy, the season of miracles. Love was the greatest miracle of all.

Chapter Seven

Jane woke to the unfamiliar sensation of something hard pressing into her cheek. For a second she was confused. Then she smiled as she envisioned the wonderful moment when Matt had placed a ring on her hand. They were engaged! Memories of Matt's face and the love that had shone from his eyes banished the last remnants of slumber. How could she sleep on this, the first day of her life as an engaged woman?

Pushing herself to a sitting position, Jane held her left hand out in front of her, admiring the diamond's sparkle and the contrast of the gold band against her skin. Had there ever been such a beautiful ring? Had there ever been such a wonderful man? Happiness, greater and deeper than she had ever known, flowed through her at the sight of this, the tangible proof that Matt loved her and wanted to marry her.

Jane tugged the drapes open. Had it been

only yesterday that she had feared she would never wear a wedding ring? How long ago that seemed. Soon she would be Matt's wife. They'd find a house and live happily ever after, just the way she had dreamed. She stared out the window at a day that was gray and overcast. Though the heavy clouds presaged snow, the ground was brown and lifeless, the trees bare. Jane was certain there had never been such a glorious morning.

She dressed quickly. Today of all mornings, she could not be late for breakfast. At the last moment before she left the privacy of her room, she slipped Matt's ring off her finger, hiding it in a pocket. There was one more hurdle to be crossed before she could openly display the evidence of their love.

Charles and Susannah were already seated in the breakfast room when Jane arrived. "Good morning," she said as cheerfully as she could. Happiness mingled with dread at the thought of Charles's possible reaction to her announcement. It would be all right, Jane told herself. Whatever his flaws, Charles wanted her to be happy. Still, she couldn't help wishing the morning were over and that Matt's ring were back on her finger.

"It was a wonderful party." Anne and Rob entered the room, hand in hand, their smiles proclaiming their happiness to the world.

Soon, Jane told herself as she buttered a piece of toast and tried to pretend that this was an ordinary day. Soon she and Matt would be able to walk into a room together and no one would question why. They would be a couple. Jane slid her hand into her pocket, touching the ring as if it were a talisman.

She must have made appropriate responses to Anne's questions and Charles's comments, for no one looked askance, but all the while Jane was counting minutes. When the clock chimed ten, her heart began to race. This was the time they had chosen. Soon Matt would be here. Soon they would make their announcement. And soon she would know Charles's reaction.

As if on cue, Megan entered the breakfast room. "You have a visitor, Jane." Though she said nothing more, the disapproval in her voice raised Jane's hackles. Megan had no right to pass judgment. Megan was not the one Jane had to convince. Charles was.

She nodded, dismissing Megan, then rose and walked to the front door. The man she loved was waiting for her. Though Matt began to smile as she drew closer, Jane read the concern on his face. Neither of them wanted this morning to turn into a confrontation, but they both feared it might. Her hand suddenly trembling, Jane reached into her pocket and pulled out the ring. "Please, Matt," she said softly as she extended her hand so that he could place the gold band on her finger. Never again would she remove it. The ring was the symbol of their love, and nothing and no one would come between them. Not even Charles.

"I love you, Matt." Slipping her hand into his, Jane managed a weak smile. "It'll be all right." Their love was strong enough to overcome every obstacle.

When she opened the door to the breakfast room, all heads turned. Predictably, Charles was the first to react. He leapt to his feet, not bothering to hide his shock. "What are you doing here?" he demanded. "The invitation was for last night only."

Susannah rose and laid a restraining hand on Charles's arm. "Please. It's Christmas."

Jane tightened her grip on Matt's hand, drawing strength from the touch of his palm on hers. They were together, and somehow they would survive this morning. "I invited Matt." To Jane's relief, her voice did not betray her nervousness. "There's something he and I want to tell you."

Entwining his fingers with hers, Matt gave Jane a quick smile before he turned his attention to the rest of her family. "Even if

Jane had not invited me, I would have come today." His head was held high, his posture that of a confident man. Knowing how much this morning was costing him, Jane had never been more proud of him.

Matt's gaze moved from Charles and Susannah to Anne and Rob. "I want you all to know that your sister has done me the very great honor of agreeing to become my wife."

The responses came at once, and for a second, it was difficult to distinguish among them.

"Wonderful!" Susannah and Rob smiled.

"Are you sure?" Anne's expression was serious.

"No! I forbid it!" Charles took a step toward Matt, his hands fisted, his stance menacing.

Though Jane felt Matt's reaction in the tightening of his grip, she shook her head slightly, telling him she would be the one to answer. She would not allow Charles's dominion to continue unchallenged.

"You may be my brother, Charles, and you may be older than me," Jane said, her voice steely with determination, "but you cannot stop me from marrying Matt." She had hoped — oh, how she had hoped! — that it wouldn't come to this, but Charles, it appeared, would not see reason. Jane faced her brother. "Though you may still view me as a child and try to treat me as one, in the eyes of the State of New York, I am an adult. I do not need your permission to marry."

Charles ignored her words as he had ignored her so many times in the past. Glaring at Matt, he said, "I wouldn't expect you to understand how such matters are handled in polite society." The insult was intentional, designed to remind Matt that he had grown up on the wrong side of the river. To Jane's relief, Matt's only reaction was a sharp intake of breath. Charles continued. "It is customary to obtain permission from the bride's father or . . ."

Before he could complete his sentence, Matt said simply, "I did."

Once again the reactions were simultaneous.

"When?" Jane asked, so stunned by Matt's announcement that that was the only coherent thought she could frame.

Anne frowned, her skepticism evident. "How did you convince him?"

Rob and Susannah remained silent. Charles did not. "You lie." His words were little more than a snarl, the tone and his stance reminding Jane of a dog defending its territory.

Matt waited until the hubbub subsided.

When he spoke, he looked only at Jane, acting as if the others did not exist. "I asked your father for permission to court you. He agreed but stipulated that I must wait until I finished law school before I spoke to you." Matt managed a small smile. "I finished."

Jane heard little beyond the fact that her father had approved of Matt. Though Papa was not here, it meant more than Jane had believed possible to know that he would have given them his blessing, that he had, in fact, given Matt his blessing. She had dreamed of her father walking down the aisle with her and giving her in marriage to the man she loved. Though that dream would not come true, Jane was filled with warmth at the realization that her father had known and approved of her husband-to-be.

"Papa agreed!" She wouldn't deny the happiness that those two simple words gave her.

Matt nodded. "He did."

"I don't believe you." Though Susannah whispered something to Charles, he shook his head at her and continued. "Your story is too convenient. If it was true, why haven't we heard it before today?"

"Charles, what you believe is not important." Matt's voice was clear and confident, the voice of a man accustomed to presenting his case before a judge and jury, the voice of a man accustomed to winning. "You would disagree with me, simply for the pleasure of the argument, if I told you your wife's name was Susannah. What is important is that Jane believes me."

"I do." As she pronounced the words, Jane's thoughts flew to the day when she would repeat those words in a different context. How wonderful that day would be! But first they had to get through today. "When did you talk to Papa?"

"The afternoon of the Harrods' anniversary party."

Jane nodded. It all made sense now. That was the reason Matt had made a special trip home and why he had spent money he could ill afford on a train ticket. He had told her the meeting with Papa was important, and, now that she knew the reason, Jane couldn't have agreed more.

"You have no proof that that conversation took place."

Matt raised an eyebrow as he looked at Charles. "And you have none that it did not."

His hands fisted, Charles rocked forward on the balls of his feet. "You will not marry my sister."

Though Charles's tone was belligerent,

Matt kept his voice firm but even. "As Jane told you, the decision is hers, and she has already made it."

Charles's face reddened with anger. "Get out!" He pointed toward the door. "You are not welcome on my property, and you never will be."

"I had hoped you would be reasonable, but some things don't change." Matt's words held both regret and resignation.

Jane tugged on his hand. "Let's go." There was no reason to remain. Though the morning had not gone the way she had hoped, she and Matt had said everything they needed to. Now what they needed was time together.

"Where are you going?" Charles demanded.

"Out," she replied. "Out with the man I'm going to marry."

As they stepped outside, Jane took a deep breath. The gray day that had seemed so glorious less than two hours earlier now looked depressing, a reflection of Charles's bitter mood.

"I didn't think it would be easy," Matt said when they had reached River Road and were no longer on Charles's property, "but this was worse than I feared. Even Anne disapproved."

Though that had hurt more than she had expected, Jane would not admit it. It had been Matt who had borne the brunt of Charles's anger, and he needed her encouragement, not further proof that the Moreland siblings' opinions could wound.

"They'll come around," she said with more confidence than she felt. "Even though they shouldn't have been, I think they were surprised, perhaps even shocked." Charles had acted like a cornered animal. Was that how he felt, as if she and Matt had boxed him into an untenable position? To give the man credit, he had always been protective of his sisters. Perhaps this was nothing more than a misguided attempt to keep her from making what Charles considered a huge mistake. But it was not a mistake. Not at all.

Jane laid her hand on Matt's arm and looked up at him, willing him to forget the unpleasantness he had just endured. "It's me you're marrying, not my family."

Matt shook his head slowly, his eyes filled with concern. "I know how important your family is to you, Jane. I don't want to be the cause of a rift."

"Family is important." She wouldn't deny it. "But you're more important. I love you, Matt. You're my new family."

"I hope that will be enough."

The news of Jane and Matt's engagement spread quickly. Jane wasn't surprised. In a town the size of Hidden Falls, the rumor mill was both active and efficient. What surprised her was Charles's reaction. She had thought that the fact that her engagement was now public knowledge would temper his anger. Instead, it had served to intensify it.

It was two days after the disastrous scene in the breakfast room. Charles had come home from the mill earlier than usual and had found Jane sitting in the parlor, working on a needlepoint purse destined to be part of her trousseau. Anne was still in town doing last-minute Christmas shopping, and Susannah was putting the finishing touches on the painting that was to be her gift to Charles. Perhaps he had known that Jane would be alone, and that was the reason he'd chosen today to speak to her.

"Everyone in town is talking about you." Charles didn't bother with social niceties but spat the words at her. "They're laughing at how far the Morelands have fallen and how desperate you must be to marry Matt."

Jane jabbed her needle into the canvas,

then rose and faced her brother. She wouldn't dispute the first sentence, for she knew it was nothing less than the truth. The second, however, made her wish she could stab Charles with something stronger than a tapestry needle. How dare he be so cruel?

"I'm afraid I don't believe you," she said, forcing her hands not to clench. "I'm certain no one said anything like that to you. They wouldn't dare risk incurring your wrath." Charles's eyes widened, telling Jane she had hit a sensitive subject. "Perhaps you'd like to believe that they said those awful things, but I don't. That's your interpretation, Charles, and it's a faulty one."

He tugged at his cravat, as if it were suddenly too tight. For a second Jane focused her attention on the yellow silk patterned with black squares. It was easier to think about Charles's tie than his hateful words.

"You're being more stubborn than usual," he said, his voice seeming to reflect frustration rather than anger. "Why can't you see that that man is wrong for you?"

"Because he's not. Only you believe that. I've never understood why you hate Matt. What did he do to you?"

Charles tugged his cravat again. "That's not important. What's important is that you're proposing to waste your life on a man everyone knows can't be trusted. How long will it be before his temper gets the best of him and he starts destroying things again?"

"That's ancient history, Charles, and you know it. Matt has changed."

"On the surface, maybe, but underneath he's still the uncouth ruffian he always was. When he doesn't get his way, he'll start using force again."

Charles's hands had fallen to his sides, but now they were fisted, as if he were preparing to defend himself. The sight triggered a memory. "Is this about the day Matt blackened your eye in the schoolyard?"

An angry flush colored Charles's face. "I told you, Jane, this isn't about me. It's about you."

She was a silent for a moment, considering his statement, wishing it were that simple, knowing it wasn't. When she realized Charles was waiting for her reply, Jane sighed. "If you really believe that, this conversation is over. Matt Wagner is the best thing that has ever happened to me."

That might be true, but Christmas was the worst holiday Jane could remember. Though it was meant to be a day of rejoicing, there was little joy at Pleasant Hill. Charles had been steadfast in his refusal to invite Matt to the family dinner, insisting that he was not part of the family and never would be. In response, Matt had suggested that he and Jane have their own dinner in the hotel's dining room. Though she knew her brother would be angry when he learned of her plan, Jane had agreed. Nothing was going to separate her from the man she loved on this the first Christmas they could spend together.

The promised snow still had not fallen, and the skies were gray. It was, Jane thought, an accurate reflection of the mood inside Pleasant Hill. Though everyone pretended to be happy as they opened the gaily wrapped packages, Charles's anger had been palpable, lines of worry marred Susannah's face, and Anne and Rob's conversation was noticeably subdued. By the time dinner was served, Jane could hardly swallow. It was good that she was having a second meal, for she'd eaten almost none of Susannah's feast.

"How was it?" Matt asked when Jane joined him at the end of Pleasant Hill's driveway. Though she had told him she could meet him at the hotel, he had been adamant. While he might not set foot on Charles's property, he would indeed escort his fiancée to their Christmas dinner.

As Jane started to reply, Matt shook his

head. "Don't lie. Your face tells me that Charles hasn't relented."

She nodded. "He hasn't. If anything, he's worse. Now he's refusing to attend our wedding."

Though Matt was normally slow to anger, the flush that rose to his face told Jane how furious that decision made him. "He should walk down the aisle with you the way he did with Anne."

Without seeming to realize it, Matt increased his pace to the point where Jane had to take two steps to every one of his. She squeezed his arm, trying to slow him. "What Charles should do and what he does are not always the same." Jane kept her voice low and calm. If Matt knew how much Charles's attitude hurt her, it would only fuel his anger. There was no need to do that. "Let's not talk about Charles. Do you know that I've never eaten in the hotel?"

"Nor have I."

Jane was silent for a second, realizing that, in all likelihood, she and Matt had different reasons for not dining at the hotel. Her parents had never seen the need to eat in a public place, but preferred to entertain at home. Matt's family, she suspected, had been unable to afford even the simplest of the hotel's meals, especially after his father was killed.

"My mother used to say that holidays should be spent with family," Matt told Jane, as if that explained why he'd never eaten at the hotel. "I wonder how many people will be there."

There were more than Jane had expected, but most, she noted, were people who had no families, confirming Mrs. Wagner's belief about where holidays should be celebrated. Jane saw the Widow Green sitting in one corner, her head held as high as if she were royalty, graciously granting the hotel the honor of her presence, rather than a woman who had no one to share the holiday with her. Mr. Ferguson, whose wife had died six months earlier, sat at a table near Widow Green, and if the looks he was sending her direction were any indication, he had aspirations of ending both of their solitary states.

Jane bit back a smile. She was becoming like Anne, turning into a matchmaker. Was this what love and the prospect of marriage did to a woman? It was true that she hoped everyone would know the happiness she'd felt when Matt had asked her to marry him. Jane only hoped they would not encounter the obstacles that blocked her own path to happily-ever-after.

The dining room reminded Jane of Fairlawn. There were the same snow-white linens — made by Moreland Mills, of course — and the same silver flatware. Someone had even draped garlands around the windows, the way Mama always did at Christmastime. Jane sighed, wishing for the millionth time that her parents were still alive. She wouldn't be in this predicament if Papa were here. Jane blinked furiously, refusing to let the tears fall. She wouldn't allow anything to spoil her day with Matt.

As the proprietor ushered them to their table, Jane saw that both Philip Biddle and Ralph Chambers were in the dining room, seated at opposite ends of the far wall. It was a bit sad, Jane thought, seeing all the solitary diners. Though all the tables could easily accommodate four, only one had more than one person. That one belonged to Reverend Collins and his wife. Jane imagined that the fancy meal was a treat for both of them, a change from sharing meals with their parishioners.

Today's meal was a treat for her and Matt, too, their first chance to be together in public. Now that they were engaged, there was no longer a need for a clandestine rendezvous. Today they could enjoy not only the food but also the opportunity to meet openly.

"Congratulations, my boy." Ralph approached their table, placing his hand on Matt's shoulder. "I always knew that when you decided to marry, you'd do it right." When Matt rose to greet him, the portly attorney gave Jane a fond smile. "There's only one problem. You picked my favorite girl. Now, who will I marry?"

Jane looked at the man who had been an important part of her childhood. No one could have asked for a more devoted uncle. She nodded. Perhaps Ralph was the answer to one of her problems.

"Uncle Ralph, you've put me in a terrible position." She kept her voice light, lest there be any thought that she was serious. "Bigamy is illegal, and Matt did ask me first." When both men chuckled, she continued. "I have a great favor to ask of you, though. Will you walk me down the aisle?"

Behind the thick spectacles, Jane saw Ralph's eyes widen in surprise. "Charles will want that honor."

Jane shook her head slowly and placed a hand on Ralph's arm. "I would like you by my side."

He blinked, and for a moment Jane feared that he would refuse. Then he smiled. "Certainly, my dear. Nothing would give me more pleasure." At the sight of the waiter approaching with Jane and Matt's meals, Ralph nodded. "We'll speak of this again. Meanwhile, tell me. Have you chosen a date?"

Matt shook his head. "Not yet. It's Jane's decision, but I can tell you that from my view, it cannot be soon enough."

Jane blushed.

The pumpkin soup they had chosen as their appetizer was delicious, and for the first time in days, Jane found herself enjoying a meal. The reason wasn't hard to find. Matt. She was with the man she loved, and when he smiled at her the way he was doing today, no matter what obstacles life — or Charles — threw at her, she could believe that miracles really did happen and that there was such a thing as happily ever after. With Matt's ring on her finger and his love in her heart, Jane felt as if she could conquer anything.

She and Matt were finishing their mince pie when Philip stopped at their table on his way out of the restaurant. Though he'd smiled a greeting when they'd entered, this was the first time he'd spoken to them. Like Ralph, Philip was dressed in his Sunday best, his collar freshly stiffened, his cravat carefully tied. Jane's eyes narrowed slightly as she recognized the yellow and black tie.

Though separated by a generation, it appeared that Charles and Philip had the same taste in cravats.

"I heard congratulations were in order." Philip shook Matt's hand, then gave Jane's a pat as he looked down at her, his expression more solemn than she would have expected. "Are you certain you want to marry this scoundrel?" Though the words could have been joking, they were not.

For a second Jane stared at the man she'd always regarded as an uncle, too shocked to speak. Why on earth was he acting this way, especially on Christmas Day? Had Charles poisoned him with his own view of Jane's engagement? Though she longed to shout her response, mindful of the fact that they were in a public place, Jane kept her voice low. "I love the man you're calling a scoundrel," she said, her voice as firm and devoid of laughter as Philip's had been.

Philip's lips curved in what could have been a smile. "I can't argue with that, can I?"

When Philip had left and he and Jane were sipping their last cups of coffee, Matt gave her a rueful smile. "When I suggested dining here, I hadn't expected interruptions. I wanted to spend some time with you . . . alone, or as alone as we could be in public."

Jane smiled at the man she loved so dearly. Though it was her family's friend who had caused the unpleasant interruption, Matt was acting as if he were responsible. "We can be alone," she said softly. "We'll walk home slowly. No one will object to that."

Matt rose and pulled out Jane's chair. "I still cannot believe it's true, that you agreed to marry me," he said as they walked toward the front of the restaurant. "What did I ever do to deserve such good fortune?"

Although his tone was light, Jane sensed Matt's seriousness. He seemed to think love was a prize to be won or a reward for good behavior. It wasn't. It was a gift.

"You didn't have to do anything other than just be yourself," she told him. "I love you, Matt. I want to be your wife."

They were standing in the vestibule which was, for once, empty. Matt held Jane's coat as she slid her arms into it. If his hands rested on her shoulders longer than simple courtesy demanded, Jane wasn't complaining. Even through the layers of clothing, the pressure of his hands was reassuring.

"You've made me so happy." Matt murmured the words.

Jane turned to face him. He needed to see her face. Surely when he saw her smile and the love in her eyes, he'd have no doubts.

"I'm happy, too." *So very, very happy.*

Though her assurance should have made Matt smile, his eyes darkened. "I hope so, Jane. More than anything on earth, I want you to be happy. I wish I could ensure that you'd always be as happy as you are today."

How could he doubt it? "We'll be together; that's all I need to make me happy." Jane looked down at the ring Matt had placed on her hand. "Have I told you that I love you?"

"Not for at least thirty seconds."

"Then it's time to do it again."

They both laughed.

Matt wasn't laughing two weeks later as he stood in the park waiting for the men to arrive. In the time since Christmas, he had had not a single client. At first he had blamed it on the holidays. Perhaps seasonal cheer kept the townspeople from having disputes. Perhaps they were simply too busy to think about legal matters. But now Matt wasn't convinced that the time of the year had anything to do with his declining business. There was something else afoot, and his instincts told him that whatever it was, he wasn't going to like it.

Today was the day Matt had scheduled the second workers' rally. As he had hoped,

Hidden Falls was in the middle of the traditional January thaw, and it was warm enough to stand outside for extended periods without feeling like an icicle. The sun was even shining, a rare event in January. It was the perfect day for a meeting, but instead of the crowd he had expected, there was one man — one solitary man — waiting for him.

"Where is everyone?" Matt asked the man.

"They ain't comin'." The man looked down at the ground, scuffing his boot in the dirt. "Reckon I shouldn't be here, neither."

As the man started to leave, Matt grabbed his shoulder. He couldn't let him go without learning why no one planned to attend the rally. He'd overheard enough conversations to know that at least some of the workers felt there was a need for reform. "What's the problem?"

The man stared at Matt for a moment, his lips pursed as if he'd eaten something distasteful. When he spoke, it was with obvious reluctance. "You, Matt. Reckon you're the problem." The man was silent for another long moment. "You talk about helpin' us, gettin' the Morelands to make the mill safer. You tell us the Morelands are the enemy, and then you go and join them." The man's eyes reflected his confusion.

"How are we supposed to trust you when you're fixin' to become a Moreland?"

Matt clenched his teeth as he realized how badly he'd mistaken the mill hands' reactions. He'd told Jane that her presence at the rally would confuse the workers. If that was true, logic said that Matt and Jane's engagement would be even more confusing. Why hadn't he seen it? The answer was simple: Matt hadn't wanted to. He'd seized on the workers' acceptance of Jane at the Thanksgiving dinner, not realizing that acceptance of Jane and acceptance of Matt weren't the same as acceptance of them together.

What could he say to dispel the mill hands' concerns? Matt focused on the crux of the man's statement. "I am not becoming a Moreland. Yes, it's true that I'm going to marry Jane Moreland, but your interests and those of all the other workers come before the Moreland family." Jane would never expect him to compromise his beliefs. Matt knew that. Somehow he had to convince the workers.

"That ain't how it looks to us." The man shook off Matt's hand and strode out of the park, leaving Matt with only the carousel animals for company.

An hour later, he sat at his kitchen table,

staring at the window. When the knock came, he ignored it. It was impossible, though, to ignore the man who walked inside, obviously unfazed by Matt's failure to open the door. Courtesy demanded that Matt rise, and he did, but he couldn't force himself to smile at Ralph, even though it was his mentor's first visit to his house.

"I'm not in the mood for visitors today."

"I figured you'd feel that way." Without an invitation, Ralph pulled out the second chair and settled in on the opposite side of the table. "That's why I'm here." He pushed his spectacles back on his nose, then peered through them at Matt. "I heard about the rally."

"You mean the rally that wasn't." Matt knew that memories of the empty park would haunt him for a long time, almost as long as the sound of the man's accusation. *You're fixin' to become a Moreland.* It was a ridiculous allegation, totally false, but if the men believed it, it was no wonder they refused to consult him.

"Don't give up, my boy." Ralph propped his elbows on the table and steepled his hands.

How many times in the past had Ralph given him the same advice? This time was different, though. "If you're going to tell me about silver linings, I'm afraid that this cloud doesn't have one." Matt scowled at the memory. "My failure is rather spectacular. There was no one at the rally. I have no clients. No one trusts me. How on earth will I be able to support Jane with no income?"

The older attorney looked around the room, and Matt guessed Ralph was comparing the simple furnishings to his own well-appointed office. "My practice generates a reasonable income. You and Jane should be able to live comfortably on it."

But that meant abandoning his hopes of helping the workers. Matt wasn't willing to do that, especially since he feared that assuming Ralph's practice would not be as easy as his mentor claimed. "What if your clients shun me the way my own have? What do I do then?"

"I don't expect that to happen." Ralph looked out the window, leaving Matt to wonder if there was a reason the older man didn't want to meet his gaze. Perhaps Ralph wasn't as certain as he pretended. "Let's wait and see what happens with your clients," Ralph counseled. "I suspect this is only a temporary setback."

"I'm not so sure."

Ralph sighed, and this time he looked at

Matt, his gray eyes registering impatience. "You're a fine man and an excellent attorney, Matt, but you have always had a tendency to magnify problems. Now, mind you, I'm not suggesting you ignore problems, but you need to keep them in the proper perspective."

"I'm not sure what other perspective there is. My life looks rather bleak." The day he'd placed his ring on Jane's finger, Matt had believed he would have everything he'd dreamed of: a successful law practice, a safer mill, and — most important — the woman he loved as his wife. Today he was afraid those dreams would never come true.

"Bleak?" Ralph almost shouted the word. "How can you say your life is bleak when the woman you love loves you? That makes you the luckiest man on earth."

"Then why do I feel like such a failure?"

"You need to eat more." Anne pushed the plate of scones closer to her sister.

Jane shook her head. "I'm not hungry." Though almost every aspect of life at Pleasant Hill had become decidedly unpleasant, meals were the worst. Charles would glare at Jane, speaking to her only when absolutely necessary, and his attitude affected

222

the others, making mealtime conversation so stilted that Jane suspected everyone suffered from indigestion. Even now, when she and Anne were alone in the parlor, Jane found that she had no appetite.

"Charles will relent. I know he will." Anne broke off a piece of scone and popped it into her mouth. "He's just being himself: stubborn."

Jane stared out the window. Though the sky was clear today, the howling wind left no doubt that one of February's legendary storms was approaching. It couldn't be more severe than the storms that raged within Pleasant Hill.

"You're more confident than I am," Jane told her sister. "I knew there was animosity between him and Matt, but I never realized Charles hated Matt."

Anne refilled Jane's teacup, gesturing again toward the scones. "I'm not so sure it's hatred. I think Charles is simply being protective of you and has gone a bit too far." As Jane picked up a scone, Anne smiled in approval. "We all want you to be happy."

"Then why don't you start by inviting Matt here and treating him like one of the family?"

Anne's sigh told Jane she also recognized the futility of that wish. "Rob and I will

welcome Matt once we move back to Fairlawn."

Though Jane knew that Anne had once
had reservations about Matt, ever since the
morning Jane had announced her engagement, Anne had supported her. "If you're
sure Matt is the right man for you," she'd
told Jane that same day, "that's good enough
for me. You deserve happiness, and so does
Matt. I just hope your marriage will be as
wonderful as mine."

Today Anne leaned forward, her expression serious. "Rob and I've talked about it,
and we wish you'd come live with us."

"I may." Though she was still concerned
about intruding on the newlyweds' privacy,
Jane knew that she could not continue to
stay at Pleasant Hill. "Charles's hostility is
upsetting Susannah, and that can't be good
for the baby."

"I agree. Mama used to tell me that
expectant mothers needed to be happy if
they wanted to have contented babies."
Anne laid her cup back on the saucer.
"Isolde and her mother are due to arrive in
a month. You know you'd enjoy being with
Isolde again."

Jane nodded. Isolde Freund and her
mother had worked at the Swiss clinic
where Anne had undergone months of treat-

ment. While Anne had been incapacitated by pain, Isolde had befriended Jane, once confiding that she and her mother hoped to someday visit America. Now they would have the opportunity to do more than visit, for Anne had offered Mrs. Freund the position of housekeeper at Fairlawn. She and Rob planned to reopen the house and move back when the Freunds arrived.

"I'll come."

Anne's smile was radiant. "I'm glad. I'd tell you it would be like old times, but it won't. It will be better. Just think, Jane. You won't have to sneak out to meet Matt anymore."

That night, when the book she was attempting to read failed to hold her attention, Jane opened her drapes and stared into the darkness, remembering Anne's words. No more sneaking. That would be . . . Her train of thought derailed as she saw a figure moving cautiously down the driveway. The woman clung to the shadows, turning occasionally to peer behind her, as if she feared discovery. How many times had Jane done exactly the same thing, slipping out of the house for a clandestine meeting with Matt? But why was this woman hiding? The dark-clad figure turned again, and this time the moonlight illuminated her face, identifying her as Megan O'Toole. How odd. Jane frowned, wondering why Megan was being so furtive. Surely there was no reason she had to conceal her departure. And where was she going this late at night?

Jane tugged the draperies closed, reminding herself that what Megan did when she was off duty was none of Jane's business. She would think of more pleasant things, things like moving back to Fairlawn. Anne was right. It would be good to no longer have to hide her meetings with Matt. Even now, though they met openly, Jane was careful not to tell Charles when she was leaving Pleasant Hill, and she hated that element of deception.

Since their engagement, she and Matt had replaced their forest rendezvous with walks in the park. Though hardly anyone was there, it felt good that their times together were no longer clandestine. Jane liked that, almost as much as she liked having Matt's ring on her finger and knowing that by summer she would be his bride. Their future seemed bright, and yet something was wrong. Though he denied it, Matt was unhappy. It was more than the failed rally. Matt had been open in his disappointment and frustration over that. There was something else weighing on him so heavily that even their times together could not erase the worry lines from his face.

Jane wanted to help, but unless Matt told her what was wrong, instead of staunchly insisting she was mistaken, there was nothing she could do. The man she loved was suffering, and Jane felt helpless. It wasn't supposed to be like this.

It wasn't supposed to be like this. Matt's feet moved sluggishly as he rounded the corner onto Bridge Street, dreading what had to be done. January had turned to February, and that short month was almost over, bringing him no clients. Not only had no one consulted him, but the workers had been open in their shunning, crossing the street to avoid speaking with him, ignoring his greetings. It wasn't the first time Matt had been shunned. He had spent his adolescence being the boy everyone criticized, the town's pariah. Though it hurt to be reminded of the past that he had tried so hard to overcome, Matt could have borne the pain of his own ostracism. What he could not bear was what was happening to Jane.

Though she told him it was simply his imagination, Matt knew it was not. He had been there when she had been snubbed. Oh, the townspeople were careful not to be overt in their treatment of Jane. She was, after all, a Moreland. Morelands, even if they showed the abysmally poor judgment of becoming engaged to a man like Matt, were due respect. But there was no ignoring the way heads turned away from Jane or the curtness of some of the conversations he'd overheard. Jane was being ostracized, and it was all his fault. None of this had happened before their engagement.

Matt clenched his fists, wishing there were something he could do to change the way the town regarded him and now, because of their relationship, Jane. But he knew there was nothing that would help. Nothing but the course he had chosen. Though it broke his heart to admit it, Matt had brought the woman he loved unhappiness. That could not continue. He would not allow it to continue, for Jane deserved better.

She was smiling when she joined him next to the carousel pavilion. "Good afternoon."

Matt could not smile. It was not a good afternoon. It was a horrible afternoon, and it was going to get worse. He swallowed, trying to dislodge the lump that had taken residence in his throat. Somehow, he had to get the words past that lump. Matt urged Jane to sit on the edge of the pavilion but refused to take a place next to her. What he had to say was best done standing.

"I wanted to find fancy words to tell you this, but there aren't any." Twin furrows appeared between Jane's eyes. She had no idea what was about to happen; she had no idea how desperately he wished it wasn't necessary. But it was. "I made mistakes, Jane, serious mistakes, and they've hurt you." He swallowed again. "I'm more sorry than I can say that that happened." He would hurt her again today, but it would be the final time. Then the healing could begin.

Those lovely blue eyes clouded. "You're scaring me, Matt." Jane rose to stand next to him and put her hand on his arm. He ought to push it away, but he didn't, not when he knew this would be the last time she'd touch him.

"What are you telling me?" she asked. "What mistakes have you made?"

Too many to count, starting with the belief that he deserved a woman like Jane. "I should never have come back to Hidden Falls." If he hadn't, he would have spared her so much anguish. "I thought I had a future here, but I was wrong. No matter what I do, it will never be good enough for the people of Hidden Falls." And that hurt more than he had believed possible. He had wanted to succeed here, to show everyone how much he'd changed. "You were right when you told me I should go to New York or Philadelphia." Matt swallowed again, not wanting to pronounce the next words. "I'm leaving tomorrow morning."

Jane nodded. He could tell that she thought she understood. She didn't. "You're right. We can make a life there."

"Not we, Jane. Me. I'm going alone." The confusion on her face told Matt she still didn't understand. He hated the pain he saw reflected in her eyes and the knowledge that he was going to make it worse. If only he hadn't come back! Matt swallowed, then took a deep breath before he forced himself to say, "I'm asking you to release me from our engagement."

"What?" The word came out as little more than a cry.

"Please don't ask me to repeat it. It was difficult enough the first time." Like knives twisting inside him, creating a pain that was almost unendurable.

Tears welled in Jane's eyes, and she blinked furiously to keep them from falling. This was the Jane he loved, maintaining a brave front, no matter what happened.

"Don't you want to marry me?"

Her question was so plaintive that it wrenched Matt's heart. Though he had known today would be difficult, he had badly underestimated the difficulty. Nothing in his life had ever hurt this much, not even his father's death. That pain had been dealt to him. Now he was the one inflicting pain, and that was unbearable.

Matt couldn't answer Jane's question without lying. Instead he said, "I was wrong. I knew there might be problems, but I thought we could overcome them. Instead, all I did was make them worse."

She stared at him, no longer trying to staunch her tears. "I love you."

The words were like a jagged sword, scouring the inside of his heart. More than anything on earth, Matt wanted to reassure Jane, to tell her how deeply he loved her, to insist that they could have a future together. But he could not.

"Forgive me, Jane. It's not enough."

Chapter Eight

Jane felt as if she'd been crying for days. Never before had she wept like this, not even the night her parents were killed and Anne was so badly burned. That night she had remained dry-eyed, though everyone who saw her had urged her to let the tears fall. "They'll help you heal," the well-meaning onlookers had told her, but she shed not a tear. Dr. Kellogg had assured Jane that this was a normal reaction, that she was still in shock. He was wrong. They were all wrong. Jane hadn't cried, because she hadn't allowed herself to cry. She didn't deserve the healing or even the simple release that tears provided. The suffering she held inside was what she deserved, for she was the guilty one. From the moment Jane had seen the scorched brick and learned the extent of the tragedy, she had known she could never be exonerated for her failure. If she hadn't been selfish, if she hadn't left the house, she could have saved her parents and prevented Anne's injuries. And so she had locked her grief deep inside her heart.

It was different this time. No matter how she tried, Jane could not keep the tears from falling. But the people who had told her that tears would heal her pain were wrong. So very, very wrong. Tears brought no relief. In the aftermath of the fire, she had been filled with guilt. This time, she was empty. At first it had felt as if she had been drained of everything important, leaving nothing but an immense void deep inside her. Then the pain had come, and Jane felt as if her very life was being ripped out, leaving jagged wounds that would never heal.

There was nothing left. No happiness, no hope, no future. Matt was gone, and he would not return. Jane brushed her hair, trying not to look in the mirror. She knew what she would see: a tear-stained, white face, the face of a woman who knew that her dreams of love had been nothing more than illusions built on the shakiest of foundations. Matt didn't love her; he never had, and that hurt more than anything else.

Jane tugged at a snarl, wincing when her brush pulled out the knotted hair. What a fool she had been! She had been so caught up in the magic of her own love that she hadn't noticed that that love wasn't returned. It was true that Matt had asked her to marry him. It was true that his kisses had been sweet and had seemed to promise love. But as Jane recalled the times they'd been together, she realized that Matt had never once told her that he loved her. She had said the words more times than she could count, but he had never repeated them.

Matt didn't love her. He didn't even know what love was, or he would never have told her that it was not enough. Love was the most powerful force on earth. It could break down every barrier, vanquish every foe. But Matt didn't know that.

Now he was gone, further proof that whatever he had once felt for Jane, it wasn't love. Perhaps it was only friendship, and he had tried to convince himself that what he felt was deeper than simple camaraderie. Jane didn't know. What she did know was that whatever he had felt, it wasn't strong enough to surmount even the smallest of obstacles. Matt didn't love her. It all came back to that. Matt didn't love her, and that knowledge felt like a rusted knife, tearing out her heart and leaving only aching emptiness in its wake.

"I wish there was something I could do to

help you." Though the others had left to go about their normal morning routine, Anne had remained in the breakfast room, waiting for Jane. Today was the last day she'd be at Pleasant Hill. Tomorrow Anne and Rob were moving back to Fairlawn.

"It's my own fault." Jane reached for a piece of toast and began to spread marmalade on it. Making a pretense of eating was better than facing Anne's censure. "How Charles must be gloating!" Jane broke off a bit of toast, trying to concentrate on the simple act of chewing. "You were right, you know, both of you. Matt wasn't the man for me." Oh, how that realization hurt. Jane felt tears begin to well in her eyes as she faced her sister. "I don't know what to do, Anne. I love him so much!"

Anne shook her head slowly as she replaced her cup on its saucer. "Charles is not gloating. He's sad and he's angry, and it's probably a good thing that Matt left Hidden Falls, because Charles has been making wild threats about killing him. 'No one hurts my sister and survives it.'" Anne parodied Charles's voice. On another day, Jane might have smiled. Today she could manage little more than a nod.

"None of us like seeing you so unhappy, least of all me," Anne continued. "You helped me through the most difficult time of my life. Oh, Janie," she said, reverting to her childhood name, "I wish I could help you." Anne paused, and Jane suspected she was trying to frame her words. Everyone, it seemed, tiptoed around Jane and her grief. "You said you didn't know what to do," Anne continued. "You may not want to hear it, but I'm going to give you the same advice that you gave me in Switzerland: think of something else."

"That's sound advice," Jane admitted, remembering the times she'd provided that counsel to her sister. "Do you have any suggestions? I've been trying to concentrate on chewing and tasting the flavor of the marmalade, but it's not accomplishing much."

Anne wrinkled her nose, obviously not amused by Jane's pathetic attempt at levity. "I'd help you if I could, but you need to find something important — not toast and marmalade — by yourself. Just remember that you're a Moreland. Mama always said Morelands were strong people."

It was a good thought. Two days later, Jane donned her coat and prepared to leave the house for the first time since Matt had broken their engagement. Anne and Rob had left. Charles was at the mill. Susannah was painting. It was time Jane did something. What she had in mind might not qualify as earthshakingly important, but it was something.

She walked briskly, refusing to look at Fairlawn as she passed it. It would be easy to spend the day there, visiting with Anne and Isolde. Jane would not do that. Instead she continued to the last house on the hill. As she turned toward Rose Walk, Brad emerged from his home, wearing a driving duster.

"Jane!" The smile that lit his face was brighter than usual. She had seen Brad only in passing when she'd been engaged and not once since then. "Dare I hope that you've come for another driving lesson?"

Jane shook her head. "Perhaps later," she said, startled by how much Brad's welcome and that broad smile lightened her mood. When Matt had left, Jane had lost not just her fiancé but also her best friend. It felt amazingly good to realize that, no matter what had happened, Brad was still her friend. "Right now, I need your mother's advice."

"Be careful what you ask for. My mother's advice is never in short supply." Brad chuckled as he extended his arm to guide Jane up the stairs. When they reached the door, he paused and raised one eyebrow in the gesture Jane knew frequently preceded a question. "Do you mind if I join you? That is, if the advice you need isn't too personal."

"It's not personal at all," she assured Brad, "but I imagine you'll be bored."

"Not if you're there. I shall bask in the radiance of your presence."

Jane couldn't help it. She laughed and was still laughing when she greeted Brad's mother.

"My dear, it's a pleasure to see you," Mrs. Harrod said as she ushered Jane into the parlor. Though the older woman studied Jane's face, she made no reference to Matt or the broken engagement. Jane almost sighed in relief. The memories of that horrible afternoon were still all too vivid, and she appreciated Mrs. Harrod's tact in not mentioning it. "A true pleasure," Brad's mother repeated.

"That's what I told her." Though the response was directed at his mother, Brad kept his eyes fixed on Jane. "I said it was a pleasure to be in the company of the most beautiful woman in Hidden Falls."

In the past, Brad's effusive compliments had made Jane uneasy. Today she accepted them as a friend's attempt to cheer her. Wrinkling her nose at Brad, she demanded,

"Are you trying to embarrass me in front of your mother?"

"I speak only the truth." He said it with such solemnity that Jane laughed again.

"Brad, dear, why don't you see if Cook can make us some tea and muffins?" When her son had left the parlor, Mrs. Harrod laid a hand on Jane's arm. "I'm delighted to have you here. Do you realize it's the first time you've come to call since you returned from Europe?"

"I'm sorry." Jane felt a twinge of regret for her poor manners.

"Don't be. I understand that you were preoccupied." That was, Jane suspected, the closest Mrs. Harrod would come to mentioning Matt. Preoccupied. What a strange way to describe being in love and having one's heart broken. Jane was so surprised by the word that she almost missed Mrs. Harrod's next comment. "You remind me so much of your mother."

This was an easier subject to address than her failed engagement. "Really? I don't think I look like Mama, though Anne certainly does since the surgery."

Mrs. Harrod scrutinized Jane's face carefully before she said, "It's your mannerisms more than the physical appearance. Just seeing you sitting here brings back happy memories of all the times your mother and I shared."

"It was thoughts of my mother that brought me here today." Though Anne's admonishment to do something had echoed in her head, at first Jane had had no clear idea of what that something should be. Then she recalled fragments of a conversation she and Anne had had, one in which Anne had claimed that Jane was destined to take their mother's place in society. That had given her the seed of an idea.

"I would like your advice about a party," Jane told Mrs. Harrod. "What I'm thinking about would be more than a ball. I'd like to arrange a whole weekend celebration." She continued, explaining that guests would be businessmen and their wives from cities like New York, Boston, and Philadelphia. "The goal is to promote Hidden Falls," Jane said. "We'll show them the goods that the mill produces, the carousel, and — of course — the fact that the Harrod railroad can transport those goods to them."

"What an excellent idea!" Mrs. Harrod's green eyes, so like her son's, shone with enthusiasm.

"I agree," Brad chimed in from the doorway. The casual way he leaned against the doorframe made Jane wonder how long he'd been there. "But why make it so exclusive?" Brad asked. He took a seat on the settee, turning so that he faced Jane. "We could invite the whole town to events on Saturday. If we close Bridge Street between Mill and the river, we could have dancing in the street."

"I like that idea." And, Jane told herself, it wasn't only because Matt would be pleased that the workers were being included. What Matt wanted and what he thought important didn't matter. He was gone, and the sooner Jane accepted that, the better. But, the fact was, if the goal was to promote Hidden Falls, it was a good idea to involve everyone in town. The visiting dignitaries would be impressed by the workers' participation.

Mrs. Harrod pulled a pen and a piece of paper from the small desk and began to write. "Have you thought of a date?"

"Possibly early May. It will be warm enough to open the carousel."

Brad's mother nodded. "What about May Day?"

"We could have a maypole."

"With more games for the children." Brad added his suggestion.

"And, of course, a party here on Saturday night." Mrs. Harrod nodded toward the ballroom that had been the site of many gala events.

The planning continued, with the three of them proposing ideas and Mrs. Harrod scribbling furiously as they made decisions. Before Jane knew it, two hours had passed, and she had thought of Matt only a few times. That was progress.

"Would you like to go for a drive tomorrow?" Brad asked as he escorted Jane back to Pleasant Hill. "The sap has started to run, and some of the farmers will be sugaring."

It had been years since Jane had watched the maple sugaring process, though an excursion to buy maple syrup had once been an annual family event. "That sounds like fun."

And it was. Brad's ready smile and his sense of humor brightened Jane's days so much that she did not object when his visits became daily. Sometimes they would ride through the countryside. Other times he would continue Jane's driving lessons. Still other days they would stay at home, playing chess or Parcheesi. It wasn't like being with Matt. There was none of the excitement, the sense of eager anticipation that had accompanied her meetings with him, but being with Brad was a pleasant way to spend the day. It helped fill the void and keep the pain at bay, if only for a few hours, and for that, Jane was thankful. Maybe, in a hundred years or so, she would have forgotten the sight of Matt's face as he'd told her that love wasn't enough.

It was late morning when Megan knocked on Jane's door. "Brad is here again." The lovely brunet flashed a saucy smile. "Sure and that man is courting you."

Jane stuck another pin through her hat. They had agreed to walk to the falls today, and the wind was stronger than normal, dictating a small-brimmed hat and extra pins. It was relatively easy to secure a hat, far more difficult to suppress Megan's curiosity. "Brad is a good friend," Jane said, refusing to address the issue of courtship. Love, marriage, and happily-ever-after were part of a dream that had been shattered. Now all Jane sought was friendship and a few hours' respite from memories that refused to fade.

"I know courting when I see it." Megan's smile changed, becoming secretive. "I've got me a suitor of my own, you know."

Jane tried not to look startled at the announcement. "That's wonderful news," she said sincerely. Though her own dreams of marriage were gone, Jane wished Megan happiness. And, though she wouldn't mention it, she was glad that Megan appeared to have recovered from her infatuation with Charles. "Who is your suitor?" Jane asked.

Megan shook her head. "I can't say. It's a secret. All I can tell you is that he's a gentleman. A real gentleman."

Jane nodded slowly, absorbing the news. A secret admirer explained Megan's furtive behavior. It also explained why she no longer gazed at Charles so longingly. But who, Jane wondered, could the suitor be, and why did he feel the need for secrecy?

"Mr. Porter wishes to see you." The clerk stood next to Matt's desk, delivering the message in such solemn tones that he might be announcing a natural disaster. Matt rose and straightened his cuffs. A summons from the senior partner in the law firm was not to be ignored.

"Good morning, sir." Matt looked at the man who had hired him, trying to gauge his mood. In the six weeks that Matt had worked for Porter and Latham, he had exchanged no more than casual greetings with the two older partners. From the first day he'd joined the firm, he'd been engrossed in a case that another attorney had abandoned, declaring it impossible to win.

Matt had worked eighteen hours a day, interviewing his client, searching reams of paper for precedents, doing everything he could to avoid another failure. For, painful as it was to admit it, he had failed in Hidden Falls. He'd failed the mill hands; he'd failed himself; most of all, he'd failed Jane.

No matter how hard he worked and how exhausted he became, Matt could not erase the memory of Jane's face when he'd broken their engagement. Shock, anger, and sorrow had crossed her face, one blending into the next like images in a kaleidoscope. But overlying every other emotion was love. Somehow, despite the pain he'd caused her, Jane loved him. If only that had been enough! But it wasn't, and Matt hoped with every fiber of his being that Jane was rebuilding her life as he was his own.

Though both Messieurs Porter and Latham had interviewed him, Matt had suspected the decision to hire him had come from Mr. Porter. The older of the two partners, he was approaching sixty, his hair steel gray, his eyes the same shade of brown as Matt's, his posture ramrod straight. It was that posture, legend said, that convinced juries to trust him. It had also convinced Matt that this was the firm he wanted to join. Though not as large and well known as some of the others he had considered, he had liked Mr. Porter's approach and the promise that there would be opportunities for *pro bono* work.

"Have a seat, Matt." Mr. Porter gestured toward one of his client chairs. Like the rest of the office, they were comfortable without being ostentatious. Though the styles differed greatly, the atmosphere reminded Matt of Fairlawn. *Stop it!* He admonished himself. *Fairlawn and Jane are the past. You have to forget them.* He focused his attention on the senior partner.

"There are several things I would like to discuss with you." The tone of Mr. Porter's voice gave Matt no clue to the nature of the discussion. Though the older attorney leaned back in his chair, clearly at ease, Matt wished he were so relaxed. Until he knew why he had been summoned, he could do little more than force himself to breathe evenly.

"First of all," the senior partner said, "I wanted to tell you that we're pleased with the work you've been doing for us. Finding that citation in the Hobbs case was a stroke of genius."

Matt took a deep breath, exhaling slowly. He wouldn't tell Mr. Porter how important the case had become to him. It wasn't simply that it had given him the opportunity to show Porter and Latham his skills, although that was undeniably important. More important to Matt had been the few hours of respite the intense work had provided. There had been times, some lasting as long as an hour, when he had not thought of Jane. He would not tell anyone that. Instead, he said, "Thank you, sir, but any attorney could have found it."

The older man shook his head. "Only an attorney with your tenacity and the ability to convince both a skeptical judge and twelve hostile jurors could have won that case." Mr. Porter glanced down at an envelope in the middle of his desk, then fixed his gaze on Matt again. "Modesty has its place, but so does pride. Never be afraid to take credit for your success, Matt. You did more than win a case that no one thought we could win. You've also brought favorable publicity to the firm."

Matt had been surprised by the articles in two of the major newspapers, describing his efforts as heroic. He had not considered his work extraordinary. The simple fact was, he had been convinced of his client's innocence and had been determined to prove it. That was, after all, the reason he had attended law school: to see justice served.

"Porter and Latham already have three new clients as a result of that publicity, and more will come," Mr. Porter continued. "The other partners and I want to show our appreciation." He handed the envelope to Matt. "Open it."

Matt's eyes widened when he saw that the amount inscribed on the bank draft exceeded what he had earned during his entire time in Hidden Falls. "That's very generous, sir."

"It's a fraction of the value you've brought to us." For the first time since Matt had entered the senior partner's office, the man smiled. "I told you there were several things I wanted to discuss with you. That was one. The second is that my wife and I have a box at the theater. We would like you to join us and our daughter next week."

Matt took a deep breath, trying to control his elation. This was what he sought: approval of the work he had done, acceptance into what Charles Moreland described as 'polite society.' This was one of the brass rings he had reached for, and by some miracle, it was now in his hand.

"I would be honored, sir."

As he dressed for the theater, Matt couldn't shake his sense of disbelief. Was it possible that he would be attending the most acclaimed play of the season? And he wasn't simply attending it. He would be seated in a luxurious box, accompanying Pamela Porter, who was widely reported to be one of the most eligible heiresses in New York. He listened, expecting a knock on the door, delivering the message that Mr. Porter had changed his mind, that he had decided Matt was not a suitable companion for his daughter. But the knock did not come.

The evening at the theater was more enjoyable than Matt had expected. The older Porters made him feel welcome, treating him no differently than they did the visitors who entered their box at intermission. No one seemed to realize that Matt was an imposter. There were no fingers pointed, no loud whispers that this was the boy from the wrong side of the river. Tonight Matt wasn't simply accepted by polite society; he was part of it. The Porters' invitation had ensured that.

Matt smiled at the woman who stood by his side, greeting visitors and introducing Matt. Pamela Porter was a lovely young woman whose pale green dress accented her dark hair. It wasn't her fault that Matt preferred blonds to brunets. She was petite, her head coming only to his shoulder. It wasn't her fault that Matt preferred taller

women. Pamela's laughter was spontane-
ous, a bit louder than Jane's. It wasn't her
fault that Matt preferred more reserved
women. There was no denying it: Pamela
Porter was a beautiful, charming woman.
Any man would be proud to have her at his
side. It wasn't her fault that she wasn't Jane.

As the curtain rose for the second act,
Matt sighed. When would he stop thinking
about Jane? He feared that he knew the
answer.

"I thought perhaps green and white." Mrs.
Harrod kept her pen poised over the paper,
ready to inscribe the decision.

"I'd prefer red and white." Though he
spoke with apparent conviction, Brad's gaze
was fixed on the floor, as if the patterned
carpet held the answers to the mysteries of
the universe. It was, Jane suspected, simply
a ploy so that neither she nor his mother
could read his expression. Surely he wasn't
serious. Red and white?

"Nonsense!" Mrs. Harrod's reaction was
instantaneous. "That would make it look
like a candy cane, not a maypole."

The way Brad's lips twitched, obviously
trying to contain a grin, told Jane her as-
sumption had been correct and he had been
teasing his mother. It was her turn now,

though she had no intention of teasing. "I like green." Jane knew it was important to express an opinion, whether or not it was ultimately accepted. If she didn't, Mrs. Harrod would become concerned, believing Jane had lost interest in the celebration. "Green is perfect for spring," Jane continued, "but I think we should use another color with it rather than white. Maybe blue or yellow."

The discussion continued for another quarter of an hour before Mrs. Harrod carefully noted that the maypole ribbons would be green and blue. Jane tried not to let her impatience show. Although she still believed that the May Day celebration was a worthwhile project, she was shocked by how many decisions had to be made and how difficult it was to reach agreement on even the simplest of things. The maypole ribbons were a perfect example. The three of them had spent close to half an hour debating the merits of various color combinations, seemingly forgetting that hardly anyone would remember what colors the maypole had worn once the twining ceremony was completed. If this was what Mama's life had been like, Jane wondered how she had survived it.

Brad appeared to be equally restive, for he

kept tapping his fingers on the chair arms. "Would you like to go for a ride when we're finished?" he asked, clearly directing his question at Jane.

"It may be a while." She knew that Mrs. Harrod wanted to discuss seating arrangements for the Saturday night dinner. With twenty-four guests expected, there were almost infinite combinations. Jane tried not to shudder.

"Nonsense!" For a second Jane feared that Brad's mother had read her thoughts, but when she smiled at her son, Jane realized that Mrs. Harrod's response was to the words Jane had spoken, not her traitorous thoughts. "I can handle the rest of the details. You two young people enjoy yourselves." She laid down her pen and paper. "Brad, why don't you bring the car around for Jane?" Something in the tone of her voice told Jane there was more to Mrs. Harrod's suggestion than simply saving Jane a trip to the stable.

"There's something I want to show you," the older woman said, "and I thought it better that Brad not be here." She reached under the chair skirt, pulling out a newspaper that had been folded to highlight one article.

Jane scanned the text, her eyes drawn to

the list of people who had attended opening night of the opera. *Miss Pamela Porter was accompanied by Mr. Matthew Wagner. Miss Porter wore . . .* Jane marshaled every ounce of self-control she possessed to keep her smile from fading. This was the third time in as many weeks that Matt's name had figured in the New York society pages, always with the same woman. As a young and ambitious attorney, it was to be expected that Matt would want to attend various social functions. After all, that was how business was done.

There could be a dozen reasons why he was always in the company of Miss Pamela Porter, but — knowing Matt — Jane was certain there was only one that mattered. He enjoyed Miss Pamela Porter's company. She was young and beautiful, and had impeccable social connections. Miss Pamela Porter would be the perfect wife for Matt. That was why he continued to escort her. Jane tried not to wince as other thoughts assailed her. Perhaps Matt had kissed Pamela. Perhaps they were on the verge of announcing their engagement.

Jane swallowed deeply as she handed the newspaper back to Mrs. Harrod. What further proof did she need that Matt did not love her, that he never had? He had left

Hidden Falls and all that was in it — including her — behind and was establishing a new life for himself. She swallowed again, trying to dislodge the lump in her throat. It was only natural that Matt was creating a new life. All she hoped was that it would bring him happiness. After all, one of them ought to be happy.

Mrs. Harrod's green eyes were serious, her forehead furrowed as she looked at Jane. "I've come to think of you as the daughter I never had, and so I hope you'll permit me to give you some motherly advice." The older woman reached out and clasped Jane's hand in hers. "Let go of the past, Jane. Find yourself a man who loves you."

Though unspoken, Jane heard the rest of the sentence. *A man like Brad.*

CHAPTER NINE

"Hidden Falls doesn't seem the same without him."

It wasn't eavesdropping, Jane told herself. Though Virginia Sempert's comment was directed toward her sister, she spoke loudly enough that all the women in the sewing circle could hear her. Jane pulled her chair closer to Mildred Hirsch and tried to focus on the young woman's needlepoint. That was the reason the dozen women were gathered in the church hall on a Monday evening. They wanted to learn how to do needlepoint.

Remembering how the Sempert sisters had admired her petit point bag, Jane had volunteered to teach a class for any of the mill workers who were interested. Though the women believed the lessons were for their benefit, Jane knew she was the one who'd gain the most from them. The classes would fill some of the empty hours in her life, for, now that the plans for the May Day celebration were complete, Jane's days felt devoid of purpose. Teaching would help. That was the reason Jane was here, not to share gossip.

"Thank goodness, I've never needed his advice," Deborah Sempert told her sister.

Jane turned to Mildred, who was frowning at the twisted yarn in her needle, and showed her how to let the needle dangle so that the wool would straighten itself. Though she and Mildred were apparently concentrating on the tangled yarn, Jane could not ignore the Sempert sisters' conversation.

"I knew I could always count on him to listen," Deborah continued. "Sometimes a good listener is all a person needs."

Virginia and Deborah were speaking of Matt. Of course they were, for there was no one else in Hidden Falls who fit the description. Keeping a smile on her face, Jane slid her chair next to Hilda Brown and demonstrated the technique for starting a new piece of yarn. Perhaps if she concentrated on teaching her students how to make perfectly even stitches, she would not have to think about how accurate Virginia and Deborah's observations were.

Hidden Falls wasn't the same, now that

Matt was gone. Some things were better. Charles's anger had dissipated, and he was more solicitous of Jane than ever before, insisting she remain at Pleasant Hill. She was thankful for that as well as her new-found friendship with Mrs. Harrod. It was good, having the advice of someone her mother's age. But those things, as positive as they were, did not compensate for the emptiness inside Jane. The initial searing pain had subsided, but the chasm it left in its wake was almost worse.

She had felt lonely when Anne had left. This was worse. The void was deeper this time, compounded by the knowledge that it was permanent. There would be no visits, no further contact with Matt. He was gone, and with his leaving, Jane had lost an important part of her life. The most important part.

"Let me see." She moved next to Virginia and looked at her canvas. "Your stitches are a bit too tight. See how the canvas is stretching." Carefully, Jane showed the sisters how to pull the yarn, ensuring that it didn't twist and that it wouldn't distort the canvas.

"You make it appear easy," Deborah said as she tried to emulate Jane's technique. "It isn't."

Jane shrugged. "I could say the same thing

about you. You make hair styling look easy, but when I try, all I get is a mess." She gestured toward her coiffure. Though she had mastered the art of arranging a pompadour, her hair never looked as soignée as Deborah's.

"It's simply a matter of practice," the young mill worker told Jane.

"So is needlepoint." Practice. Maybe that was the key. Maybe with enough practice, Jane would be able to get through a whole day without wishing she were sharing it with Matt.

Spring had always been her favorite season. Jane loved the promise of renewal that it brought, and nowhere was that promise more evident than in a garden. A bubble of happiness rose inside her as she knelt in the flower bed, cutting a bouquet of daffodils. How many times had she helped her mother do exactly this? How many times had Mama told her that the daffodil blossoms were trumpets, announcing to the world that spring had come? This wasn't Mama's garden, and spring hadn't brought everything Jane had expected, but there was no denying the joy of seeing green shoots emerge from the apparently bare ground. She smiled and reached for another flower.

"I thought I might find you here."

Startled out of her reverie, Jane turned to see her sister. Though Anne was wearing her everyday coat and hat, her expression was one Jane had never seen. Anne's eyes sparkled even more than they had on her wedding day, and her smile, though as sweet as ever, held a hint of mystery. If Jane had had to describe her sister in one phrase, she would have said that she glowed. "You're looking especially beautiful this morning."

Anne wrinkled her nose as Jane rose to her feet, laying the basket of daffodils on the ground. "I'm not feeling beautiful," she said, and this time her smile was wry. "I'm feeling a bit queasy, but . . ." Anne hesitated for a second, then smiled again. "Oh, Jane, I'm so happy. I'm going to have a baby!"

Her own heart filling with gladness, Jane hugged her sister. "What wonderful news!" Spring truly was the season of birth. "When is the baby due?"

"Dr. Kellogg thinks it'll be around Christmas."

"It sounds as if you and Rob are giving each other the perfect gift." Jane stepped back and studied her sister. Though it was too soon for physical changes to be evident, Anne's smile left no doubt that she was thrilled by the prospect of motherhood.

"First Charles and Susannah, now you and Rob. Oh, Anne, I'm going to have such fun being an aunt."

Anne gestured toward the wrought-iron bench where Susannah and her mother used to sit. "I tire more easily these days," Anne said as she seated herself. "I'm not used to this, but Dr. Kellogg says that will pass, along with the queasiness." She closed her eyes for a second, and Jane knew she was picturing herself holding her child in her arms. "You'll be a wonderful aunt," Anne said as she opened her eyes, "but you ought to be a mother, too."

Those were thoughts Jane had relegated to the back of her mind. Though her dreams of Matt had included marriage, a small house, and three or four children, Jane knew those dreams would not come true. There was no point in wishing for what could not be. "I need a husband first."

Anne shifted on the bench so that she was facing Jane, her expression serious. "I know you once had . . ." She hesitated, as if searching for the correct word. ". . . feelings," she said at last, "for Matt."

Feelings. Though it was a better term than Mrs. Harrod's *preoccupied*, it didn't begin to describe Jane's love and the horrible pain she'd endured when she'd realized that

Matt did not love her. "That's over." There was no recapturing those first few days of excitement, of believing that there would be a happily-ever-after for her and Matt. Reality was very different from dreams. "Matt made it clear that he doesn't love me." And that still hurt, more than Jane would admit to anyone, even her twin.

"Brad loves you. I know he does. I see it on his face every time he looks at you."

Jane had seen the same expression. At first she had told herself it was friendship, but Jane knew that was not the extent of Brad's feelings toward her. He loved her, and she . . . "I don't know, Anne. What I feel for Brad isn't what I felt for Matt."

"Mama used to say there were many kinds of love and that a good marriage was based on friendship as well as physical attraction." Anne stared into the distance for a moment, then turned back to Jane. "Brad loves you. He'd be a good husband and father."

"I know." And that made it worse. Brad was a wonderful man, one whose company she enjoyed. He would be a good husband and father. Jane knew that, just as she knew it wasn't his fault that he wasn't Matt.

"Are you ready for another lesson?" Brad stood in the front hall of Pleasant Hill, his usual grin lighting his face.

Jane smiled, noting that Brad's freckles, which had made him the object of frequent teasing when he was younger, seemed more prominent than normal today. Would his children have freckles? Ever since Anne had raised the subject, Jane had tried to picture herself as Brad's wife. It was not an unpleasant picture. Oh, there was none of the excitement that had accompanied thoughts of marriage to Matt, but images of a future with Brad brought Jane comfort.

She nodded at the man whose invitations had become so frequent that even Jane could not deny they were part of a courtship. Today's invitation, she knew, was not simply for a driving lesson. Brad always found something extra for them to do, once fatigue returned Jane to the passenger's seat. He seemed to take great pleasure in discovering spots in the countryside that Jane had never visited. They'd done things as diverse as watching maple sugaring and helping to feed orphaned goats. The excursions, Jane knew, were a way of extending their time together so that it encompassed the entire afternoon. And that, she reflected, was not bad.

When they reached the deserted section of Forest, Jane settled herself behind the steering wheel and began to practice the turns that had once stymied her. It was a measure of Brad's skill as an instructor that she now felt comfortable with the Model T, even when she placed it in reverse. It was another measure of his skill that she was now able to let her mind wander while she drove, for the movements of the pedals and the hand lever had become instinctive.

Today she thought about the time they had spent together. The excursions had done more than show Jane the countryside. They had revealed new aspects of Brad. Though he was quick with a grin or a joke, Jane learned that Brad possessed a serious side. He confided how frustrated he was at not having an active role at the railroad and admitted that he was considering leaving Hidden Falls if his father did not allow him to assume some responsibility.

That revelation had shocked Jane, making her realize how much she valued Brad's friendship. She couldn't bear the thought of losing another friend. But Brad, she knew, wasn't simply her friend. He was also a special man, a man filled with kindness and with love. To Jane's amazement, that love was given freely, asking nothing in return.

Brad knew how she felt about Matt and did not expect her to forget her first love.

He would, she knew, be content with whatever she could give him. Anne was right; so was Susannah. Brad might not be Matt, but life as his wife would bring Jane happiness.

"I think it's time to tell Charles."

Jane's eyes widened in surprise, and she felt the blood drain from her face. "What?" Though thoughts of marrying Brad occupied more and more of her time, she wasn't ready to tell Charles. She needed a few more weeks to be certain this was the best thing for both of them. Besides, Brad had not asked her, other than the joking proposal at Anne's wedding reception. Why was he suddenly insistent?

Brad shrugged, as if the answer should be apparent. "You're doing so well that I thought we'd invite Charles for a ride — with you as the driver."

"Oh!" Jane took a deep breath, then released it slowly. Of course Brad wasn't talking about marriage. How silly of her to think otherwise. Unlike Matt, he would probably seek Charles's permission before asking Jane to marry him; he'd never surprise her brother with an unexpected announcement.

"It's the perfect day for a ride." But not for an engagement. Jane pulled the car to the side of the street and stopped it. "You'd better drive to the mill, so we don't spoil the surprise. I don't want someone running ahead and telling Charles."

As Brad drove slowly down Mill Street, Jane tried to relax. How odd to realize that while she had no doubts whatsoever about what Charles's response would be if she and Brad were announcing their engagement, she wasn't certain how he would react to the knowledge that she had learned to drive. Would he be annoyed that she was driving before him? Would he, like Uncle Philip, think it an unseemly pastime for a woman? Jane settled back in the seat, continuing to take the deep breaths that she knew would help quell her worries.

Though filled with workers four times a day, the street was almost deserted now. All the mill hands were working, and few other residents had a need to traverse Mill Street. Idly, Jane noticed a woman half a block ahead of them. While others might walk briskly, she was sauntering, her gait almost a strut. Who was she? Her walk looked familiar. Jane's eyes widened as the car drew closer and she recognized the bonnet the woman was wearing as Jane's favorite chapeau, a one-of-a-kind model. The stranger, it appeared, had copied it.

The woman turned slightly, giving Jane a

view of her profile, and as she did, Jane caught her breath. The stranger was no stranger. She was Megan O'Toole, and Jane would bet almost anything that the hat was no copy. If she was right, Megan had "borrowed" it, probably to meet the mysterious admirer who she mentioned to Jane almost daily. Why hadn't she asked? Jane exhaled slowly, remembering the day she had thought she believed Megan was wearing Charles's signet ring. Were these "borrowings" isolated incidents or the sign of something more serious?

Matt stared at the letter that he had tossed onto the dresser, though his instinct was to crumple it and hurl it into the wastebasket. He shook his head in disgust as he reached for a clean shirt. There was no point in destroying the letter, for the words were etched on his brain.

I hesitate to repeat gossip, Ralph had written in his precise script, *but the tales are so pervasive that I believe them to be true. Brad Harrod is reported to be courting Jane Moreland. According to the stories, an announcement is expected to occur at the May Day celebration she and his mother are planning.*

Matt buttoned his shirt, then slid a cufflink into one sleeve. The news shouldn't have surprised him, and indeed it did not. It did, however, disturb him. Matt gritted his teeth, trying to bite back the pain that thoughts of Jane and Brad together induced. He wanted Jane to be happy. Of course he did. That was the reason he had broken their engagement and left Hidden Falls. Matt knew that Jane's path to happiness involved marriage, and that no matter how desperately he wanted it, that marriage could not be to him. But knowing that and accepting the reality were two different things. Two very different things.

I do not presume to advise you, Matt's mentor continued, *but I wish to remind you that it is still my intention to retire, and my offer to have you assume my practice remains open.*

As he stared into the mirror, tying his cravat, Matt frowned. If only that were the solution to his problem. Unfortunately, it was not. Matt had already tried life in Hidden Falls, and it had proved a dismal failure for him and for Jane, at least when she had him at her side. That was why Matt had left. He couldn't remain; she couldn't leave. And so they had no future together. Matt had known that in February. He knew it today, just as he knew there was no point in wishing for things that could never be. As painful as it was to think of Jane as Brad's wife, that was the best thing for her. Brad could give her the life she wanted and deserved. But, still . . . Hopes and dreams were slow to die.

Two hours later Matt stood in the doorway to the senior partner's office.

"Come in, Matt." When Matt was seated, Mr. Porter leaned forward, closing a bit of the distance between them. "I have a new case for you." Matt was surprised, not by the new case, since he had completed his last one, but by the fact that Mr. Porter was assigning it. Normally a junior partner handled distribution of work.

"You know the firm does *pro bono* work," Mr. Porter said. "When I heard about this matter, I realized that you were uniquely qualified to handle it." The older man handed Matt a small stack of papers. "A man was killed in the Webster Textile Mill. His widow believes the accident was caused by neglect."

Textile mill. Man killed. Matt felt the blood drain from his face as images of the day his father had died flooded through him. Matt had been the one who'd opened the door when they'd brought Pa's lifeless body from the mill. How had Mr. Porter learned of his father's death? When he had applied for the position with Porter and Latham, Matt had made a conscious decision to tell no one of his past other than that he had once lived in Hidden Falls. He had wanted to leave the town behind him in every way possible. Coming to New York was his chance for a new beginning. It was his chance to be accepted for what he had done with his life, rather than the accident of his birth.

Matt swallowed, realizing he needed to respond. "I'm honored by your confidence, sir, but I'm not certain this is the best case for me." How would he face the widow, remembering all that had happened to his mother after Pa's death? An attorney needed to remain impartial. How could he possibly do that?

"Of course it is, Matt. Growing up as you did in a mill town, I'm certain you know more than anyone else on the staff about the workings of a textile factory. I'm confident you'll determine whether or not our client has a valid case, and — if she does — that you'll be able to convince a jury to award her a settlement."

There was no way to refuse, short of revealing a part of his past that Matt wanted to remain hidden. "I'll do my best, sir."

The senior partner smiled. "Your best has never disappointed me." He cleared his throat, then steepled his fingers as he leaned back in his chair. "Lillian and I have tickets for the symphony next week." Lillian, Matt knew, was Sidney Porter's wife. "I admit I'll probably fall asleep during Beethoven, but Lillian and I need to attend the concert. It is one of those social obligations that come with being part of this firm." Mr. Porter gave Matt a wry smile. "We would like Pamela to accompany us, but she has announced that she will not go unless you escort her." The older man's smile broadened. "You've made quite an impression on my daughter."

"And she has made quite an impression on me." It was not an exaggeration or flattery designed to placate her father. Pamela was a beautiful, charming woman, and the more time Matt spent with her, the more he liked her. She might belong to the highest echelon of society, but there was nothing haughty about Pamela Porter. Though he had once feared that conversation with Pamela would be awkward, that had proven not to be the case. To the contrary, Matt found himself both comfortable in her company and eager to spend more time with her. As for Pamela, the smiles she gave him told Matt she was not indifferent to him.

Matt rose and returned to his desk, pondering the invitation. The fact that Mr. Porter had presented it as his daughter's request told him that the elder Porters would not object if Matt began to court her. He pretended to study the papers Mr. Porter had given him, while his mind whirled, considering the possibilities. Marriage to Pamela Porter. It wasn't what he had once dreamt, and yet he could not deny the appeal. Marrying Pamela could give him a close to perfect life. He was already living in an exciting city, doing stimulating work. With the right wife, one with social connections, his career would know no limits.

Matt stared sightlessly at the papers, unable to concentrate on anything other than thoughts of marriage. Though he had dreamed of marrying Jane, that dream would never come true. Jane was about to marry Brad Harrod, while Matt . . .

Matt clenched his fists. It was time to change his dream. He had once thought love and marriage to Jane were what he sought, but they had not brought happiness. The true brass ring, it seemed, was a successful career and marriage to a woman he respected. As Matt had told Jane the day they'd parted, love wasn't enough.

■ ■ ■ ■

"You're more beautiful than ever, Miss Moreland."

"Why, thank you, Mr. Harrod. You're looking quite handsome yourself." Jane glanced down at her gown, an emerald green silk concoction she had had made especially for the ball. Had she told Brad that she would be wearing green? She could not recall having done so. Perhaps it was his mother's doing that his cravat matched her gown, making them look like a couple.

It was not coincidence, Jane suspected, that Mrs. Harrod had placed her next to Brad in the receiving line. The elder Harrods were the first to greet guests, followed by Brad, then Jane and the rest of her family. Though the reason that she preceded Charles and Susannah might be because of the work she had done organizing the weekend festivities, Jane didn't doubt that Mrs. Harrod's matchmaking instincts had also been involved. The older woman had said nothing directly, but had hinted that she and her husband would favor Jane as their daughter-in-law, and Anne had reported that the rumor mill was predicting an imminent announcement of Jane's engagement to Brad.

For once, the rumor mill might be accurate. Though he had never given Jane the traditional gifts of flowers, books, and candy, Brad was definitely courting her. There had even been times when the expression on his face had made her think he was about to propose, but something had stopped him. Perhaps it was timing. On several occasions Brad had mentioned that Anne had been married almost half a year, and the way he had said it told Jane he had taken seriously her lighthearted comment about no Moreland weddings for at least six months. Perhaps he was waiting for that amount of time to elapse before he declared his feelings.

Six months ago, marrying Brad had been the furthest thing from Jane's mind. Now . . . So much had changed in half a year! She wouldn't think about those changes, any more than she would think about the answer she had decided she would give Brad when he asked the all-important question. Instead, she would focus on greeting the guests and ensuring that tonight, the culmination of the weekend celebration, was a resounding success.

The guests from New York, Boston, and Philadelphia had arrived Thursday evening.

While the women had played bridge on Friday, the men had toured the mill, rejoining their wives for a scenic train ride followed by the grand reopening of the carousel. Judging from the comments Jane had overheard, all the events had been well received, as had today's unveiling of the maypole and the other activities that had included the entire town. Jane couldn't help smiling as she recalled the townspeople's enthusiasm as they'd joined in games, a picnic, and dancing in the streets. The gaiety and camaraderie had exceeded even the Thanksgiving dinner. And throughout it all, Brad had been at her side. If rumors hadn't been flying before, they surely were now.

"I hope you will give me the honor of the first dance," Brad said during a lull in greeting guests.

"It would be my pleasure." Though the reply was conventional, it was also the truth. Jane liked to dance with Brad. It was one of the many things they did together that she enjoyed.

"And the last one."

Jane nodded slowly. Hidden Falls tradition said that the last dance was reserved for a special man, either the woman's husband or her fiancé. If she had neither and did not want to favor a single man, she would dance with an elderly man who could not be considered a suitor. By agreeing to share the last dance with Brad, Jane would provide additional grist for the rumor mill.

"That would also be a pleasure," she said firmly. She had made her decision. There was no point in dissembling.

As she and Brad whirled around the room during the first dance, Jane saw that the elder Harrods were smiling with approval. So, too, were Anne and Rob. And, though Charles and Susannah remained on the sidelines due to Susannah's "delicate condition," there was no ignoring their smiles. Everyone, it appeared, approved. Everyone, that is, except Ralph and Philip. As Jane passed them, she saw a faintly disapproving look on both men's faces. How odd. Surely they wanted her to be happy, and Brad would make her happy. She knew he would.

"You're the perfect partner." Brad whispered the words so softly that he could not be overheard, but the warmth in his eyes brought a flush to Jane's cheeks.

"Thank you. Dare I remind you that you once had a different opinion?"

As she had hoped, Brad laughed and changed the subject, but he twirled her with more vigor than normal, as if to show her that, no matter what he did, she would be able to follow his lead. Jane found herself laughing with pleasure.

The song was ending and Brad was preparing to make his bow when Jane saw a familiar figure moving behind him. Today Megan wore her black serving dress, its white apron stiffened with starch, her hair partially hidden under a white cap. When Jane had confronted her about the hat, Megan had been apologetic, explaining that she had wanted to impress her suitor. Since that day, there had been no more incidents of missing items, and for that Jane was thankful.

She looked at Megan, remembering Anne's wedding reception. Tonight was different. Tonight Megan's face was flushed with happiness, not longing. Tonight the lovely brunet did not fix her gaze on Charles. Instead, she barely seemed to notice that he was in the room. And that, Jane thought, was reason for celebration. Whoever Megan's secret admirer was, he had successfully ended Megan's infatuation with Charles. Wonderful!

When Brad returned Jane to the side of the dance floor, Ralph rose and requested the next dance.

"You and Brad make a handsome couple," he said as they glided around the room.

There was something in his voice that made Jane think he wanted to continue the sentence with a "but." Though he said nothing more, Jane was reminded of Ralph's congratulations and obvious pleasure when he heard of her engagement to Matt. Tonight was different. While he might not openly disapprove, Jane sensed that he had reservations about her marrying Brad.

"I enjoy dancing with Brad," she said lightly. "Almost as much as I do with you."

The gray-haired attorney shook his head slightly, his expression telling Jane he realized she was trying to redirect the conversation. "You know what I mean, Jane. It's a serious step you're considering. I want you to be sure you'll be happy."

"I will be." Marriage to Brad would give Jane what she had always longed for, a family of her own. And, if Brad wasn't the man she had first dreamed of, well . . . sometimes it was necessary to change one's dreams.

Though Ralph nodded, behind his spectacles, his blue-gray eyes were serious. "I hope so. I know your parents would say the same thing if they were here. We all want you to be happy."

"I will be," she repeated. Jane was filled with a sense of relief when the dance ended. Though Ralph had said little more about

Brad, instead telling her that he hoped to retire soon if he could find someone to take over his practice, at times Jane had felt as if she were a witness being cross-examined. It was not a comfortable feeling.

As Ralph moved to claim another partner, Jane returned to the sidelines, where Susannah sat, flanked by two empty chairs. "Where is Charles?" Jane asked her sister-in-law. There had been heated discussions at Pleasant Hill about tonight's dancing, with Charles insisting he would not dance, since Susannah could not, and his wife arguing that he had an obligation to their guests. Though Jane believed that Charles had won, the fact that he was no longer at Susannah's side made her think he had reconsidered.

"I'm not sure," Susannah said. "He excused himself for a few minutes. I thought he'd be back by now."

Jane gestured toward the seat on the other side of Susannah. "Since Uncle Philip is gone, too, I imagine they're outside, talking about something."

"More likely Philip is smoking his pipe, and Charles is keeping him company. I don't imagine there's a lot of talking going on."

Jane smiled, picturing the scene just as

Susannah had painted it. "You're probably right. I wouldn't be surprised if Charles is thankful for a little silence. All he's heard all weekend has been how much the guests are enjoying their time in Hidden Falls."

"He's heard even better news than that," Susannah confided. "He's gotten promises of new orders for the mill, and I overheard one of the women telling her husband that they should commission a carousel for the park near their home."

Jane's smile widened, threatening to crack her face. This was why she had organized the celebration. She had wanted to help both Charles and Anne, and it appeared that her plans had succeeded. Though she had failed her family the night of the fire, at least she had not failed this time.

Half an hour later when Jane was waltzing with one of the gentlemen from New York, she glanced toward the row of chairs that lined the perimeter of the room. Both Charles and Philip had returned and, judging from the way they were laughing, they were regaling Susannah with an amusing tale.

Jane smiled when she saw that Ralph's chair was vacant. She'd expected that. Though the older man was not the best of dancers, she knew that he enjoyed the conversation that came with dancing almost as much as the dancing itself. Jane looked around the ballroom, wondering who his partner was this time. How odd. Ralph didn't seem to be on the dance floor, and neither did Brad. Although it was normal to leave during one of the brief intermissions, both men had told Jane that they planned to dance every dance. She smiled at her partner, responding automatically to his questions while she wondered where Brad and Ralph were. Had they, like Charles and Philip, found something fascinating outdoors? Perhaps she and Susannah should venture outside and see what was luring the men away from the festivities.

"Can you help me solve the mystery?" Jane asked Philip a few minutes later when she seated herself at his side. Though she knew Philip would not ask her to dance, she owed him the courtesy of her company for the length of a song, particularly since she had danced with Ralph. As part of one of her many etiquette lessons, Jane's mother had impressed on her the need to treat both men equally.

"I never fancied myself a Sherlock Holmes, but perhaps I've missed my calling." The former banker raised an eyebrow. "What mystery do you want to solve?"

Jane sipped her punch before she said, "I noticed that you and Charles, now Ralph and Brad, all went outside and stayed there for some time. What's the allure?"

Instead of answering, Philip stared at the floor, then cleared his throat. For some reason, Jane's question appeared to have made him uncomfortable. "Oh, my dear, I fear you've placed me in a bit of a predicament," Philip said at last. "I don't want to lie to you, but I fear that the reason I went outside will cause you distress, and that is not my intention. Not at all."

Though Jane tried to mask her surprise, she suspected that she failed. What she had thought was an innocent question had turned into something different. Perhaps she should change the subject rather than open what might be Pandora's box. But Jane had never been one to dodge unpleasant situations. "What is it, Uncle Philip?"

He cleared this throat again and kept his gaze focused on the floor, obviously uneasy with whatever he was going to say. "You'll think me a foolish old man," Philip told Jane, "but I thought I heard the crackling of flames. I tried to convince myself that it was simply my imagination, but I couldn't help remembering that awful night and the sound of the fire." Philip gripped the chair arms so tightly his knuckles turned white. "I'm sorry, my dear, but I went outside to convince myself that I was mistaken and that Fairlawn was not burning again."

Jane felt the blood drain from her face. Would the reminders of that night ever cease? She hadn't realized that Philip and the others at the Harrods' party had been able to hear the fire. Since she'd been so far away, Jane had seen the smoke and the ominous color of the sky; she had smelled the acrid odors of burning wood, but she had heard nothing until she and Matt reached Fairlawn. Perhaps the wind had made the sound travel in this direction, and that was why Philip had been aware of crackling.

"I'm sorry I asked," she said faintly. Tonight was supposed to be a night for happiness and dreams of the future, not memories of the time she had failed so miserably.

"And I regret that I answered." Philip patted her hand. "Let's find something more pleasant to discuss."

By the time the next dance started and Jane moved into Mr. Harrod's arms, she had pushed the unhappy memories aside and was once more smiling. Her smile broadened when she saw Brad reenter the ballroom, his gaze searching for her, his own smile brightening when their eyes met.

"I hope that smile is for my son," Mr. Harrod said as he expertly led Jane around the dance floor. "His mother and I have great expectations for him. And for you."

Jane had no doubt what those expectations involved, for she shared them. She chatted with Brad's father, then touched his shoulder softly. "Something seems to be amiss." Mrs. Harrod was standing at the entrance to the dining room, her expression telegraphing annoyance. "I'd better go to her."

"What's wrong?" Jane asked when she reached the older woman. The consummate hostess, Mrs. Harrod had been schooled to hide her emotions. The fact that she was obviously frazzled concerned Jane.

"It's that girl. I can't find her anywhere." Mrs. Harrod looked around the room.

"What girl?"

"Megan O'Toole. She's supposed to be putting out trays of food." Brad's mother gestured toward the dining room, where the long buffet held only two silver platters. It should, Jane knew, be filled with food and beverages.

"I can help."

"Nonsense. You're a guest."

"I'm also one of the planners. I want

tonight to be perfect, and that means we need to serve the food."

Slowly, Mrs. Harrod nodded her assent. When Jane entered the kitchen, she discovered that Moira O'Toole, Megan's mother, wore the same look of concern that had been etched on Mrs. Harrod's face.

"I don't know where she's gone," Moira said without being asked. "She looked flushed and told me she was stepping out for some air."

"Then she'll be back soon." Whatever other faults she had, Megan was not irresponsible. But as the hours passed, Megan did not return. Annoyance mingled with concern as Jane did her best to cover the young woman's absence. She must have succeeded, for, oblivious to the worry that filled the air in the kitchen, the guests savored the food, then returned to the ballroom for the final hour of dancing.

When the conductor announced the last dance, Brad came to Jane's side. "I believe this one is mine," he said, taking her hand and leading her to the center of the floor. For a few moments, they danced, then Brad's steps changed, and Jane realized that almost imperceptibly he was edging toward the French doors. She felt a fleeting sense of amusement that, although she and Susannah had not gone outside together, she and Brad were headed there. The amusement disappeared when Jane saw the earnest expression on Brad's face, and her pulse began to accelerate as she realized why Brad wanted to leave the ballroom. The time had come.

Brad relinquished Jane's hand for a second, opened the door, then guided her onto the terrace. The night was cool but clear, perfumed with the scent of late-blooming hyacinths. Though the crescent moon provided scant illumination, light spilled from the ballroom, highlighting Brad's face. Jane's pulse accelerated again when she saw that his eyes were more serious than ever, and she felt the trembling in his hands as he gripped hers. Though Brad should have known what her answer would be, it appeared that he was nervous.

"I've rehearsed this all day," Brad said in a voice that quavered almost as much as his hands. "I wanted everything to be perfect, but now I can't remember any of the flowery phrases I practiced." He tightened the grip on her hands. "Jane, I love you. Will you marry me?"

It was the question she had expected, the one she had been waiting for. Jane looked at the man who stood in front of her, his expression so earnest, the love shining from his eyes. This was Brad, the man who had been her friend for years, the man whose unwavering friendship had helped her survive the pain of Matt's leaving, the man who was now offering her his name, his heart, and a chance at happily-ever-after.

As her heart continued to race and her mouth turned unexpectedly dry, Jane studied the face that had become so dear to her. Brad was a good man. A kind man. An honest one. He would be a fine husband to her and a wonderful father to their children. Marriage to him would bring Jane two of the things she most wanted: a home of her own and children. She knew all that, just as she knew what her answer would be. She loved Brad, and there was no denying that the future he offered was one she wanted.

Jane swallowed deeply, then moistened her lips. She opened her mouth, fully intending to say "yes." But when the words came out, she heard herself saying, "I'm sorry, Brad. I can't."

He stared at her for a moment as shock registered on his face. "I don't understand. I thought you loved me."

"I do." And that was the problem. In the second when her heart refused to do what her mind was urging, Jane had understood the meaning of love. It was more than making herself happy. It was doing what was best for both of them. That was what Matt had tried to tell her the day he'd left. Jane hadn't understood it then. She did now.

"Oh, Brad, I do love you. The problem is, I love you as a good friend or a brother, but not as a husband." She swallowed again, searching for the words to help Brad understand. "If I married you, I'd be cheating you, for you deserve more than I can give. You deserve a wife who will love you with her whole heart. I'm not that woman."

Brad shook his head slowly, and Jane hated the pain she saw in his eyes, the pain she had put there. "It's you I want, Jane, no one else. I want you to be my wife and the mother of my children." He tightened the grip on her hands, almost hurting her. "We'd be happy together. I know it."

"I'm sorry, Brad." And she was, so deeply sorry that it almost broke her heart to see him standing there, hurt and confusion reflected on his face. "I wish I could give you a different answer."

He pulled her into his arms and hugged her, his voice fierce with love and longing. "I'll wait. I'll wait as long as it takes for you to see that we're meant for each other." Brad paused, and she heard him swallowing. Oh, why, did she have to hurt him? He was such a good man!

"I love you, Jane. I always will."

As she pulled herself from his embrace and blinked her eyes to keep the tears from falling, Jane winced. Why couldn't it be Matt who had said those words?

CHAPTER TEN

It was earlier than usual when Jane descended the stairs the next morning. Though the ball had lasted late and she had been tired, she hadn't slept well. She had tossed and turned, remembering the shock and sorrow on Brad's face and wishing she had been able to give him a different answer. Why did love have to be so painful? How Jane longed for a magic wand that she could wave to introduce Brad to a woman who would give him the love he deserved. And while she had it, Jane would wave the wand at herself. Somewhere there had to be a happily-ever-after for her.

But she had no magic wand, and so she'd spent a sleepless night. So, too, it appeared, had Moira O'Toole. When Jane entered the kitchen, she found the housekeeper staring at the stove, her eyes red-rimmed and dark-circled.

"I'm worried," Moira said, pouring a cup

of tea for Jane. "Megan didn't come home last night."

Jane felt a pang of remorse. Thoughts of Brad had been foremost in her mind, and she'd almost forgotten Megan's absence from the party. When she hadn't returned by the end of the evening, Jane had assumed Megan was with her secret admirer and would sneak back into Pleasant Hill before dawn. Though that hadn't occurred, there might be an explanation that would ease Moira's worries. Perhaps when Megan left, she had had no intention of returning. "Are you certain she did not leave a message?" If, as Jane suspected, Megan had eloped with her mysterious suitor, surely she would have left a note for her mother.

Moira shook her head. "Not a word. Miss Jane, I don't know what to do. Megan's always been a good girl. Where can she be?"

Though Jane wanted to reassure the older woman, she could think of no reason why Megan hadn't told her mother where she was going. A knock on the kitchen door saved Jane from having to murmur platitudes. She raised an eyebrow, wondering who was calling. Visitors came to the front door, and tradesmen made no deliveries on Sunday. As Moira opened the door, revealing Mayor McBride, Jane's heart sank. The distinguished man's expression boded no good.

"Come in, Mr. McBride." It was Jane who issued the invitation, gesturing toward a chair at the table.

"Good morning, Miss Moreland, Mrs. O'Toole." He remained standing, his clenched fists revealing as much as his solemn mien. "I'm afraid this is not a social call." He nodded at Moira. "We found your daughter."

"Saints be praised!" Moira clapped her hands. "Sure and she had me worried."

Furrows appeared between the mayor's eyes. "You may want to sit down, Mrs. O'Toole." He pulled out a chair for her and waited until she was seated before he continued. "Two workers found your daughter this morning when they were sweeping the park." Frowning, he shook his head. "There's no easy way to say this. They found her on the carousel." He swallowed deeply, his reluctance to complete the tale obvious. "Your daughter is dead, Mrs. O'Toole. Murdered."

As Moira began to keen, the mayor turned toward Jane. "I need to speak with your brother."

It was a beautiful Monday morning, the

kind, he had heard, that made May one of the best months of the year. As he sat in the back of the hansom cab on his way to the Webster mill, Matt told himself that he should think about the weather or the case he was undertaking or even Pamela Porter. He should think about anything other than the fact that the Hidden Falls May Day celebration was now concluded and, if the rumor mill was correct, Jane was officially engaged to marry Brad Harrod.

Matt gritted his teeth. He didn't want to think about Jane's engagement. Though the prospect of her marriage caused his insides to knot, he could not change it. Matt had had his chance. For a brief, wonderful period, he had been the one planning to marry Jane, and look how that had ended. He loved her with all his heart and she loved him, but it wasn't enough. Though Matt wished it were otherwise, love did not guarantee happiness.

The cab had left the tree-lined streets that surrounded his boarding house and was now in an area of seedy buildings and dilapidated warehouses. Matt stared out the side window, reflecting that though the portion of Forest where he had lived was considered the worst section of Hidden Falls, it appeared prosperous in comparison to these buildings. Surely this wasn't where the Webster mill hands lived.

"How much further?" he called to the driver.

"Another ten minutes." Good. By then, the neighborhood would have had a chance to improve. Matt didn't expect palatial conditions, but he did expect that the workers' accommodations would be comparable to the ones in Hidden Falls.

Hidden Falls. No matter what he did, no matter how hard he tried, his thoughts returned there, to Jane and the life he'd once longed for. That was gone now. The dream of marrying Jane and building a life together in their hometown was over. Jane's engagement to Brad concluded that chapter of Matt's life. It was time to begin a new one.

Though he wrinkled his nose at the unpleasant smells of rotting garbage and streets that had not been cleaned in months, Matt could not deny the feeling of anticipation that swept through him as he thought of the case he was now handling. While his initial reaction had been dismay, Matt had to admit that Mr. Porter had been correct. It was the right case for him. He'd known that from his first meeting with the widow.

Matt couldn't bring Mrs. Preble's husband back. No one could. But he had a chance to right wrongs, starting today. If Mrs. Preble was accurate in her description of the working conditions at the mill, Matt would have the force of the law behind him as he ensured that she need no longer worry about where she would live and what she would eat. The woman's plight had touched Matt in ways he hadn't expected. Instead of sorrow, it had brought anger and the realization that not every widow was as fortunate as his mother.

Fortunate? Matt blinked in surprise. It was the first time he could recall using the word *fortunate* in conjunction with thoughts of Moreland Mills. But what he had learned about Mrs. Preble's situation told Matt that John Moreland had been unique in his willingness to continue to provide housing for the mill hands' widows and schooling for their children.

"This is it, sir." The driver stopped the cab in front of a red brick building that reminded Matt of the factory that had taken his father's life. It was the same shape and size as Moreland Mills, even the same shade of brick. The difference was that whereas Moreland Mills' brick had been broken with large windows, the five stories of this building had no openings. The only windows were on the two story section that, if the layout was the same as the factory in Hidden Falls, held the owner's office.

A thin man of slightly less than average height greeted Matt, introducing himself as Harold Ketch. "Mr. Webster was called out of town," he explained as he ushered Matt into the factory. "He asked me to show you around."

Matt nodded. Though he had hoped to meet the owner, he might learn more from one of the employees. They were often less schooled in choosing their words carefully. "You know why I'm here," he said, keeping a smile on his face.

It was Mr. Ketch's turn to nod. "That unfortunate accident," he said solemnly. "Workers can be so clumsy."

Though bile rose to his throat, Matt bit back his angry retort. He would accomplish nothing by alienating the man. "I would like to see the weaving room where the . . ." He paused slightly. ". . . unfortunate accident occurred."

His sarcasm was wasted on Mr. Ketch. "Are you certain, sir? It's a noisy room, not the sort of place a gentleman like you is accustomed to."

Gentleman. Matt kept his expression neutral as he reflected on the difference a hundred miles made. No one in Hidden Falls would have referred to him as a gentleman, despite his law degree and the finely tailored suits he'd worn when he established his practice.

"Be that as it may, I need to see the room. It's necessary to satisfy the widow." *And myself.* Though Matt knew he needed to remain impartial, his pulse raced at the thought that he might be able to achieve here what he had failed to do in Hidden Falls.

His reluctance obvious, Mr. Ketch led the way up the main stairway. "Certainly, sir."

When his guide opened the door and ushered Matt into the weaving room, it was all he could do to control his reaction. Matt thought he knew what to expect. He had, after all, spent a considerable amount of time in the weaving room at Moreland Mills. He'd worked there for a year after his father's death before John Moreland had insisted that he return to school. Matt knew the Moreland Mills weaving room. This one was different.

He forced his face to remain impassive as he looked around. The looms appeared to be the same type that Moreland Mills used. The difference was that here there were at least a third more in a room the same size.

Matt stared at the scene before him, wondering how the workers were able to move between them to tie on new warp. An average-sized man would have difficulty maneuvering. One with unusually broad shoulders would bump into the neighboring loom.

The crowding was appalling and dangerous, but it was the noise of the additional looms that disturbed Matt even more. Though it was difficult to hear in the Moreland Mills weaving room, this thumping and banging was truly deafening. Even shouted warnings would be lost in the din the machines created.

And then there was the lighting. Or, more precisely, the absence thereof. With no windows to provide natural illumination and only half the number of lights in the ceiling, the room was considerably darker than Moreland Mills. The hand signals the workers used to communicate would be virtually useless here. Matt tried not to let his dismay show. The question was no longer how Mr. Preble had died but, rather, how the others managed to avoid serious injuries.

Mr. Ketch smiled broadly. "As you can see, Mr. Webster insists on the most modern equipment. Why, he had those lights put in last month." He gestured toward the few electric fixtures.

"What was there before?" Mr. Preble's death had occurred two months earlier, before the pitiful attempts at improvements had been implemented.

"Why, gaslight, of course. The new ones are much brighter."

"I see." And Matt did.

As he settled in the hansom cab for the ride back to his office, Matt reflected that his eyes had been opened, both literally and figuratively. As much as he hated to admit it, Charles had been telling the truth when he said that Moreland Mills was better than most mills. Charles had also been right when he had accused Matt of chasing ghosts.

How much time he'd wasted! He'd been so blinded by his grief over his father's death that he'd let sorrow fester, turning to anger. That was bad enough. Even worse was that, in the grip of that anger, Matt had sought to assign blame. He had wanted someone else to suffer the way he had. The truth was, John Moreland could not have saved Pa's life. Accidents *did* happen, but John Moreland and now his son had done their best to prevent them.

Matt's smile was rueful. The workers knew the truth. That's why they hadn't been interested in organizing against the mill. It was only Matt, chasing ghosts, who had thought there was a problem.

By the time the driver stopped in front of the building that housed Porter and Latham, Matt's smile had become genuine. If he had needed further proof that he was not needed in Hidden Falls, today had provided it. There was little for him to change there, but here . . . Here he could make a difference. Here his efforts to improve mill conditions would have an effect. Jane was right. This was where he needed to be.

"I didn't do it."

"Of course you didn't." Jane took a sip of the cocoa that Anne had prepared, insisting that Mrs. Enke's remedy would help. It didn't. Nothing could change the fact that Charles had been accused of murder and that only his standing in the community kept him from being locked in the town's one jail cell.

Jane looked around the small parlor where she had sat so often since she had moved to Pleasant Hill. It was a bright, cheerful room, upholstered in shades of blue and green, a darker blue carpet on the floor. Normally she enjoyed sitting here and found it a peaceful place to rest. Today it was anything but peaceful. Charles and Susannah sat on one settee, their arms wrapped around each other as if that would ensure they would not be separated. Anne and Rob occupied the other settee. Though they remained a proper six inches apart, their hands were clasped, and Jane knew that Anne was seeking comfort from her husband. Jane had positioned her dark green wing chair between the two settees, trying to ignore the fact that she sat alone. Like her siblings, she needed comfort and reassurance, but refusing Brad's proposal meant that Jane had no one in Hidden Falls who could provide it.

"You couldn't kill another person anymore than I could," Jane told her brother. As soon as Mr. McBride, who served as Hidden Falls' policeman in addition to being its mayor, had accused Charles, Jane had called Anne. Charles needed his family's support. Now, two days later, it appeared he needed much more than that.

"We know Charles is innocent, but no one will believe us." Anne's voice trembled, signaling that she was once more close to tears. They had all reacted differently to the news of Charles's implication in Megan's murder. Anne cried; Jane raged; Charles remained so calm that Jane suspected he was still in shock.

Though lines of strain marked his face, Charles's voice did not break. "Even I have to admit that the evidence appears incriminating. Megan was strangled with my tie, and she had my ring on her finger."

"Why wouldn't the mayor believe me when I told him that the tie was gone?" Susannah's frown mirrored her frustration. "Even though it was Charles's favorite cravat and I knew he'd miss it, it was so badly stained that I threw it out weeks ago." Susannah looked at Jane, her love for her husband and concern for his welfare evident. "How did the murderer find it?"

"Perhaps Megan took it out of the trash," Jane suggested. "I know I saw her wearing Charles's ring several months ago, and she borrowed my best hat one day. It's possible she saw the tie and wanted it. But that doesn't explain why she had it with her that night." Nothing made sense unless Charles was the murderer. Since he wasn't, the only other explanation was that someone wanted to frame him.

Rob, who had been sitting quietly, spoke for the first time. "Unfortunately, it's not just the evidence. Charles also had the opportunity to kill Megan." The murder, they had been told, had occurred during the ball.

"A lot of people know that he was absent from the party for a while." Though Charles had explained that something — perhaps the punch — had upset his stomach and he'd wanted fresh air to clear his head, Mr. McBride had not believed him, especially when Susannah had reluctantly admitted that Charles had not told her of his illness. The fact was, Charles had been gone long enough to kill Megan.

Jane laid her cup on the table with so much force that cocoa sloshed onto the saucer. "Charles might have been gone, but so were Brad, Uncle Philip, and Uncle Ralph. No one's accusing them."

"There's no reason to," Charles pointed out with disturbing logic. "It wasn't their cravats or their rings that were found at the murder scene. Everything points to me." Someone wanted Charles accused and had gone to great lengths to ensure that he was.

"But opportunity's not everything. There has to be a motive." Anne brushed a tear from her cheek, then gripped Rob's hand again as she faced her brother. "Why would anyone think you'd wish Megan dead?"

"I didn't."

Jane managed to swallow a sip of cocoa. Though she knew Charles was innocent, the rest of Hidden Falls did not. "Unfortunately, Megan told me she had a secret admirer who was going to marry her. An 'important gentleman' is the way she described him. Apparently, she told others the same story."

"And Charles was supposed to be that 'important gentleman'? Absurd!" Anne scoffed.

"We all agree that it's absurd," Susannah said quietly, "but the fact is, it's common knowledge that Megan set her cap for Charles before we were married."

Rob's expression revealed his skepticism. "Do they think he promised marriage, then changed his mind and killed her so she wouldn't tell anyone? Absurd!"

"It may be absurd," Charles said in a strained voice, "but if I can't prove my innocence, I may go to jail — or worse — for a crime I didn't commit."

It was a nightmare. That was the only way Jane could describe living under a cloud of suspicion with the very real fear that Charles would be convicted of Megan's murder. There had to be a way to prove his innocence, but though they'd spent hours talking, no one in the family could find it. They needed help.

"I wish I could help you, my dear," Ralph said when Jane consulted him. The portly attorney's face was more serious than Jane had ever seen it. "I will, of course, defend Charles if it comes to that, but I must admit that the situation is not a good one." Ralph polished his spectacles, then replaced them on his nose. "I've spoken to Mr. McBride, and he believes his case is a strong one. It's not simply that all the evidence points to Charles, but also there are no other suspects."

"What about the man Megan had been seeing, her secret admirer?"

Ralph shook his head slowly. "There's no proof that Charles wasn't that admirer."

"He wasn't!"

Ralph's expression was grim. "You and I know that, but knowing and proving are two very different things." Hidden Falls' only lawyer crumpled a piece of paper in obvious frustration. "It pains me to admit it, but I fear this case is beyond my expertise. Charles needs an attorney who knows criminal law better than I do."

Jane closed her eyes, not wanting Ralph to see the despair in them. She had to save her brother. She had to. And that meant finding another lawyer. Jane clenched her hands, then relaxed them slowly as she admitted that there was a possible solution. There was someone who could help Charles. He had the training and, if the newspaper articles were accurate, recent experience. The question was, would he?

CHAPTER ELEVEN

"You did what?" Charles's face, which had borne a grayish pallor ever since Mayor McBride had announced that he was the primary suspect in Megan's murder, turned an alarming shade of red. Jane leaned back in the chair, trying to distance herself from her brother's anger. She had known he would not be pleased, but she had not expected such an extreme reaction.

"You heard me the first time, Charles," Jane said as calmly as she could. Mama had told her that the best way to diffuse anger was to speak quietly. "I sent Matt a telegram, asking him to help us." She wouldn't tell Charles how much courage she had had to muster to draft that telegram, after what had transpired between her and Matt the last time they'd been together. He might refuse. He probably would refuse. But still she had to ask. And, miraculously, Jane had received a response the same day, indicating that he would arrive on the next train.

"I don't want him here." Charles sprang up from the chair where he had been sitting and began to pace the floor. It was strange. Charles had been almost unnaturally calm when the mayor had accused him of murder, but the thought of Matt's defending him had caused his anger to flare.

"I'm afraid you have no choice, Charles." It was, Jane realized, the first time she'd seen her brother pace. Perhaps it wasn't simply anger at Matt that propelled his steps. Perhaps this was also his way of venting frustration that he'd been placed in this situation.

Though she was addressing Charles's back, Jane continued, "I will not let you be convicted when I know that you didn't kill Megan."

Charles stared out the window, then pivoted on his heel and glared at Jane. "Just what will Matt Wagner do? The man would like nothing better than to see me hang."

Jane resisted the urge to ignore her brother's ranting. If Matt was going to help him, he needed Charles's cooperation. "Can't you forget your silly quarrel for even a minute?" she demanded. "Matt's a lawyer — a very good one — and that's what you need right now."

"There are other fine attorneys in New York state. Ralph would have found one for me."

But no one else knew Charles. No one else realized that, whatever faults he might have, Charles was not a murderer. She and the rest of the family would waste precious time convincing a stranger. "Stop being so stubborn." Jane wanted to shake some sense into Charles. She clasped her hands together to keep them from trembling. "Don't you understand that I want to help? It's time I did something good for this family."

Charles stared, his expression one of bewilderment. "What do you mean?"

"Oh, Charles, don't you see? Maybe if I can help you, I'll be able to forgive myself for the fire." Though she hadn't meant to utter them, the words were wrenched out of Jane.

"What are you talking about?" Charles stopped his pacing and loomed over her, his brow wrinkled with concern. "What does the fire have to do with Megan's murder?"

"I should have been there." They were simple words. Five words, five syllables: an elementary concept. What they represented to Jane was anything but simple. Hearing her speak those words, she doubted anyone would guess how deeply the thought had haunted her, how it had turned into a burden of guilt so heavy that at times it threatened to crush her, how it had filled her days with regret and her nights with unspeakably painful dreams. "If I had been home when the fire started, I could have saved Mama and Papa, and Anne wouldn't have been burned."

Blood drained from Charles's face, and his eyes widened in shock. "I can't believe you blame yourself for the fire!" He tugged Jane to her feet and wrapped his arms around her. Jane couldn't remember the last time Charles had done anything so physically demonstrative. He was a man who rarely displayed emotions other than anger. "Oh, Jane! If only I had known that you thought you could have changed what happened that night!" He patted her back, as if he were soothing a colicky baby. "For the longest time I thought the same thing. I was convinced that if I hadn't argued with Father, the fire wouldn't have started."

Jane caught her breath and looked up at her brother. Not once had it occurred to her that Charles believed he shared the blame for the fire. He had been miles away when it started, and in all the intervening months he had said nothing that had indicated he felt more than the normal sorrow over the events of that horrible night.

Charles placed his hand on Jane's cheek. "I wish I'd known what you were going through. I might have been able to help. It took me a long time to accept it, but the truth is, none of us could have stopped it. Someone set that fire and meant for it to be deadly." Charles tipped Jane's chin so that he could look into her eyes. "I've made my peace with what happened, and I hope you can, too. Now all I wish is that I knew who set the fire."

Jane shook her head slowly, still trying to make sense of what Charles had said. "That's not important anymore. All that matters now is proving your innocence. Matt will do that."

Clackety-clack. Clackety-clack. The sound of the train wheels formed a chorus, seeming to echo the thoughts that reverberated through his mind. *You're a fool. A colossal fool.* Clackety-clack. Matt sat in the crowded train compartment, ignoring the other travelers' attempts to engage him in conversation. Though on another day he might have spoken, today his thoughts made him an unfit companion. What a fool he was! When he had left Hidden Falls, Matt had sworn he would never return, yet here he was, only a few minutes away from the town that held so many memories. His resolve, which he had believed as strong as the train rails, had melted like snow on a summer day. All it had taken was one plea from Jane.

What a fool he was! Matt closed his eyes in a vain attempt to block the thoughts that rushed through him. It was bad enough that he would have Charles as a client. Though Matt's lips curved in a wry smile at the irony of being in a position to defend his childhood nemesis, the smile quickly turned into a frown at the realization of what returning to Hidden Falls meant. It wasn't only Charles he would see. There would also be no way to avoid the sight of Jane and Brad together. By now their engagement would be public knowledge. Jane would be wearing Brad's ring, and that lovely smile that had once greeted Matt would be lavished on Brad. How would he bear it?

Matt gripped the edge of the seat. What a fool he was! He should have refused. He should have sent a polite but firm refusal, citing a pressing client load. That wouldn't have been a lie. Matt did have important cases to prepare for Porter and Latham, and it had been with obvious reluctance that Mr. Porter had granted him a leave of absence to return to Hidden Falls. Matt should have refused Jane's plea, and yet he could not.

He stared out the window. When he had left, the trees had been bare; now they sported the fresh green of new growth. The seasons had changed, but he had not. Though he had thought he'd put Hidden Falls and Jane behind him, his reaction to her telegram demonstrated the fallacy of that particular thought.

Unbidden, Matt recalled the night of Anne's wedding when Jane had met him at the site of the old gazebo, demanding that he dance with her. He hadn't wanted to dance with her, not there. Their first dance should have been in a ballroom, not on an old cement platform. But he'd agreed, telling Jane that, like Charles, he was unable to resist a Moreland woman's plea. Half a year had passed, and their lives, which Matt had once thought would be entwined forever, had gone in different directions. He had believed he'd changed. Perhaps he had, but one thing had not changed: Matt was still unable to refuse one of Jane's requests. That was why he was on his train, pulling into the Hidden Falls station. That and the fact that no matter what else he might be, Charles Moreland was not a murderer. Matt would stake his reputation on that.

As the train screeched to a halt, Matt

made his way to the door. The sooner he was off the train, the sooner he could begin his defense of Charles and the sooner he could return to New York. That was what he wanted: to spend the minimum time in Hidden Falls, the minimum time with Jane. Matt's lips curved in a rueful smile. He was deluding himself if he claimed he didn't want to see Jane. He did. What he didn't want to see was Brad Harrod's fiancée.

Gripping his suitcase, Matt descended the iron steps, trying to ignore the way his pulse leaped when he spotted Jane. She looked older than the last time he'd seen her. Strain, Matt knew, could do that to a person. Today she was soberly dressed in a dark blue frock and matching hat. Her normally impeccably-coiffed hair appeared a bit lopsided, as if she hadn't been able to focus when she was arranging it. The biggest sign of the strain was her eyes. Ringed with circles, they bore a haunted expression that reminded Matt of those first few terrible days after the fire when Jane and her family tried to make sense of lives that had been turned upside down. She looked tired and strained, and yet, despite everything, Jane was the most beautiful woman he had ever seen.

What a fool he was! Matt clenched his

fists, trying to quell the longing that welled up inside him. He should not have returned to Hidden Falls. There was nothing here for him but memories of what could never be. He'd made his decision that gloomy February day. He should not have come back.

"Thank you for coming." Jane extended her hand, as if he were a casual acquaintance, not the man she had once promised to marry. Matt bit back his disappointment. What had he expected? Brad's fiancée would hardly welcome him effusively. Even if he and Jane were still engaged, the fact that this was a public place would have constrained their greeting.

Jane tugged her hand slightly, telling Matt he had held it longer than simple courtesy demanded. As he released it, she continued, "I didn't know where else to turn."

Jane's words confirmed what Matt had suspected, that only desperation had caused her to contact him. Though the knowledge stung, it was no more than he deserved. He had, after all, been the one who had broken their engagement. Though the decision had been made to protect her, he had been the one who had uttered the final words. He had been the one who had brought anguish to those lovely blue eyes. He had been the one who had rejected the love she had offered so freely.

"I hope I'll be able to help." While he longed to ask her whether she was certain life with Brad would bring her happiness, Matt dared not. It was safer to speak of the murder. That, he reminded himself, was the reason he'd returned to Hidden Falls. Only that.

Matt walked at Jane's side, his eyes widening when she gestured toward a motor car and climbed behind the wheel. "I didn't know Charles had bought a car," Matt said as he settled in the passenger seat, "and I certainly didn't know you could drive."

"It's Brad's car," Jane said as she started the motor.

Brad. Of course. Matt tried not to think of the other luxuries the heir to the Harrod fortune was able to lavish on the woman he loved. Undoubtedly, the ring he had given her to celebrate their engagement boasted a diamond the size of one of the Model T's headlights, whereas the one she had once worn held only a chip.

Matt closed his eyes briefly, remembering the day he had bought the ring and the joy that had filled him when he had slid it on Jane's finger. He should have returned it to the jeweler and gotten his money back. A sensible man would have done that. Matt had always thought he was a sensible man. But if he was, why was the ring Jane had once worn tucked into his suitcase?

"Brad taught me how to drive."

From a distance Matt heard Jane's words, and as he did another memory surfaced, the memory of Jane and Brad together in the motor car, Jane laughing with apparent pleasure. At the time, Matt had believed that Jane's pleasure was caused solely by Brad's company, and spears of jealousy had pierced him. Had he been wrong? Was Jane's apparent glee the result of learning to drive?

Matt recalled the day he had taught Jane to fish and the cries of delight she'd uttered when she had hooked her first trout. She had always enjoyed learning new things. Was the fact that he was teaching her the reason she had spent so much time with Brad? Matt gave himself a mental shake. He was being foolish again. If Jane's friendship with Brad was nothing more than driving lessons, Ralph would not have called it a courtship.

"I'm impressed," Matt said as Jane expertly negotiated the turn out of the train station. When she smiled in apparent pleasure over the compliment, Matt changed the subject. It was far too dangerous to watch Jane smile and to be reminded of the life he'd once envisioned.

"Tell me everything you know about the case," he urged. Her telegram had said only that Charles was accused of Megan O'Toole's murder and that Jane needed Matt's assistance in proving her brother's innocence. Now, as she recounted the events, Matt tried not to frown. Though Jane already knew how damning the evidence was, he didn't want her to see how difficult he feared it would be to exonerate Charles. "The first thing I want to do is talk to your brother," Matt said. "I want to know every detail of what he did outside the Harrods' house. Perhaps someone saw him and can establish an alibi."

Jane's feet moved on the pedals as they climbed the hill to River Road. "It won't be an easy conversation," she cautioned. "Charles is unhappy that I asked you to help."

"I'm not surprised. I knew you must be desperate if you contacted me." She would not have asked him if she had had any alternatives.

Jane shook her head slightly, taking her eyes off the road to look at him. "It was more than desperation, Matt. I know there are other attorneys — Charles has certainly reminded me of that particular fact — but it's you I trust."

The rush of satisfaction that her words brought startled Matt by its intensity. Jane trusted him. Surely that was a good sign. Only a foolish man would have expected her to say that she had asked him to return because she still loved him. Matt shook himself mentally. Even if Jane did love him, nothing had changed. They had no future in Hidden Falls. Both he and Jane would be miserable if they tried to build a life together here. It was Brad who could bring Jane happiness.

But as they entered the gray house that was Charles Moreland's new home and Jane removed her hat and gloves, Matt was unable to deny the bubble of happiness that rose within him. Jane wore no rings.

He looked different. Jane darted another glance at the man who walked at her side as they climbed the front steps to Pleasant Hill. It was not simply the more fashionable hair cut and the new suit. Matt's whole demeanor seemed to have changed. She'd seen it the instant he emerged from the train car and descended the iron steps. There was a new confidence in his gait and the way he held his head. Gone was the faint diffidence that had clung to him, even after he'd returned from law school. In its place was an undeniably cosmopolitan air. New York had changed Matt, and — though she had not thought it possible — made him even more attractive.

Jane swallowed deeply. How could she have considered marrying Brad, even for a moment? Matt was the only man she would ever love, the only man she could ever marry. She swallowed again, forcing back the bitter knowledge that that man did not love her.

"Susannah, we're here!" Jane kept her voice as light as she could and led Matt into the parlor. This was, it seemed, where the family spent most of its time. Anne and Rob came at least once a day, sometimes joining them for a meal, and Susannah no longer painted. She was, as she had told Jane, unable to concentrate on anything other than proving her husband's innocence. For his part, though Charles went to the mill each morning, he spent the majority of his time here with Susannah.

As Jane and Matt entered the room, Charles rose and glared at Matt. "I won't welcome you."

"Charles, please!" Jane and Susannah's exclamations formed a duet.

Matt shook his head. "It's all right, Jane," he said, his eyes meeting hers, the expression telling her that Charles's rudeness bothered Matt less than it did her. "I didn't expect anything else from your brother." Matt shrugged. "This is the first time I've had a hostile client, but I suspect it will not be the last." When Jane was seated, Matt took the place next to her on the settee. Though they were a decorous distance apart, Jane found comfort in the fact that Matt was here. If anyone could save Charles, it was the man at her side.

Though Matt had pulled out paper and a pen, he did not uncap the pen. Instead, he leaned forward slightly, addressing Charles. "Before we begin, there's some old business I want to settle. I want to apologize."

Apologize to Charles? Why? Jane stared at the man beside her, not believing her ears. Why would he believe he owed Charles an apology? Was it somehow related to their childhood animosity?

Matt's voice was earnest as he said, "I didn't want to believe you when you told me your mill was the safest in the country. I was wrong, Charles. It is."

Jane could only guess how much it had cost Matt to admit that. She looked at her brother, hoping he would accept the apology in the spirit it was offered, but Charles merely glared at Matt.

"Save your breath. It was your interference that put me in this predicament. If you hadn't stirred up the workers, the town wouldn't be so willing to believe I'm capable of murder."

Jane heard Matt's intake of breath and saw his knuckles whiten. "That's ridiculous, Charles, and you know it," Jane said, her voice seething with anger at the undeserved accusation. The workers, far from condemning Charles, were convinced of his innocence, declaring that a man who worried about their safety would not kill anyone. It was the mayor and the town council who believed Charles culpable.

Ignoring Jane's protest, Charles pointed a finger at Matt. "You probably came here thinking that if you helped me, I'd consent to your marrying Jane."

This time it was Jane who gasped.

"I told you once that I didn't need your consent," Matt said, as coolly as if they were discussing the weather. "For your information, I came here because I believe in justice. You may be an ungrateful wretch who doesn't deserve a sister like Jane, but I know you are not a murderer." Matt crossed his ankles in an apparently casual gesture, the rigidity of his fingers the only clue that he was not as calm as he seemed. "As soon as your case is closed, I will leave Hidden Falls, and I promise you that I will not return."

Matt's words were like a vice, squeezing Jane's heart. She had thought the wounds Matt's leaving had inflicted had healed and that she could regard him as nothing more than a friend and the one person she trusted to defend Charles. How wrong she'd been! Seeing Matt again only strengthened Jane's love for him and her longing to be his wife. It was foolish, for they had no future together. Matt had made that clear when he'd broken their engagement, but oh, how it hurt to hear him declare it again.

Jane bit the inside of her cheek in an effort to not cry out and forced herself to concentrate on the questions Matt asked Charles. This was what was important, not Jane's foolish heart clinging to impossible dreams.

An hour later, Matt had completed what he called his initial interview with Charles and had covered several pages with notes. Both Charles and Susannah had pled other business, leaving Jane and Matt alone in the parlor. Jane suspected that Susannah feared another outbreak of hostility and wanted to separate Charles from Matt, for though Charles had answered Matt's questions, it had been with obvious reluctance.

"The situation is bleaker than I feared," Matt told Jane as he rifled through his notes. "Charles was gone long enough to have committed the crime, and — even though we know he didn't do it — we have no proof."

Jane tried to swallow her disappointment. She had hoped that somehow, someway Matt would find something they'd overlooked. The truth was, Jane had hoped for a miracle, and miracles didn't happen, at least not to her. "I'm convinced the murderer was Megan's mysterious suitor," she said. "The problem is, I don't know who he is."

"Or if he really exists."

Jane looked at Matt in surprise. "What do you mean?"

"The suitor might have been a figment of Megan's imagination. Maybe she thought Charles would be jealous if he believed he had a rival."

"But Charles didn't care about Megan, at least not romantically."

"And we can spend all day speculating about what Megan thought. Unfortunately, there's no value in that." Matt rose and extended his hand to Jane. "I'd like to look at the evidence. I'm surprised none of you have done that. There may be a clue there."

Once again, Matt's words surprised Jane. No one had felt the need to examine the evidence, because Mayor McBride's description left no doubt about what he had found. Still, it couldn't hurt to see it. Even if this visit proved to be another dead end, Jane would have the satisfaction of knowing they'd done everything they could. That would, however, be faint consolation if the jury convicted Charles of a crime he hadn't committed.

As she guided Brad's car back into the center of Hidden Falls, Jane refused to speak of the murder. Perhaps she was being foolish, but she needed to pretend — if only for a few minutes — that she and Matt were not involved in the most serious matter of her life. And so she turned toward him. "I hear you've been very successful in New York." That was a neutral topic, less painful than thoughts of her brother's situation and far less painful than the knowledge that Matt did not love her.

"The work is immensely satisfying." Matt's expression as well as the tone of his voice confirmed his words. "You were right when you told me I should move to a large city. Porter and Latham is giving me the opportunities I've always dreamed of."

Jane couldn't help wondering if one of those opportunities was being able to court Pamela Porter. "So you caught the brass ring?" she asked.

The corners of his mouth quirked upward. "Let's say that it's within reach."

Of course. The courtship wasn't complete. Matt would have the brass ring in his hand only when Miss Pamela Porter became Mrs. Matthew Wagner. Would Pamela's parents insist on a lengthy engagement, or would she become a late summer bride? Jane pushed those thoughts firmly aside as she parked the car in front of the small building that served as the mayor's office. The only reason Matt had returned to Hidden Falls was to prove Charles's innocence. There was no point in thinking of other times they'd been together or wishing for things that could never be.

"I'm glad to see you again, Matt," the mayor said when he had greeted Jane and ushered them into his office. "I've been following your career with interest."

So had Jane, although for different reasons.

"Thank you, sir. I'm enjoying practicing law, but I must admit I never thought my first murder case would be in Hidden Falls."

Mr. McBride's face turned stony. "It's appalling what a man will do when he's angry."

Though Matt had counseled her to remain silent and let him do all the questioning, Jane could not allow the statement to go unchallenged. "Charles didn't kill Megan," Jane said, her voice as steely as the mayor's face.

Mr. McBride's expression was slightly condescending. "I admire your loyalty to your brother, but the evidence says otherwise."

Before another angry retort could cross Jane's lips, Matt spoke. "May we see the evidence?"

"Certainly." The mayor rose and disappeared into an adjoining room. When he returned he was carrying a small box. He made a process out of opening it and consulting a sheet of paper that Jane assumed was a listing of the contents. "This is the ring we found on Miss O'Toole's hand," he said, holding out the signet ring that Charles had once worn. Jane noticed that the mayor was addressing Matt and studiously ignoring her. She wouldn't let his attitude annoy her. Too much was at stake.

Matt held the ring, carefully examining each side. "I've seen this many times," he said, his tone conversational. "I also know that Charles stopped wearing it five or six months ago. There had been an accident at the mill, and he instituted a new policy, forbidding the workers to wear anything other than plain bands."

Mr. McBride nodded. "Precisely. That's the reason we believe he gave it to Miss O'Toole."

"That ring is an heirloom," Jane cried, unable to contain her anger that the mayor wasn't listening to reason. "Charles was saving it for his oldest son. He would never have given it to Megan."

Matt laid his hand on Jane's, silently urging her to say nothing more. This was, he had tried to impress on her as they drove into the center of town, their opportunity to learn facts, not to convince a judge or jury.

Ignoring Jane's protests, the mayor reached into the box. "And this is the murder weapon." He unfolded the yellow and black cravat, displaying it to Jane and Matt.

Jane stared at the piece of silk that had once been tied around Charles's neck. She had seen that cravat many times, for, as Susannah had said, it was Charles's favorite. Though it had been nothing more than a fashion accessory when Charles had worn it, someone had turned that fashion acces-

327

sory into a garrote to choke the life from an innocent woman. Jane shuddered.

The mayor draped the silk over his hand, extending it toward Matt. As he did, Jane studied it. Something was wrong. Her eyes narrowed as she looked at the beautiful piece of silk. Something was missing, something important. Jane stared at the yellow and black print. Was it possible? For the first time since Mr. McBride had told her of Megan's murder, she felt a stirring of hope.

"I feel faint." Jane leaned back in the chair and laid her hand against her cheek, as if trying to keep from swooning. "May I have a glass of water?" As she had hoped, Mr. McBride rushed to comply. As soon as he was out of the room, Jane turned to Matt.

"This isn't Charles's tie."

Jane wasn't certain which surprised Matt most, the fact that she was not about to faint or her assertion. "What do you mean?"

"Charles's tie was stained. That's why Susannah threw it away. Look at this one. There's not a spot on it."

Matt examined the cravat, turning it over to ensure that there were indeed no stains.

"Is it possible that there's a second tie in Hidden Falls like this one?"

"Yes," Jane said with certainty. "And I know whose it is."

CHAPTER TWELVE

"Why did you do it?" Though Jane's voice was remarkably devoid of emotion, Matt could only imagine the thoughts that must be roiling in her head, knowing that a man she had considered an honorary uncle had killed a woman and then tried to implicate her brother for the murder. Were he in Jane's position, Matt wasn't certain he could sit so calmly. Even now, his hands itched to throttle the man, to show him a bit of the fear Megan must have felt, to cause him a fraction of the anguish he'd inflicted on the Morelands. Jane appeared to have none of those primitive instincts. She sat with her hands clasped in her lap, her head held high, as if this were nothing more than a social call.

"I hated him." The words were filled with venom. When Jane and Matt had reached his house, the man had admitted them with no more than mild curiosity, ushering them into his parlor, apologizing that he had no tea to offer. Even when Matt had presented the evidence, he had said little. Only at the end had he reacted, and when he did, his reaction had surprised Matt. For instead of displaying remorse, the man had appeared to be gloating. He was proud of his crime. "I hated him," he repeated.

Jane's face paled, and Matt saw that her hands were now clenched. "I don't understand. What did Charles ever do to earn your hatred?"

The silence lasted so long that Matt feared the man would not answer. Looking around the beautiful room, Matt wondered what drove a man whose life appeared to be close to perfect to commit murder. He understood disliking Charles. He'd spent a lifetime doing that. But murder? Never!

The man stared at Jane, then blinked, as if he'd suddenly heard her question. "Charles? It wasn't Charles. I hated John." For the first time in Matt's knowledge, Philip Biddle's polished veneer cracked, and he began to laugh, a laugh that bore no mirth, only a hint of madness. "John stole the only thing I ever wanted."

Whatever it was, it must have been valuable. Matt considered the possibilities. Only one made sense. "Mary." If his conclusion was correct, Philip was nursing anger and enmity caused by unrequited love.

The tall, distinguished man who was both a pillar of Hidden Falls society and a confessed murderer nodded at Matt. "That's right, young man. Mary would have married me," Philip said fiercely. "I know she would have. But John interfered."

Matt heard Jane's quick intake of breath. "You thought my mother loved you?" There was a note of incredulity in her question that Matt understood, for anyone who'd seen Jane's parents together knew the love they bore each other.

"We all loved her. Ralph, John, me. But I was the one Mary favored. She would have married me if John hadn't turned her away." Philip glared at Jane, his expression so menacing that Matt wanted to place himself between them as a shield. "John told her lies about me. I couldn't let him go unpunished."

"Naturally not." Matt saw Jane's back stiffen, and he knew she wanted to dispute his assertion. How painful it must be, hearing Matt appear to agree with a murderer. He gave her a quick look, reminding her of the plan they'd developed on the short drive to Philip's house. Matt would lead the interrogation, using techniques he'd been taught at law school.

"What did you do first?" he asked, as casually as if he'd been inquiring about the kind of fuel Philip used for his Model T.

Philip appeared to relax. That was the key, Matt knew. Disarm the witness, let him trust you, and he'd reveal more than he planned. "I set out to destroy him." Philip turned toward Jane. "Do you remember the investments that failed?" He had to be referring to a series of companies that had gone bankrupt in quick succession, taking the life savings of many of Hidden Falls' citizens. It had been a major scandal a few years earlier, in great part because John Moreland had advised his friends to invest in those companies. "I was the mastermind," Philip said with obvious pride, "but John took the blame. He never knew I was responsible." Philip's laugh made the hair rise on Matt's neck. No sane man would laugh like that, but Philip wasn't totally sane. He couldn't be to have turned his disappointment in love into an excuse for murder.

"You deliberately destroyed people's fortunes and let my father suffer the consequences?" Though Jane had promised to remain silent, this was more than she could bear.

Philip's blue eyes glittered. "John deserved

to suffer. Nothing I did to him compared to the way I suffered every time I saw him with Mary. She should have been my wife. You and Anne should have been my daughters."

As Jane shuddered in horror, Matt spoke quickly, trying to divert Philip's attention. The last thing he needed was to have Philip's madness turned toward Jane. "What an ingenious form of revenge." Matt forced admiration into his words as he measured the distance between Philip and Jane. If the man made a sudden move, Matt needed to be prepared to block him.

"You think so?" To Matt's relief, Philip appeared to relax and began to preen. "Unfortunately, the shame didn't have the effect I had expected. I thought John would be so despondent over his failure that he would kill himself, and then Mary would turn to me for consolation, but he didn't."

Philip had obviously not understood the man he had tried to destroy. John Moreland was a man of honor and strength. He would never have considered suicide.

"I imagine you had another plan ready to be executed."

"Indeed I did, my boy. I set the fire at Fairlawn."

Jane gripped the chair arms, and Matt sensed that she was trying desperately not to jump to her feet and claw at Philip's face. "You killed my mother, too!"

Nodding as calmly as if he were admitting to a minor peccadillo rather than a monstrous crime, Philip said, "It was necessary. Mary had her chance to come with me and refused. She had to pay for that."

The man was mad. It was the only explanation for his twisted idea of revenge. There was no doubt, no doubt at all, that Philip Biddle was guilty. Even if a jury granted him leniency because of his obvious instability, Matt could ensure that Philip spent the rest of his life locked away where he could harm no one else.

"I understand your reasoning," Matt said, though in truth he could not understand killing innocent people because of unrequited love. "Why did you need to punish Charles? It was John who wronged you."

Philip gave Matt a look that said the answer should be obvious. "Charles bears the Moreland name. I couldn't let any Morelands remain in Hidden Falls." Philip rubbed his chin, as if pondering something. He was silent for a moment before he said, "I tried to sabotage the mill, thinking Charles would leave Hidden Falls when he was forced to cease operations." Philip laughed again, that horribly disturbing laugh that chilled Matt almost as much as the man's recitation of his diabolical schemes. "I would have succeeded if Brian O'Toole hadn't bungled the mill fire." Philip shrugged his shoulders. "It's so difficult to find competent arsonists."

Though Jane had been in Switzerland, Matt had seen the aftermath of the fire. It took an almost superhuman effort not to react to Philip's cavalier attitude.

"Brian died in that fire." Though Matt had bit back his retort, Jane was unable to remain silent.

Philip raised one eyebrow in a gesture of supreme insouciance. A casual observer would never have guessed that Philip was discussing matters of life and death. "That's the price of failure."

"Understandable," Matt said in his most placating tone. Though he wanted to yank the man from his chair and haul him off to jail, Matt needed the answer to one more question. "I'm not certain, though, that I understand why Megan had to die."

"She was a pawn." It was a measure of Philip's madness that he considered human life of no consequence. "I knew Charles had spurned her. That made it easy to convince her that I was different and that I would marry her. The fool! She was just like her father. She'd do anything I asked."

Matt had heard laughs described as blood-chilling. Philip's was one of those. "You must admit that it was quite brilliant the way I implicated Charles in the murder. No matter how well respected he was in Hidden Falls, I knew he would hang. It was the perfect plan." Philip laughed again.

"It might have succeeded if you hadn't worn the cravat on Christmas Day." Jane spoke so softly that Matt wasn't certain Philip heard her.

"It was such a nice piece of silk. It reminded me of a dress Mary once wore. I couldn't resist."

Matt pulled out a piece of paper and began to write. "You know it's over."

Philip appeared to have no curiosity about what Matt was writing. "It's never over," he said. "This town will never forget me."

"Indeed, sir, they will not." Matt blotted the last line, then handed the sheet of vellum to Philip. "If you would be so kind as to read this and sign it."

For the first time, a hint of confusion crossed Philip's face. "What is this?"

"It's a recounting of everything you've done. A legacy for posterity." A confession, although that was a word Matt chose not to use.

"Very good, my boy." Philip glanced at the page, then signed it with a flourish.

"And now we should pay a visit to Mr. McBride." Matt nodded toward Jane.

An expression Matt could not identify flitted across Philip's face. "Certainly." He rose and walked toward the door. "Let me get my hat."

Matt heard footsteps, a door opening and closing, then a long silence. "I wonder . . ." Before he could complete the sentence, a single shot rang out.

Jane's face turned pale, and she began to tremble at the realization of what Philip had done. Gently, Matt drew her into his arms. "It's over, Jane. It's finally over."

"It's difficult to believe Uncle Philip was responsible for all those terrible things." Anne sat on one of the settees, Rob's arm around her shoulders.

After they had summoned Mr. McBride and presented him with Philip's confession, Jane and Matt had returned to Pleasant Hill, where they'd found Anne and Rob already gathered with Charles and Susannah. Jane was thankful for that. It would be difficult enough, recounting the scene at Philip's house with its tragic ending once. She didn't think she could bear to repeat it.

Though Matt had told her that the nightmare was over, Jane knew there was some truth to what Philip had said. It would never be completely over. The tentacles of Philip's evil had touched many lives, changing them forever. Memories would fade, but they would never totally disappear.

"Some people are good at hiding their true selves."

Jane looked at Matt, who sat on a chair beside her. Was he one of those people? Watching him in Philip's house, she had been amazed at how skillfully he had drawn the confession from Philip, how calmly he had faced a murderer and managed to gain his confidence. This was a side of Matt she had never seen. What else had he managed to keep hidden?

"It seems I owe you thanks." Charles nodded at Matt, his voice betraying the reluctance with which he uttered the words.

Matt shook his head. "I told you before. I wasn't doing this for you. I simply wanted to see justice served."

Justice. Of course. Though she had harbored the hope that Matt had come back to Hidden Falls at least in part because he wanted to see her, his words showed Jane the fallacy of that thinking. What they had shared was over. Perhaps that was what

Matt had meant when he had held her in his arms. She had thought he was referring only to Philip's reign of evil, but perhaps she was wrong. Perhaps Matt was also telling her that his last tenuous connection to Hidden Falls had been broken. Perhaps now that his exoneration of Charles would gain him the approval of the townspeople, Matt no longer had anything to prove here. He could return to New York, unencumbered by regrets or unfinished business.

Fixing his gaze on Charles, Matt said, "I don't need your thanks, but I would like to know one thing before I leave. Why have you always hated me?"

Jane nodded slowly. It was as she'd thought. Matt wanted to tie up every loose end before he climbed onto the train.

If the question surprised Charles, he gave no indication. Using one of Matt's techniques, he responded with a question of his own. "Wouldn't you hate someone who tried to usurp your position not just in this town but — more important — in this family?"

The confusion Jane felt was reflected on Matt's face. What on earth did Charles mean? Matt had never been part of the family, and he most certainly had not been accepted by the townspeople.

"I'm sorry, Charles, but I have no idea what you're talking about." Matt's voice, which had been perfectly calm when he'd faced Philip, was tinged with emotion, telling Jane how important this conversation was to him.

Brushing off Susannah's restraining hand, Charles rose and glared down at Matt. "Don't you think I knew about all the times you visited my father in his office? He was too busy to teach me to ride a horse, but he had time to spend with you." Charles's voice seethed with resentment. "Until you started going to school, I was the top of the class. Then you came, and no matter how much I studied, I could never measure up. Believe me, I heard about that."

"I never heard Papa criticize you for being second." Jane couldn't let Charles continue with his distorted view of the past.

"Maybe not, but I'm sure you recall the times he talked about the brilliant future Matt would have. Matt was the son he wanted."

"Charles, that's not true." Jane's eyes filled with tears as she realized how Charles must have suffered from the imaginary slights. "I heard Papa tell Mama how proud he was of you for following your own convictions. It would have been easy to stay here and work at the mill, but you didn't choose the easy path. You wanted a different future, and you succeeded at it."

"That's right," Anne chimed in. "You weren't here, but Papa would tell anyone who'd listen about you and all you'd accomplished."

Jane looked at the two men she loved most. Matt sat quietly while his lifelong nemesis bared his soul. Charles, on the other hand, had begun to pace, as if the activity would settle his inner turmoil.

"It sounds as if we need some explanations." Matt spoke for the first time since Charles had begun his accusations. "It's true that I went to your father's office every day after school, but I assure you it was not of my own volition. Your father insisted on it." Matt gave Jane a wry smile. "Mr. Moreland claimed it was to ensure I did my homework, but I wouldn't be surprised if it was his way of protecting the mill. After all, I couldn't set fire to bales of cotton if I was in his office." Shaking his head slowly, Matt looked at Charles. "You may not believe me, but there was nothing parental in our relationship. For years, I considered your father my truant officer."

Charles was silent for a moment, his expression pensive. "Be that as it may, it always seemed that you were trying to outdo me and that you wanted me to fail."

"I *was* trying to outdo you," Matt admitted. "Remember, Charles, that I was the boy from the wrong side of the river. I had to prove that I was as good as or better than you. That doesn't mean I hated you, and it certainly doesn't mean that I was trying to usurp your position." He swallowed, and Jane thought he had said all he intended. But Matt continued. "Even though I wouldn't admit it at the time, I always wondered what it would be like to have you as a brother."

Jane looked at her brother, whose expression left no doubt that he was uncomfortable with the direction the conversation had taken, then turned to look at Matt. "You mean that this enmity that's lasted more than half your lives would not have happened if you'd ever talked to each other?"

The two men stared at each other and shrugged. "Twelve-year-old boys don't talk. They use their fists." It was Matt who ventured the explanation.

Susannah shook her head. "Men!"

Matt strode down the street as quickly as he could without actually running. The train would leave in less than half an hour, and he had no intention of missing it. He placed one foot in front of the other, trying to erase the memory of Jane's eyes when he had refused her offer to accompany him to the station. She had been hurt and confused. He couldn't blame her, but he also knew that he couldn't say farewell to her at the train station. It had been easier — safer — to bid her good-bye with the rest of her family at her side. That way there was no opportunity to say things that were best left unsaid.

He slid his hand into his coat pocket, fingering the small box. He wasn't sure why he'd taken it from his suitcase, any more than he understood why he'd brought it with him in the first place. It wasn't as if he were planning some grand gesture, like tossing it from the train window, and he had no intention of offering it to Jane again. So, why was he carrying it with him? Matt shook his head. He couldn't explain it.

It was fitting that he be alone when he climbed onto the train. That was the way he had left Hidden Falls the last time. It was the way he should depart today, figuratively brushing the dirt off his shoes, never to return.

Matt breathed in the fresh May air. Now that the trees had begun to leaf out, song birds were returning. His hometown — his former hometown, he corrected himself — would soon reach the height of its beauty. The fact that he would not be here to enjoy that beauty should not bother him. He had made his choices. New York might not have the same pastoral beauty, but it was where he belonged.

Matt inhaled again, savoring the scent of moist earth and newly sprouted grass. He should be happy. He *was* happy. He had proven Charles's innocence and put an end to the hostility that had separated them for so long. He was on his way back to New York City and the life he found so satisfying. That was his choice. It was the right one.

Matt turned right onto Bridge Street. In a few minutes, he'd be at the depot with time to spare. Soon he'd be on the train, headed east. Life in Hidden Falls would continue. The mill would prosper. Charles's son or daughter would be born. Jane would marry Brad. That was as it should be.

No, it was not!

Matt clenched his fists, trying to fight back the bile that thoughts of Jane and Brad together created. He had been in Hidden Falls less than a day. Matt forced his fingers open and stared at them. He could count the hours he had spent with Jane on one hand. Five hours. That wasn't very many, and yet it had been enough. More than enough, in fact, to show him how wrong he had been.

Matt clenched his fists again as he crossed the bridge where he and Jane had stood on Thanksgiving evening, admiring the reflection of stars in the water. That had been the night they'd shared their first kiss. Matt knew he'd never forget that, just as he'd never forget the anguish in Jane's eyes the day he'd broken their engagement.

Swinging his suitcase with more force than necessary, Matt hurried across the bridge, trying to banish the memories. He failed, utterly and completely. How could he have ever thought that life without Jane could satisfy him? He'd been deluding himself. It was true that he enjoyed working at Porter and Latham and that his cases there were more satisfying than any he'd have in Hidden Falls. It was true that he enjoyed the acceptance he'd found in New York. But those few hours he had spent with Jane had shown Matt another truth. What he had in New York was an existence, not a life. The pleasure, the contentment, the sense of satisfaction that he found there was nothing — nothing at all — compared to what he felt when he was with Jane. Only Jane could fill the empty spaces inside him. Only Jane could turn contentment into joy. Only with Jane was he truly alive.

Matt stared at the depot. The train was there. He had his ticket. All he had to do was climb aboard. As he reached into his pocket, touching the square box, he knew that he could not board the train. Jane might refuse him. She had every right to after the things he had said to her. Matt knew that, but he also knew that he had to try again.

He turned around.

Jane stared sightlessly out the window. She knew that she could see Fairlawn in the distance, just as she knew that she could not see the depot where even now Matt was probably boarding the train. He was gone, or he would be in a few minutes. He had accomplished everything he had come for. Now he was returning to New York and the life he deserved.

Jane gripped the windowsill, trying to quell the pain that thoughts of Matt leaving Hidden Falls brought. Going to New York was the right thing for him. He deserved the challenges the city could provide. He deserved the success and acclaim he found there. He even deserved Miss Pamela Porter, although it hurt almost unbearably to admit it. Jane closed her eyes, in a vain attempt to block images of Matt and the lovely debutante. He deserved a future filled with success, happiness, a wife and family. No one deserved it more. Jane simply wished she could be part of that future.

At the sound of a bird's trilling, she opened her eyes. The day was beautiful as only a day in May could be. It was a day made for happiness, for singing aloud at the sheer pleasure of being alive. But Jane was not singing. Instead, she felt as if her heart were breaking.

She and Matt had spent only a few hours together, but oh, how wonderful it had been to be with him! Though they'd been engaged in the most serious of endeavors, there had been a sense of excitement as they had worked together. For a few hours, Jane had felt as if she and Matt were partners, two halves of a whole. Separately, neither of them could have exonerated Charles. Together, they had accomplished what others had considered impossible.

Jane smiled at the memory. It had felt so good, being with Matt. Today had been unforgettable, both exhausting and exhilarating as she had experienced the whole spectrum of emotions. Fear had turned to anger, then sorrow, all culminating in overwhelming happiness that Charles was safe. And through it all, Jane had been with Matt. He had helped to lessen her fears and heighten her joy simply by being at her side.

For the first time in months, Jane had felt alive — truly alive. Being with Matt had shown her that everything she had done since he had left Hidden Falls had been nothing more than an attempt to rebuild her life. Today was proof of how badly she had failed. The simple fact was, she couldn't have the life she wanted unless Matt was part of it.

Jane took a deep breath as she watched two birds squabble over a twig, then both abandon it. Had she been like that, giving up too easily? Matt had once asked her what her brass ring was. At the time, Jane hadn't been certain. Now there was no doubt. The brass ring she sought was a life with him. She wouldn't be like the birds. She wouldn't abandon her dream.

Jane heard the hall clock chiming and felt a frisson of fear. Now that she'd made her decision, would she be too late? Would the brass ring continue to elude her? She had no way of knowing how today would end. What she did know was that she couldn't let Matt leave Hidden Falls without telling him once more that she loved him.

She ran down River Road, not caring that dust was covering her skirts, not caring that her hat was probably askew, not caring that anyone who saw her would think she had lost her mind. None of that mattered. All that mattered was seeing Matt again. Jane heard the train's warning whistle. In five minutes, it would depart. She willed her feet to move faster. Somehow, she had to reach the depot before the train left. If only she had Brad's car, but he had already reclaimed it. Though her side ached and she was gasping for breath, Jane continued to run. She was almost at Bridge Street. Once she turned there, she could make it. She had to.

Her heart pounding wildly, Jane careened around the corner onto Bridge. Faster, she urged her feet. Faster. And then she saw him. A man was at the bottom of the hill, racing toward her. Matt!

Jane stopped and tried to catch her breath, but she was still panting when he reached her. "The train's the other direction," she said. It wasn't how she had meant to greet him, but suddenly words deserted her. Though she wanted to believe the fact that Matt was not on the train meant he had changed his mind, Jane didn't dare. There could be other reasons why Matt was hurrying up the hill, although at the moment she could think of none.

"I couldn't leave without seeing you again," he said. The words made it clear that he was still planning to return to New York. Jane tried to bite back her disappointment. Just for a moment she had been filled with elation and the hope that Matt had decided he could not leave her. It was a foolish hope. He had simply decided to take the next train. Still, his delay would give her the chance she sought to tell him one last time that she loved him.

"Let's go to the park," Matt suggested.

Jane hesitated for a second, remembering that the park was where Matt had broken their engagement. The carousel she had once loved had become the source of unhappy memories. She started to protest, then nodded slowly. Perhaps it was fitting that this meeting, which might be their last, take place there.

Jane and Matt crossed the street together and entered the park. At this time of day, the carousel was open but empty. Once the mill closed, there would be riders, but now the animals stood motionless. To Jane's surprise, Matt urged her to mount one of the horses. Was it because he — like Jane — cherished the memory of the time they'd ridden the carousel?

Jane noted with bemusement that the horse Matt had chosen was the one she had ridden that magical night when they'd first operated the merry-go-round. Matt had taken the horse next to her that night. Today he stood at her side, looking so serious that Jane's heart contracted with fear. Why had he brought her here? She took a quick breath, trying to dismiss the thought that Matt was preparing to tell her of his engagement to Pamela Porter.

But when he spoke, it was not about the New York debutante. "I used to dream about carousels," Matt said. "In my dreams, I was riding the fanciest horse, and I always caught the brass ring." He laid his hand on the painted pony's neck, then looked up at Jane, his brown eyes serious. "I was about to get on the train, when I realized that I couldn't catch the brass ring unless I reached for it." He swallowed deeply, and she sensed his hesitation. "It's taken me a long time to realize it, and I've made some foolish mistakes along the way, but now I'm sure. You're my brass ring, Jane." He paused again before he asked, "Can you forgive me for all the pain I've caused you? Can you possibly forget that long enough to marry me?"

Marriage! Matt wanted to marry her! Jane looked at the man she loved so dearly, scarcely able to believe what she'd heard. *Yes! Yes!* she wanted to shout. Instead, she paused. This time she had to be certain that the ring she caught was brass and not tin.

"I gave you my answer once," Jane said quietly. "It wasn't enough for you then. What's different this time?"

Matt laid his hand over hers. "You're right to ask that question. What's different is me. I've had a chance to try the things I thought would make me happy. I won't lie to you, Jane. I enjoyed the life I had in New York, but I realized that wasn't enough." He laced his fingers with hers. "I need you to be part of my life if I'm going to be truly happy."

Jane nodded slowly. She needed Matt, too. Without him, her life was incomplete. But she also needed something he hadn't offered. She needed love. Jane started to speak, but before she could utter a word, Matt continued.

"I know how important living here is to you," he said. "Hidden Falls is your home, and I wouldn't ask you to leave it." He gestured toward the center of town. "Ralph wants to retire and has offered me his practice. I won't be able to give you all the luxuries you had at Fairlawn, but we should be able to live comfortably on the income from Ralph's clients."

Jane caught her breath at the realization of what Matt was willing to do for her. Assuming Ralph's practice would mean giving up the challenging cases he'd had in New York. Recalling the obvious pleasure she'd seen on Matt's face when he'd spoken of his work for Porter and Latham, Jane shook her head. "That's not what I want. I don't want you to sacrifice your career for me." She looked down at their hands. They were joined, just as she wanted their lives to be. "You said you've changed. I've changed, too. You were right in saying that Hidden Falls has always been my home. I never thought I'd live anywhere else, but the last few months have shown me the truth of the adage, 'home is where the heart is.' I realized I don't need to stay here. I could be happy in New York if that was where my heart was."

"Oh, Jane!" Matt's eyes shone as he smiled at her. "Dare I hope that your heart would be with me? I promise I'll do everything in my power to make you happy." He paused, then repeated his question. "Will you marry me?"

Jane was tempted to nod, but she could not. She had made that mistake before. This time she wouldn't settle for anything but the real thing, the brass ring of love. "More than almost anything on earth, I want to say 'yes,' but I can't."

Matt's face reflected his confusion. "Why not? Do you think Brad or anyone else can love you more than I do? They can't."

Love. Matt had finally said the word. Jane's heart filled with a happiness so deep that she had to catch her breath. She wanted to proclaim to the world, "Matt Wagner loves me!" but she had to be certain.

"Do you love me, Matt?"

He blinked. "Of course I do. I've loved you since you were a little girl in pigtails." Matt drew Jane's hand to his mouth and pressed a kiss on it. "I was sure you knew that."

She shook her head slowly. "You never told me you loved me, not even when you asked me to marry you the first time. Then when you broke our engagement, I thought it was because you realized you didn't love me." Matt stared at her, his shocked expression telling Jane how wrong she'd been. "I love you, Matt. I've always loved you, but one thing I learned when you left me was that I can't marry a man who doesn't return my love."

Matt released her hands. "What a fool I was!" Before Jane knew what he intended, Matt was kneeling next to the painted pony. He looked up at her and took her left hand in his. "I love you, Jane. I love you more than I thought it was possible to love a person. I love you with all my heart, with every fiber of my being. I will love you every day of my life." He smiled at her, and the love shining from his eyes made Jane's heart skip a beat.

"Will you marry me?" he asked.

"I will."

Matt pulled a small box from his pocket. Slowly, he unbuttoned Jane's glove and freed her hand from it. "This time is forever," he said as he slid the ring onto her finger. "Our love is forever."

Jane smiled as she slipped off the painted pony and into the arms of the man she loved. It had been a long and bumpy ride, but she and Matt had done it. They'd caught the brass ring.

AUTHOR'S LETTER

Dear Reader,

I hope you enjoyed Jane and Matt's story and that you've come to love the town of Hidden Falls almost as much as I have. As I promised you in *Painted Ponies,* there are many more tales to come.

Both *Painted Ponies* and *The Brass Ring* feature Hidden Falls at its zenith. The carousel is new; the mill and the whole town are prospering. Flash forward almost a hundred years, and the situation is vastly different. The carousel has been dismantled; the mill has long since closed; and the residents of Hidden Falls fear that their town will soon disappear. High school teacher Claire Conners is determined that that will not happen and will do anything — including butting heads with land developer John Moreland — to prevent that. Look for *Dream Weaver,* Claire and John's story, publishing soon.

If this is your first Hidden Falls romance, I encourage you to read *Painted Ponies.* You may be surprised by the problems Anne and Rob encounter on the path to happiness. And, if you — like me — feel sorry for Brad and wish he'd find true love, I can promise you that Brad will have his own book, as will his and Charles's friend Anthony. The saga continues.

Happy reading!

Amanda Harte

ABOUT THE AUTHOR

A chance encounter with a merry-go-round horse in — of all places — a highway rest area led to **Amanda Harte's** incurable case of carousel fever. She's been planning stories about painted ponies and the people who love them ever since and is delighted to share the next *Hidden Falls Romances* with you.

Amanda is a charter member of Romance Writers of America, co-founder of its New Jersey chapter and an avid traveler. She married her high school sweetheart, who shares her love of travel and who's driven thousands of miles to help her research her books. They've recently fulfilled a long-time dream and are now living in the American West, where they're continuing to search for antique carousels.

The Brass Ring is Amanda's ninth romance novel for AVALON and the second book in her *Hidden Falls Romance Series. Painted*

Ponies is the first. In addition to her highly acclaimed *War Brides Trilogy (Dancing in the Rain, Whistling in the Dark* and *Laughing at the Thunder),* she has written three *Unwanted Legacies* books *(Strings Attached, Imperfect Together* and *Bluebonnet Spring)* as well as *Moonlight Masquerade,* the story of a romance writer with a problem.

Amanda loves hearing from readers and encourages you to visit her website at:

www.amandaharte.com.